Yuma had been alone and lonely for far too long,

lost in a dark nightmare created in a faraway land. He had lived in a prison cell of the mind and spirit, and suffered the tortures of the damned inside his own head. Wendy, lying at his side, was a touch of sunlight and warmth, a human touch. A womanly, soft, caring touch.

He might curse himself for the rest of his days, but he could not refuse himself this one taste of light and life and warmth.

Damn, she was soft. She curled into him, melted into him—as if she belonged there.

And that was what shook Yuma back to reality.

Dear Reader,

The holiday season is here, and as our gift to you, we've got an especially wonderful lineup of books. Just look at our American Hero title, another "Conard County" book from Rachel Lee. *Lost Warriors* is the story of a heart that returns from the brink of oblivion and learns to love again. That heart belongs to rugged Billy Joe Yuma, and the saving hand belongs to nurse Wendy Tate. To learn more, you'll just have to read the book. Believe me, you won't regret it.

And here's another special treat: Judith Duncan is back with *Beyond All Reason,* the first of a special new miniseries called "Wide Open Spaces." It's set in the ranch country of Alberta, Canada, and will introduce you to the McCall family, a set of siblings you won't soon forget. More miniseries news: Marie Ferrarella completes her trilogy about the Sinclair family with *Christmas Every Day,* Nik's story. And the month is rounded out with books by Christine Flynn, a bestseller for Special Edition, Alexandra Sellers, and a second book from Julia Quinn called *Birthright.*

So from all of us to all of you, Happy Holidays—and Happy Reading!

Yours,

Leslie Wainger
Senior Editor and Editorial Coordinator

AMERICAN HERO

LOST WARRIORS

Rachel
Lee

Published by Silhouette Books
America's Publisher of Contemporary Romance

ISBN 0-373-07535-9

LOST WARRIORS

This edition published by arrangement with Harlequin Enterprises B. V.

Printed in U.S.A.

Books by Rachel Lee

Silhouette Intimate Moments

An Officer and a Gentleman #370
Serious Risks #394
Defying Gravity #430
**Exile's End* #449
**Cherokee Thunder* #463
**Miss Emmaline and the Archangel* #482
**Ironheart* #494
**Lost Warriors* #535

*Conard County series

Silhouette Shadows

Imminent Thunder #10

RACHEL LEE

wrote her first play in the third grade for a school assembly, and by the age of twelve she was hooked on writing. She's lived all over the United States, on both the East and West coasts, and now resides in Texas with her husband and two college-age children.

Having held jobs as a waitress, real-estate agent, optician and military wife—"Yes, that's a job!"—she uses these, as well as her natural flair for creativity, to write stories that are undeniably romantic. "After all, life is the biggest romantic adventure of all—and if you're open and aware, the most marvelous things are just waiting to be discovered."

To Debbi Brod, a wonderful friend.
This one's for you!

ACKNOWLEDGMENTS

Thanks to Bob Hill, Elaine Charton and Laurie Miller for racing to the rescue when I hollered for help on P*.

Special thanks to Buck Parker of Casper, Wyoming, for coming up with facts and e-mailing them when I begged for help. Hope the hunting in Hungary is fantastic.

And a very extraspecial thanks to Debbi Brod, an EMT who gave tirelessly of her time and expertise in answer to my dumb questions. And who came up with one of the most invaluable reference books I'll ever own.

You were all great . . . and the mistakes are purely MINE.

Chapter 1

"Yuma, old son? You got a minute or two?"

At the familiar sound of Sheriff Nathan Tate's deep, gravelly voice, Yuma felt an instant lightening of his spirit. It was always good to see Nate, the only man on the face of the earth that Yuma counted as a true friend.

"Just give me a minute to tighten up these bolts, Nate." He was lying on his back on a dolly beneath the belly of Conard County's emergency helicopter. Smeared with grease and oil, he was performing routine maintenance. Heat rose from the pavement around him, summer's dying breath.

"Got any coffee inside?" Nate asked.

"Need to make it."

"I'll just go do that, then, while you finish up, son."

Nate's boot heels thudded on the cement as he walked toward the hangar and the office of the Emergency Response Team. It was quiet today in Conard County, Wyoming, a nice afternoon so far undisturbed by anything of importance. Nate nodded at Ben Grissom and Cal Simmons, the two EMTs, emergency medical technicians, on duty. They were keeping busy drinking pop and polishing the wax on the ambulance.

A good day to go fishing down by the creek or walking along some backcountry road. Maybe he could coax Marge into it, Nate thought as he stepped into the cool office. Not that Marge seemed to want to do a whole lot lately, he admitted. Maybe it was getting on high time he asked her if something was wrong.

The coffeemaker stood on a file cabinet beside Yuma's desk. It was reasonably clean; a man didn't have to be reluctant to touch it to fix a pot. It hadn't always been that way around Yuma, Nate recalled with a slight shake of his head. Not always.

Just as the coffee was finishing up, Yuma stepped into the office, wiping his hands on a rag. He was a tall, rangy man with a ravaged face and a limp he couldn't always conceal. Looking at Yuma, a man knew he was looking at someone who had an intimate acquaintance with hell.

His hair was still dark, though, and he'd filled out some in the past few years, and his color was healthy as a man's ought to be, Nate thought. Yuma was on the mend physically, at least. Well, mentally, too, or he wouldn't be piloting the county's Medevac chopper.

Yuma scrubbed up quickly in the men's room and then joined Nate for a fresh cup of coffee at the desk. Putting his feet up, he gave Nate a faint, cockeyed smile. "Just don't tell me the budget's been cut. We're on a shoestring already."

Nate shook his head. "Nothing so terrible. At least, not yet."

Yuma wasn't fooled. For Sheriff Nathan Tate to come out here in the middle of the day, during duty hours, meant he was here on business. Obviously it wasn't an emergency, but it was important or Nate would have picked up the telephone. When the radio on his hip squawked, Nate turned it down. No interruptions. Yuma tensed inwardly, knowing somehow that he wasn't going to like this at all.

"There's been some theft at some of the outlying ranches," Nate said. "More than the usual stuff, I'm afraid. And folks are blaming your friends up in the hills."

Yuma's "friends up in the hills" were homeless Vietnam veterans, men who had been unable to readapt to society and a normal way of life. Until a few years ago, Yuma had been one of them. Now, recovering, he did whatever he could to help them out.

"Nate, damn it, you know—"

Nate interrupted. "Calm down, son, and just listen. For some time now folks have thought those vets were responsible for the occasional missing item. Clothing, meat, sometimes a sickly steer. And most of the time folks turned a blind eye. We got good, charitable folks in these parts, Yuma, and you know it as well as anyone."

Yuma nodded. "Some are. Yeah."

"As long as the things that turned up missing were something those guys really needed, most folks just chalked it up to neighborly charity. Hell, son, you've carried the Christmas and Thanksgiving baskets from the churches up to those men yourself."

Again Yuma nodded. No point telling Nate just how galling that charity could be, because unless you'd ever been forced to accept charity, you had no idea what it did to your pride. Yes, he'd carried the baskets up there, baskets full of smoked turkey and canned goods, candy and blankets. The local folks meant well, and like most Westerners, they didn't scorn veterans, even sick ones.

"Anyhow," Nate said, taking a hefty swig of hot coffee, "something's changed. I'm not saying it's your friends. To tell you the truth, I don't really think it's them at all. But lately some valuables have turned up missing at a few of the outlying ranches. Some high-quality hunting rifles. Tools. Some jewelry. Nothing really big, but all of it good for pawning. And folks are starting to point at the guys in the hills."

Yuma regarded Nate grimly. "I can't do a damn thing about what folks think."

"No, but you can talk to your friends, warn 'em, suggest they keep a low profile."

"If folks are going to point the finger at those guys, I doubt there's a damn thing they can do about it."

"Just warn 'em, Yuma," Nate said harshly. "Warn 'em. I'll do my damnedest to head the trouble off at the pass, but they can damn well disappear deeper into the woods until I get a handle on it."

Yuma didn't move a muscle for the longest time. When he spoke, he sounded bitter. "You know, most of those guys collect a VA disability check every single month. It goes automatically into a bank account they never touch because they can't make themselves come out of the woods. Most of 'em could come out of those hills tomorrow and buy every one of the things that's been stolen. They got no interest in that crap, Nate. None. They don't care about money. They care about being left alone, because it hurts too damn much to be around other folks. It hurts like being skinned and having nothing but bare nerve endings all over you. I seriously doubt they're responsible for *any* of the thefts, including clothes and food. Those men are trained in survival to a level few people ever achieve. I doubt there's a thing on earth they need or want...except to be left alone."

Nate rose and carried his coffee over to the window. Outside, the concrete apron baked in the late afternoon sun, and beyond it was visible the blue line of the western mountains. Beautiful country. God's country. Nate sighed. "I'm worried about vigilantes, Yuma. Good folks won't get involved, of course, but there are some..." Shaking his head, he turned from the window and faced Yuma. "But there are others, and you know it as well as I do. So ask your friends to back off and keep clear until I can find out who the hell is behind the thefts."

After a moment, Yuma nodded. "Okay."

"I know you resent the hell out of it, man. I don't blame you."

Yuma shrugged. There was nothing more to be said. Justice and reality were often worlds apart.

Nate resumed his seat and sipped again at his coffee. Yuma shoved a box of doughnuts toward him. The sheriff shook his head. "Nope. Gotta take off twenty pounds." He patted his softening middle.

One corner of Yuma's mouth lifted. "I thought you said you'd earned it."

"I figured I had, but Doc Randall doesn't think so." And Marge wasn't interested in sex much anymore. He couldn't help but think maybe she wasn't finding him attractive these days. But he left that thought unspoken. "Twenty pounds by Christmas. Think I'll make it?"

Yuma cracked a faint smile. "With Thanksgiving in the middle? You might have to do it twice."

Nate chuckled deeply and lifted his mug yet again.

Nate was stalling, Yuma realized. The bad news wasn't finished with yet. He reached for a doughnut powdered with confectioner's sugar and bit into it, watching the sugar sift down onto the front of his sage-green flight suit. He seldom wore anything else, just flight suits and combat boots. The uniform felt comfortable. Familiar. Like himself. And he sure as hell didn't have anybody to impress.

Nate drained his mug and filled it again. Yuma's tension grew with each passing minute of delay. Damn it, he wondered, was the sheriff here to fire him?

"How're Marge and the girls?" he finally asked to fill the silence. Nate had six daughters, ranging in age from twenty-four to twelve.

"Fine. At least, the girls are. Marge I'm not so sure about." Nate wandered to the window again, steaming mug in hand. "The chopper's okay?"

"Yeah. I was just doing some routine checking. What do you mean, you're not sure about Marge?"

Nate shrugged one shoulder, keeping his back to the room. "Just a mood, I guess. It'll pass off. Listen, I figure I owe you a little advance warning on something."

Yuma put his feet down on the floor and sat up straighter in his chair. "What?"

"The hiring committee settled on a new flight nurse to head up the Emergency Response Team."

"Well, it's about time. We've been dragging like a bird with one wing ever since Steve quit two months ago." Why should he need warning about this?

Nate faced him. "Yuma, old son, they chose Wendy."

Wendy? Fully ten seconds passed before Yuma made the connection. When he did, his stomach sank like lead. "Wendy? Your daughter Wendy?"

Nate nodded. "Look, she's six years older. She swears she got over her crush on you. It'll be a purely professional relationship. You fly, she nurses. No big deal."

No big deal? No big deal? Six years ago Wendy Tate, freshly out of high school, had stalked him from one end of the county to the other and had nearly seduced the socks off him. No big deal? "Damn it, Nate!"

Suddenly Nate laughed. It was a good, hearty belly laugh.

"What the hell is so funny?" Yuma demanded.

"Life," came the answer. Nate chuckled again. "Son, I'm the father of six young, beautiful girls. They could have any man in the county—probably any man in the country—if they crooked their little fingers. It beats the hell out of me why Wendy ever wanted you, but I'll never in all my days understand why you ran so hard."

Was he losing his grip on reality? "She was just a kid, Nate. She's still just a kid. And I'm—well, you know."

"What I know is that you're one hell of a chopper pilot, and there're hundreds of guys out there who never would have come home from Nam if not for you. What I know is you flew into heavy fire all the time in that Medevac chopper and you couldn't even shoot back. What I know is you spent two years as a POW. What I know is you volunteered for all that when you were a conscientious objector and never even had to go at all. Now, to my way of thinking, that adds up to a hero, son. Maybe not a guy I want for my daughter, but a hero anyway."

Yuma muttered another curse. "Look, Nate, all that's ancient history. Let's stick to the present problem. If I'm not a guy you want for your daughter..." He trailed off, not sure what he wanted to say, knowing only that it felt as if life were dealing him yet another unfair blow. Wendy Tate? How was he going to stand having that girl prancing around out here day in and day out?

"I'm not sure you are," Nate admitted quietly, settling back into his chair. He set his mug down on the desk and regarded Yuma straight on. "I always wanted my little girls to find men with clear eyes and a good sense of humor. I want my girls to have someone who doesn't live with a passel of demons. Someone who isn't so locked up in the prison of his past that he can't see he has a future."

"You don't have to warn me—"

"I'm not warning you, son," Nate interrupted ruthlessly. "I know I don't need to warn you. You did everything short of strangling her to keep her away." He sighed and shook his head. "I'd like her to have someone her own age, not someone who's almost *my* age. I'd like her to have some young guy who could get as excited about every little thing as she can. Somebody still fresh enough to think life's a miracle."

Yuma listened silently, taking it on the chin. Hell, he already knew all this, in a general way. He was poison. Pure poison.

"But," Nate continued, fixing him with a hard stare, "should it happen she's still got her little heart set on a friend of mine, I'm counting on that friend to keep one thing in mind—I don't want her hurt."

Ten minutes later Yuma was alone at his desk, staring at a bottle of Jim Beam. That bottle had been keeping him company for more than six years now, and he still hadn't broken the seal. Would never break the seal. He kept the bottle only because he knew that if the craving ever became intolerable, it was there and he could get to it. Like a security blanket. Because in some crazy way, it was easier to tell himself no when he knew he could say yes at any time. So far the craving had never gotten so bad that he had given in.

That bottle was just one of the ten million reasons why he would never have anything to do with Wendy Tate—or any other honest woman, for that matter. Sighing now, he put it in the bottom drawer and shoved the drawer closed. The bottle, the memories, the nightmares—the list just went on and on. Billy Joe Yuma, who answered to nothing except Yuma, had enough trouble keeping his head above water as it was.

He closed his eyes, leaned back in the creaky old chair with a sigh and gave up fighting the memories. Wendy Tate had turned his summer crazy six years ago, until he had finally flat-out called her a baby and told her to grow up. Nate Tate had tried to discourage his daughter from pursuing Yuma, but there was just no stopping a woman who thought she could save a man's soul, and the younger the woman was, the more apt she was to be a zealot. Wendy had definitely been a zealot.

In spite of himself, Yuma smiled, just a faint lift of the corners of his thin mouth. She had been something else. Yessiree. Only, instead of coming after him with talk of fire and brimstone, cries of temperance and demon rum, she had talked of love—and just about succeeded in seducing him.

As he'd remarked to Nate at the time, when Wendy had been doing her level best to drive him crazy by wearing short shorts and halter tops, "My mind may be a mess, but my body parts are in perfect working order. *All* of them."

That was still the problem, Yuma thought. It was always the problem. If his body had just given up and died years ago in that hellhole, his mind wouldn't be a mess right now, would it? Of course not.

From graduation day until she left for college late in August, it had seemed that wherever Yuma looked, Wendy Tate had been waiting. Nor had the girl made any secret of what she was doing. She was stalking Yuma and she didn't care who knew it. She even told her own father, when he had ordered her to leave Yuma alone, "But, Daddy, don't you see? Yuma needs me."

Yeah, the way he had needed another hole in his head, or a frontal lobotomy, or a case of the crabs.

Nate had finally shrugged and told Yuma, "I can't get through to her, son. You try. Be rough if you have to. It's for her own good."

So he'd been rough, telling her she was a baby, that she might as well be in diapers for all he cared, and that she'd better go away and grow up before she called herself a woman. God, how he had hated to do it! Every time he remembered the look in her innocent brown eyes when he cut her to ribbons, he felt sick to his stomach. Even all these years later. And that night, Jim Beam had looked awful good. That was the closest he'd ever come to opening that bottle.

And Wendy Tate wasn't the first woman who'd thought her love could heal him. Others had tried over the years, but Yuma never gave them the chance. The one woman whose love should have healed him, the woman who had waited throughout his long years in Vietnam and in the POW camp, the one woman he honestly believed really *had* loved him, had walked out finally, unable to take any more.

That was another one of the ten million reasons why he wanted Wendy Tate out of his hair. Carla's desertion had come after a long fight to hold their marriage together. If Carla couldn't stand him, couldn't make it work, then nobody could.

The bottle and Carla. Two reasons. That left 9,999,998 reasons to go. He wanted Wendy Tate to leave him alone so that he wouldn't have to enumerate them, either to her or himself.

But most especially to her.

He knew she was there before she made a sound. The next morning, as he stood at the filing cabinet, pouring the day's first cup of coffee, he felt her behind him as if a breeze had whispered through his mind, his heart, his soul. It had always been that way with Wendy Tate, even when she was at her most maddening. Once he'd even been crazy enough to wonder if they didn't have some kind of unfinished business from another life between them.

What he knew for sure, though, right now, was that her return to his life was God's punishment on him for past sins. He was going to pay for every wayward thought, every stupid choice, every dumb thing he'd ever done, by having to look at Wendy Tate every day. By having to deal with her.

Because his body had never stopped wanting her.

He set the mug down on top of the filing cabinet and turned to face his doom.

"Hi, Yuma," she said. Softly. Quietly. She didn't step any closer.

Oh, God, he thought, she'd grown up. She really *had* grown up. In all the right places, which not even the modest khaki jumpsuit could conceal. But more, she had grown up inside. He could see it in her tentative posture, her incredibly soft brown eyes, in the short, stylish cut of her honey-brown hair.

Suddenly, in an almost-flashback, he remembered the first time he'd seen her. He'd been in Nate's jail, having slept off another drunk. He'd been hung over, red-eyed, sick as a damn dog, and he'd looked past Nate to see sixteen-year-old Wendy Tate looking at him. Not with disgust or loathing or even shock, but with a compassion that had seared Yuma's brain and left scars on his heart. He'd gone on the wagon at that very instant, and had backslid only once since.

He remembered her, so young, fresh and untouched, her long hair draped around her shoulders, her jeans and T-shirt molding a body that had only just started to bloom. He hadn't noticed she was female. He'd seen a kid. What had killed him was that a kid felt compassion for him. A kid. Damn it, that had been one of the bitterest moments of his life.

Now she was standing here years older, looking at him as if he might bite. With justification. When had he ever behaved like anything but a rabid dog around her?

The moment called for a friendly, casual smile, an equally casual hello and an invitation to come on in. He couldn't manage it. He just couldn't manage it. Instead he stood staring at her with about the same feeling he would have felt toward his executioner and said only, "Wendy."

She took a step toward him, a determined step, then stopped. He saw her hands clench into fists just before she spoke. "I acted like a crazy child six years ago," she said to him, only the faintest tremor in her voice to betray her agitation. "I—It still embarrasses me to think about it. I'm sure it embarrasses you, too. I just want you to know...I'm not a kid any longer. I won't act that way anymore. I'm here to work, nothing more."

He managed a nod. He needed to say something, he realized. If he didn't say the right thing now, the past would never be left in the past but would always loom miserably between them. This girl—woman, he amended honestly, for she surely was a woman now—this woman had done nothing except care about him. She didn't deserve his bitterness, his scorn or his lousy temperament. "Forget it," he managed finally. "Forget it. It was probably the sweetest thing anybody's ever done for me in my entire life, but past is past."

Then, realizing one thing more was necessary, he stepped forward and offered his hand. "Welcome aboard," he said as they shook.

If only it would be this easy from here on out. But he knew better. He never dealt with Wendy Tate without feeling as if he were juggling nitroglycerin. He didn't want to hurt her, he didn't want to hurt Nate, and he didn't want to get hurt himself. It was a hell of a triangle of fears to be racked on. "Let me show you around."

She smiled. "Sure."

Conard County's Emergency Response Team was necessarily small, partly because of budgetary restrictions and partly because demand wasn't heavy. All the sheriff's deputies and volunteer firemen were trained in first aid and CPR and could handle most medical emergencies until the

ERT could respond. Similarly, a group of trained volunteers stood ready to answer calls for rescue and disaster assistance.

Which left only a few full-time positions. Yuma filled one. He piloted and maintained the Medevac helicopter that was so necessary in the vast distances served by the emergency team. He also maintained all the medical equipment and the ambulance. Two emergency medical technicians also filled full-time slots, as did Wendy now, and there were four other part-time positions.

Wendy's job would involve a lot more than nursing. Not only would she head up the team, but she would be responsible for training volunteers, organizing them and soliciting donations for the unit. A little of everything.

The first thing Yuma did was hand her a pager. "Don't let it out of your sight," he said. "You're on call all the time unless you arrange something else first."

She nodded and hooked the small box to the inside of her pocket. That had been the first thing the hiring committee had warned her about. It was the primary reason Steve Wohler had left after only a year.

Yuma wore a pager, too, she noticed. But of course he would. He was always on call, as well. Nobody else could fly that Huey. She watched him bend over to pull a file from a lower drawer and wondered if he ever wore anything besides sage-green flight suits. She couldn't remember ever having seen him in anything else, not even jeans. And laced-up black boots, never cowboy boots or regular shoes.

She turned away swiftly and looked through the open door into the huge, empty hangar. God, was she crazy? What the hell difference did it make what he wore? None. Absolutely none!

"Wendy?"

He had come up right behind her, and his voice was a low, rough sound in her ear that made her shiver. Quickly, she stepped forward and turned around to face him. Instinctively, she folded her arms across her chest.

"Your desk is over here," he said, pointing with a file folder to a gray metal desk in the back corner. "This file should give you an overall rundown on what's what, and Steve left some stuff in the drawers he thought you could use."

Reluctantly, she unfolded her arms and accepted the folder.

"Bathroom's through there," he continued as if he hadn't noticed her reluctance, "and there's a cot in the back room if you need a nap sometime. Feel free to use it."

She suspected he spent most, if not all, of his nights there.

"Come on. I'll show you all the supplies and equipment. You ever use a computer?"

The time came when there was nothing more he could tell her until she started asking questions. She sat at her desk across the room from him and appeared to be absorbed in the files and notes Steve had left behind. Good, he told himself.

But was anything ever that easy? Of course not. She drew his gaze as if she were some bright, shiny object in an otherwise dull world. Inevitably, he remembered how she had felt in his arms...because naturally, she had managed to get herself there more than once that long-ago summer. Once, he'd nearly had to bite his tongue to keep from asking her if she had a balance problem of some kind, the way she was always tripping, stumbling, falling....

He felt the corners of his thin mouth lift at the memory. In retrospect it was funny. Cute, even. How many times had he caught her and found her breasts pressed to his chest? Her hip pushed into his groin. With all the innate instinct of any female animal, she had known how to flaunt her assets and arouse a man. At times that summer, he could have sworn he'd walked around in a perpetual state of arousal.

But Wendy deserved better than that, and he didn't have anything better than that to offer.

He didn't even have to close his eyes to remember how his wife, Carla, had wept when she left, her heart sundered, her grief as real as a stabbing wound, begging him to understand that she just couldn't handle it anymore. She just couldn't handle it.

At the time he had felt distant from Carla, from her leaving, from all the grief he'd caused her. A normal reaction of post-traumatic stress disorder, he had been told. To feel removed from things and people that had once been vitally important. Normal or not, he suspected that the coldness inside him had been at least as responsible for Carla's departure as anything he had done. As responsible as the whiskey, as responsible as the rages and the nightmares.

A good thing in the end, he told himself. She'd gotten out. For whatever reason, she had managed to save herself from him. She was happily married now, with two kids and a normal husband, and he told himself he was happy for her, that she deserved every good thing that came her way.

But inside... inside he resented it. He hated her for abandoning him. He hated that he had driven her away and cost himself the only happiness he'd ever known. Childish, normal, selfish feelings. Poison. Just some more of the many things that made him poison.

"Yuma?"

He glanced up and found Wendy looking at him from across the room. "Yeah?"

"What happens when you take time off? Can somebody else fly?"

He nodded. "Derek Locke fills in." Locke was a local insurance agent. "He flew Hueys when he was in the army, and he volunteers so I can have time off. He'll be on call tomorrow, as a matter of fact. I've got some business to take care of." In the hills. With men who hadn't been quite certain of him since he had left their ranks and begun his return to the world.

"You're going up into the mountains?"

Startled, he peered at her. "What do you know about that?"

She gave a small shrug and a smaller smile. "Dad mentioned it. He's right, you know. There are some nasty things being said. I've heard some of them, and I've only been back in town for a week."

"What've you been hearing?" Unconsciously, he leaned forward, his every protective instinct aroused. Those guys in the hills had nobody who gave a damn about them; somebody had to feel protective.

"Just grumbling." She sat up straighter and put a file to one side. "Some of the troublemakers at the bars are talking about fixing wagons. That kind of thing. Usually nothing comes of it. Usually."

Her brown eyes met his green ones straight on. "Can I do anything to help? You always take food up there, don't you? Why don't you let me help you shop for it later?"

"Why should you?"

As soon as the words were out, he wanted to recall them. They were a challenge, an insulting challenge he really had no business throwing, except that Wendy Tate's presence had left him feeling unsettled and unsure.

Wendy stood up abruptly, shoving her chair back so hard that it banged against the wall. "You know, Yuma, I've had six years to think about a lot of things. One of them was how bad a time I gave you that summer after I graduated. Another one of them was you. You've got the natural temperament of an ornery rattlesnake! You're right! There's no reason on God's earth why I should help you with a damn thing! I'll be outside talking to the guys."

She slammed the door behind her.

Oh, hell, he thought, and threw a battered old paperback across the room. Oh, hell!

How many years of this was he supposed to take? What was she—his personal nemesis? Why couldn't she have stayed in L.A. the way most kids did these days once they got away from home? Nobody came back to Conard County... nobody under thirty, anyway. Kids her age were supposed to be seeking the bright lights and all the fun they could find, not burying themselves in dusty old offices in the middle of nowhere with crusty old vets who were hanging on to their sanity by mere threads.

He swore, but it didn't make him feel any better. It never did. Every time he cursed he tasted soap, thanks to his mother and grandmother. Most people got over that, but not Yuma. Not him, with his outsize Quaker conscience and the feeling that he'd failed at everything he'd ever been meant to accomplish.

Now he was picking trouble with a woman he had to work with, for God only knew how long. How stupid could he get? She'd made a friendly offer, and he'd hurled it back in her face like...like a rabid dog who didn't want the damn bone anyway.

Not very charitable, kind or courteous of him. But then, he'd been a Judas to himself and his beliefs so long ago that he sometimes gave up all attempts to redeem himself. Sometimes he just wallowed in his iniquity.

Sometimes he hurt people who didn't deserve to be hurt. That was his specialty. And it seemed he was going to hurt Wendy even if he kept as far away from her as he could. Maybe he should just quit, move on, let Wendy Tate have Conard County and go find some other hole-in-the-wall for himself.

And then he thought of the guys up in the hills. Of Artie and Vance, Crazy and Boggs, Hotshot and Cowboy. What the hell would happen to them if he moved on? Because sure as hell nobody else would care about them.

So maybe he'd better mend his fences with Wendy.

Hell, this couldn't be any easier for her than it was for him. Harder, probably. She was probably still terribly embarrassed, and his rejection probably still hurt, and now she was sitting at a desk facing him....

Yeah, this was tough on her, too. The least he could do was get it under control. Maybe take her up on her offer to help with the shopping. Maybe buy her a cup of coffee and pie at Maude's. Make it clear they could be friends and that the past was dead and buried.

Yeah.

Except that Yuma, like most other vets, knew the past had a hellish way of resurrecting itself. Some little thing and there you were, mired in a memory like quicksand.

But this was different. The memories between him and Wendy weren't hellish, just... bittersweet. They could handle it. *He* could handle it.

And, damn it, he *would* handle it.

When Wendy returned to the office, her hair was windtousled and she was still smiling over her conversation with the two full-time EMTs, Ben Grissom and Cal Simmons. But then, as a rule, she liked emergency medical people. They dealt too closely with life and death and split seconds to have time for things like ego and rank that could make the average hospital a small hell sometimes. The team sense was strong in Ben and Cal, and probably would be in the parttimers, too, and that was a good sign for the future.

Turning toward her desk, she found herself face-to-face with Yuma. Not fair, she found herself thinking. Not fair that he should look better now than six years ago. The first time she'd seen him, he'd been an old man with a sick face and reddened eyes. Six years ago he'd gone on the wagon and had been regaining his health, but now...now he looked good. Too good for her peace of mind. He should have aged and shrunken.

"Yes?" she asked, keeping her tone courteous. She absolutely refused to apologize for her little temper tantrum earlier.

He looked down at her and cocked his head to one side, as if the words he wanted wouldn't quite come.

"Look," he said finally.

She waited, but he said nothing more, so she gave a little shrug and hoped he couldn't tell how hard her heart was hammering. "At what?"

"Me," he said gruffly. "Jackass extraordinaire."

She bit her lip and looked quickly away, trying to repress a sudden urge to laugh. She didn't want to laugh, damn it.

He hadn't been very nice earlier. But the laugh escaped anyway, a soft, reluctant sound.

"That's better," he said. "Okay, I'm a crud, and I'm sorry, and maybe it would be... politic if we had dinner together and ironed a few things out. Just something quick and easy at Maude's. Nothing fancy. I mean..." He sighed and ran impatient fingers through his hair. "Damn it, Wendy, we're stuck working together, and for the sake of both our sanities, we need to find some kind of... of..."

"Comfortable equilibrium," she supplied. He was right, of course. Heck, she'd taken this job as a cure. After six years she figured it was high time she got over her childish crush on this man, so she'd come back here to get a good look at his feet of clay. And they were clay, all right. Dinner with him would probably be another step in the right direction. "Great idea. Maude's for steak sandwiches?"

"Sounds good to me."

She gave him a polite smile and stepped past him. "I'll be ready in just a minute, if you want to go now."

"Sure." He watched her cross to her desk, watched her bend and start putting things away in drawers. She had a nice, full, rounded rump, he saw as she bent. A woman's butt. Any man in his right mind would want to get his hands on her. Why wasn't she married? Why hadn't some guy snatched her up and staked a claim?

She straightened and found him watching her, and it was as if everything in the universe stilled for a moment. She drew a long, deep breath. "Yuma?"

"Will you tell me something?" he asked abruptly, his voice as harsh as steel dragging over gravel. "Just one thing."

She nodded, aware that her heart was climbing into her throat. His green eyes were so intense, almost hard. This was no casual question.

"What the hell did you ever see in me?"

She looked down at her desk for a moment, then slowly lifted her head, meeting his troubled gaze. "A good heart," she said quietly. "A good heart that's been savagely wounded."

Before he could do more than draw a sharp, stunned breath, her whole expression changed. She bent and scooped up her purse. "I'll drive," she said, "but you buy."

And then she walked out of the office as calmly as if she hadn't just stripped him emotionally naked.

But she had. And he felt it all the way to his soul.

Chapter 2

Maude's Diner was not too busy when they arrived. As they stepped through the door, Yuma was momentarily grateful for the near-emptiness of the place. In all his years in Conard County he hadn't gone anywhere with a woman, and he could just imagine all the tongues wagging when word got around that he'd taken the sheriff's daughter to dinner. Well, at least he wouldn't have to hear it. And with the diner so empty, he would avoid all the looks they would otherwise have gotten.

Except from Maude, who made no attempt to disguise the speculative gleam in her eyes. Hell, Yuma thought, he should have asked the rest of the crew. But it was too late now, and suddenly Wendy was hurrying across the room toward the back corner, saying, "Ransom! Mandy! Oh, is this the baby?"

Yuma followed almost reluctantly. He didn't know either Ransom or Mandy very well, though he'd had dinner at the Tates' house with them not too long ago, and he was never quite easy with strangers. Old paranoias came back to haunt him, a subtle irritation. As for kids... well, he could take 'em or leave 'em.

Wendy did the expected thing, though, picking up three-month-old Justin Laird and cooing and gurgling the way women always did. Yuma shifted uneasily and managed a cockeyed smile as he agreed the kid was beautiful, perfect, absolutely adorable.

Long ago, when he'd been young, long before Vietnam had marked him, he'd looked forward to having children someday. He'd actually had a few stupid Hollywood notions of taking kids down to the creek to fish, out into the mountains to camp—all those "Mayberry, R.F.D." ideas. That was another dream that had gone out the window. He would make a lousy father. Hell, he was unfit for parenthood. No kid needed an old man who was so screwed up he couldn't always remember what year it was.

But Justin was a cute little bugger, and Yuma was prevailed upon to touch the soft little chin with his forefinger and admire the kid's big smile. And he didn't mind it when the little fellow grabbed his forefinger in a death grip and didn't want to let go. Something about the way those four little fingers curled around him, barely spanning the distance between his knuckles, touched him.

It was a relief, though, when the Lairds excused themselves to go home, and he and Wendy were finally alone in a booth. He looked uneasily at Wendy, expecting to see that goopy look women got when they wanted a baby of their own. Much to his surprise, she didn't have it.

"Just the steak sandwich and fries, Maude." She smiled at the old woman. "And some of your great coffee. You'll never know how I missed it while I was away."

Maude harrumphed. "Shouldn'ta stayed away so long, then. What's it for you, Yuma?"

"Same, please, but I'll have pie later."

"Made you some blueberry, special," Maude told him. She had a reputation for being one of the nastiest people in the county, but for a few favorites she made special pies. Evidently Yuma had somehow become one of them.

"Boy, don't you rate," Wendy whispered when Maude disappeared into the kitchen.

Yuma shrugged. "I eat here at least five times a week."

"Didn't anybody ever tell you about saturated fats?"

His smile broadened. "I don't believe in them. Besides, Maude's the best damn cook in the county. Hell, maybe in the entire state."

"That's because she fries everything. Everybody knows fried foods taste best." She felt herself smiling back, though, and mentally threw out all the nutritional habits she'd tried to maintain since the start of her nursing career. Tonight she was eating the best damn steak sandwich and fries this side of the Mississippi. "Dad said he's going on a diet."

Yuma nodded. "Something about Doc Randall. Remind me to keep out of his way. People who are starving to death tend to be rotten and nasty."

She laughed then, the first honest, comfortable, easy laugh that had ever escaped her around Yuma, and it seemed to drive away the last of the lingering tension between them. "I feel sorry for Mom, if you want the truth. I don't know how she's going to stand it. I've seen him in bearlike moods in the past."

"Yeah. I can remember a few myself."

"But *you* didn't have to live with him." Her smile faded, and she leaned back to allow Maude's waitress to serve her.

And suddenly the tension was back, as thick as the sandwiches on the plates before them. Yuma reached for the saltshaker and then just held it as if it were a lifeline. Six years ago, he hadn't told Wendy anything except that she was a baby, that she had been wearing diapers when he'd been rotting in that stinking POW camp, and that the generation gap between them was insurmountable.

But she was older now, much more mature, and those excuses didn't sound half as convincing now. The same twenty years separated their ages, but those years didn't seem quite as significant as they once had. God, he thought, this was going to be a living hell.

"I'm sure we can just be friends," Wendy said finally, breaking the tense silence between them. "Really, Yuma. It'll just take time to get easy together, that's all. A week, maybe two, and we'll just be old co-workers."

He didn't say anything, because he didn't have anything helpful to say. The bottom line was that she couldn't see herself through his eyes, could never know what a temptation she had always been to him. She always affected him like a promise that life hadn't kept, like something he should have had but had lost.

There was, however, something he owed her. Something that had been troubling him for six solid years. Maybe if he told the truth, things between them would be easier. Determined, he put the saltshaker down.

"Six years ago I called you a baby and said some pretty nasty things about your immaturity," he said. He didn't want to look at her while he made these uncomfortable statements, but he owed her that, too.

It crossed his mind to wonder why he never seemed to be able to take the easy way out with anything. All the way back to Nam, when his religion had given him an automatic draft exemption most young men his age would have given an arm or a leg to have. No, he'd had to volunteer to go as a noncombatant, as a medical corpsman. Instead, they'd taught him how to fly the Medevac choppers. Then he hadn't been content to fly his assigned missions but had volunteered to fly extra ones, night after night. Of course, if he'd ever slowed down long enough to actually *think* about what he was doing, he might never have been able to climb into the cockpit again.

And now he could just let the incidents of six years ago die a natural death in his memory, could just leave her believing what he'd said to her. It had worked, after all.

But his damn conscience wouldn't let him. He needed to tell her the truth, and she needed to hear it. Now she was looking at him warily, her dinner forgotten. Damn it, he'd put that wariness there, and it made him feel sick.

"About what I said," he began again. "It wasn't—you weren't— Ah, hell, Wendy, if you'd been twenty years older it wouldn't have made any difference. I'm poison to a woman. Absolute poison, and I know it. So your youth wasn't so much a problem as it was an excuse. And . . . hell, it probably protected you from me. I'm no saint, baby. What you were offering . . . well, it was damn hard to resist, and if I hadn't known I'd burn in hell for taking your innocence, I might have—might have—" An explosive but quiet curse escaped him, and he averted his face as he tried to finish. "Hell, I'd probably have done something I'd still be hating myself for."

He waited tensely for her response, for any response, thinking that somebody should have shot him ages ago. It would have saved so many people so much misery if Billy Joe Yuma had just never come home from Southeast Asia. His parents, who still couldn't look him in the eye. His ex-wife, who could have buried him for once and for all.

"Yuma? Why did you tell me this?"

As if his neck were rusty, he turned his face jerkily toward her. "Because I need you to know there's nothing wrong with *you*. Nothing. It was all wrong with *me*."

Wendy swallowed visibly and looked down at her plate. Long moments passed while neither of them said a thing. At any moment, Yuma thought, Maude was going to come busting out of that kitchen demanding to know what was wrong with the damn sandwiches. Only she didn't, and the painful silence dragged on.

Until at last Wendy lifted her head and looked straight at him with soft brown eyes that were too sorrowful for someone so young. "I acted like a child. I saw something I wanted, and I went after it with no thought to the consequences. No thought to how I might be hurting *you*. I deserved everything you said to me, and more. Much more."

"Wendy—"

She shook her head sharply, silencing him. "You had your say. Now I get mine. After—after you said those things I was pretty cut up. I went running to Dad, of course, and found him very unsympathetic. According to him, I didn't have the compassion, the wisdom or the experience to deal with somebody like you, and I'd gotten just what I deserved."

"Wendy, I—"

"Just wait." She bit her lip for a couple of moments before she continued. "I had a lot of time to think about it after I left, Yuma. I told you that earlier today. And I realized...I was telling you that I loved you, but the whole time I didn't love you enough to put *you* first. I was selfish, self-centered and totally thoughtless. I was typically eighteen. So I forgave myself eventually. And I forgave *you* ages ago." She gave him a small, sad smile. "Let's just move forward from here, okay? No regrets, no apologies, no more hurt feelings. I'm the flight nurse, you're the pilot, and if we work at it, we might even get along pretty well."

She was still young, he thought. Only someone so young could dismiss the power of the past so easily. Well, it wouldn't hurt to pretend to agree with her. If it wasn't going to work out as easily as she believed, she would find out for herself soon enough. "Okay," he said.

"What's wrong with them sandwiches?" Maude demanded suddenly, startling them both.

"Not a thing," Yuma said, turning to smile up at the old dragon. "We just got talking about work and forgot we were eating. They're fine, Maude. Honestly."

Maude humphed and headed back to the kitchen.

"God," Wendy whispered, "she hasn't mellowed one bit, has she?"

"I don't think she ever will." He bit into his sandwich and gave some thought to another thing that needed discussing. "About the guys in the hills..." he said presently.

Wendy looked up, all attention.

"I...don't like to talk about them much. I get a little...sensitive when the subject comes up. I didn't mean to snap your head off earlier."

Wendy nodded. "Well, I guess I came off a little like Miss Wendy Do-gooder when I just jumped in where I wasn't asked." Suddenly she gave him a rueful smile. "I guess some things *haven't* changed."

And damned if he didn't feel himself smiling right back. Maybe they could manage it after all.

A couple of weeks later, he was actually allowing himself to believe that they *had* managed it. He gave another swipe with the hammer, hitting the handle of a wrench in an attempt to loosen a bolt that had seized up. The old Huey's engine was getting cranky with age, and he seemed to be spending an awful lot of time on it lately.

He swore and took another swipe with the hammer, then wiped his brow with his sleeve. Damn bolt just wasn't going to do it the easy way. He loved working on engines, but he was sure Wendy didn't believe it. Twice this afternoon she'd come into the hangar when his language had turned particularly vicious.

"If you hate it so much, why don't you get somebody else to do it?" she'd asked both times.

And both times he'd said, "I don't hate it. I love it."

He *did* love it. He could gain more satisfaction from getting a cranky old engine to purr than he got out of anything else in his life. Turning the air blue with curses was just part of the process.

The hangar door was open, and as he paused to cool down a little, he looked out across the apron and open fields to the mountains. Twilight was falling, giving the peaks a violet glow against the fading pinks of the sunset. Soon there would be snow up there again, he thought. Confectioner's sugar powdering would appear in the highest places one of these mornings, a sign that autumn had truly begun.

He had to get some more blankets for the guys, he thought as he turned back to scowl at the recalcitrant bolt. Maybe he could swing some cold-weather gear, too. Artie's boots were looking ready to fall apart, and Vance's jacket had been on its last legs last year. He would have to go up there again soon, he decided, and see what they needed.

He figured he'd been pretty lucky himself, compared to some of those guys. Some of them *never* came out of the mountains. Yuma had gone up there only when he couldn't stand it anymore and had spent the rest of his time working whatever jobs he could get... until another binge got him fired. He had kept trying to pick up the threads of his life, and had kept stumbling.

Until the morning Wendy Tate had followed her father into the jail and looked at him as if... as if he were a wild thing caught in a trap and gnawing off his own leg.

Which, he found himself thinking now, was exactly what he had been.

"Yuma?"

Wendy's voice called to him from the office, and he straightened, wondering what she was still doing here. Bud and Cal, the two EMTs who were on duty tonight, had gone out an hour ago to help a woman in labor at a ranch just a few miles out of town. With the helicopter temporarily out of commission, there wasn't a whole lot for Wendy to hang around for. If an emergency arose, she could be paged by the sheriff's office, after all.

"Yuma? Could you come in here a minute?"

He put the hammer down and picked up a rag to wipe his hands with as he strolled toward the office.

"What the hell's going on?" he asked as he stepped through the door. "I didn't hear the radio or the pho—"

His words stopped as he saw the man standing in the outside doorway, a man wearing woodland camouflage and pointing the muzzle of an AR-15 straight at Wendy. Wendy stood backed up against a filing cabinet, hands held high.

Yuma froze, raising his hands, still gripping the oily rag. "What's up, friend? You need food? Medical help?"

The man's eyes swept over him. "You're Yuma?"

"That's right."

"Artie busted his leg bad," the man said.

"Did you bring him in?" Yuma asked.

"Won't come. No way."

"Hell." Yuma dropped his hands and looked at Wendy. "Is the standby unit ready to roll?"

"For what? Who's Artie, and why won't he come? Do you have any idea of the complications that can come from—"

"Save it," Yuma said sharply. "Argue with me later." He looked at the man. "Artie absolutely won't come in for help?"

"Man, he's got a grenade, and he said he'll blow himself to kingdom come before he lets another sawbones put hands on him."

Wendy's gasp was drowned out by Yuma's oath. He looked at her. "Can you set a leg?"

"No. Absolutely not! In an emergency—"

"Consider this an emergency. Grab the backpacks from the storage closet, all of them. We're going up into the mountains."

Wendy shook her head. "But he has a grenade! We're not supposed to go into situations like that!"

Yuma glared at her. "I'll be damned if I'll let Artie die. You bring what you need for his leg. *I'll* take care of the grenade!"

Ten minutes later the appropriate people had been advised, the backpacks were stowed in the back of the standby ambulance, and they were on the highway headed straight for the mountains. They followed the red taillights of the motorcycle driven by the man who had come for them. Just before they left, he had told Yuma his name was Gruber.

"Wherever Artie's at," Yuma told Wendy, "we're going to have to carry him out the hard way. These guys don't hang around near roads."

"Great! How the hell are the two of us going to get him out of there? Assuming, of course, that he gives up on the grenade and allows us to treat him. Damn it, Yuma, the law says people have a right to refuse treatment! This Artie obviously—"

"This Artie," Yuma said with heavy sarcasm, "is very likely having a flashback and is living out what happened twenty-five years ago when he stepped on a booby trap. The way I see it, I can talk to him and try to make him see reason. You're just along in case he agrees. Got it? In fact, I want you to stay well back until we get that grenade away from him."

A soft, quiet sound of protest escaped her, but she didn't respond. He could feel her tension, though, could feel her desire to argue with him as if it were a strain in the atmosphere.

"What do you know about me?" he asked her suddenly. "I mean, *really* know."

"Facts, you mean?" She turned her head and looked at him, picking out his features in the pale glow from the dash lamps. "You flew Medevac helicopters in Nam, you were a POW for nearly two years. You're divorced, no kids. And you curse like a pro."

"Did your dad ever tell you I'm a Quaker?"

She turned so she could look straight at him. "You know Dad doesn't gossip, Yuma. Otherwise I'd know an awful lot more about you."

"I guess." His hands tightened on the steering wheel, and he wondered why he felt it necessary to tell her about himself to try to make her understand Artie. She didn't need to understand Artie at all. All she would need to do was stabilize him for transport—if they could talk him into accepting medical help.

But he talked, anyway—maybe because every time something happened to remind him, his mind fixed on the subject and wore it to death. He was going to think about it, so why not talk about it?

"I didn't have to go to Nam," he said after a moment. "Because of my religious affiliation, I was automatically draft-exempt as a conscientious objector."

"Were you?" she asked quietly. "I mean, were you honestly a conscientious objector?"

"Yeah. For real. I soaked it up with my mother's milk. But I was also young, idealistic, patriotic and stupid, so I volunteered to go as a noncombatant, as a medical corpsman. I figured I could do some good, save some lives, really *help*. Uncle Sam, in his infinite wisdom, decided to turn me into a helicopter pilot and have me fly Medevac."

"That was helpful, wasn't it? I mean, transporting the victim is as essential as treatment."

He nodded, remaining silent for a few moments. "You think you're going to do some good. But nothing, absolutely nothing in the world, can prepare you for the reality of it. Nothing. And some people never learn to cope with it. It's as if...as if because you can't absorb the experience and put it away somewhere, you never stop living it."

Wendy said nothing, but he could feel her attention, her intensity, as she waited for him to speak further.

"Everybody has some nightmares. Nearly everybody has at least a few flashbacks. Some, like your dad, somehow manage to deal with it and put it away pretty quickly. At least, they appear to. Others . . . well, others never do. They call it post-traumatic stress disorder. PTSD."

"I know." She spoke quietly.

He glanced her way. "Yeah. I keep forgetting you're a nurse. Anyhow, they say that if it hits you hard and fast, right away, you'll probably be over the worst of it in six months or so. But if it takes longer to surface..." He shook his head. "Then it's going to last years. Twenty or more is a good average. So the guys who came home and were all right at first, the ones who kissed Mom and hugged the wife and tossed the kids in the air and acted like they'd been on a vacation . . . they're the ones who got it worse in the end.

"It showed up later, maybe five, six years later for some of them. That's why you didn't hear much about it until long after the war was over. So many guys just got on that plane in Nam and buried it . . . and then found it all surging up years later, like a damn backed-up sewer. . . ."

For long, long minutes there was no sound in the cab save the rumble of the ambulance's engine. Finally Wendy spoke.

"Was that... how it was for you?"

"Yeah. I came back from the POW camp feeling like king of the world. I was free, safe. And I'd learned how to play mind games with myself. Good mind games. I learned to imagine things so intensely that I could be out of that camp in an instant, totally unaware of the place. I learned to escape inside my head. They could put me in the hole for days, and I'd just fly to the moon. In real time. I don't mean any ten-minute dream, I mean a minute-by-minute real-time experience. Once I built a house nail by nail. It took me seven months."

"I can't imagine it."

He looked over at her and then returned his gaze to the road. "Most people can't. Don't even try. Anyway, that kind of stuff has a price. I buried it all so deep that it was four years before the sewer backed up. I remember the first time I had a flashback. Carla—my wife—came home from work and found me in the backyard dug in behind the rosebushes and curled up in a fetal ball. I thought the chopper had just crashed and I was hiding from the VC. I couldn't even hear her when she talked to me."

He braked to follow Gruber's motorcycle as it turned onto an old logging road. They jolted down the rutted road for a while before he spoke again.

"That's what you need to understand, Wendy. If you understand nothing else about a flashback, you need to know that it's real. It's not a dream. The person having it is really *there,* as if he'd slipped his place in time. His body is here, but his mind is very much in the other time and place. It's real, it's now, and you don't even exist for someone who's having one. And to the person who has them, it's as if he has no anchor in time. One minute he's here, the next he's there. And he never knows when the shift will happen."

"Like being a time traveler out of control."

"That's one good way of putting it."

They drove several miles along the old logging road before a flare of brake lights warned them that Gruber was stopping. The moon was full, bright, giving helpful illumination as they pulled to a halt along one side of the road.

Gruber came round to Yuma's door. "We walk from here."

"How far?" Yuma asked.

"Maybe two klicks."

Yuma looked at Wendy. "A little over a mile. Can you make it?"

"Of course." Lugging backpacks, back boards, equipment cases, oxygen. Sure, a mile would be a snap.

Gruber helped. Among the three of them, they managed to carry everything Wendy felt she would need to immobilize the fracture, relieve pain and treat shock—even though she considered shock highly unlikely now. If Artie was going to suffer from it, he'd probably have done so long since and it would be too late to help him.

The hike through the woods was strange, silent. Gruber wasn't talkative, and Yuma seemed to have sunk deep into thought. Gruber picked a relatively easy trail, though, requiring little climbing or expertise, though it was far from an easy stroll. The moon rose higher and higher, and the shadows grew more and more dense.

It was eerie, Wendy thought, this dark walk through dark woods at night. It felt almost as if she were leaving her world behind and passing through a tunnel to another reality.

Which, she realized with sudden force, was exactly what she was doing. These men didn't live in her world. Hadn't lived in her world since the day they shipped overseas.

Post-traumatic stress disorder was a fancy name for minds and souls that had been shattered by violence. Rape victims frequently suffered from it. Why should it be hard to understand that men who had lived through endless days of hell should suffer as much or more?

"Easy." Yuma caught her arm as she stumbled on a small boulder.

Dragged out of her thoughts, she was suddenly aware again of the dark forest around them, of the restless sighing of the wind in the treetops, of a distant owl's haunting cry. It was cold, dark and desolate. As cold, dark and desolate as the lives of the men who lived out here. God, couldn't anyone help them? A shudder ripped through her.

Suddenly Yuma, still holding her arm, halted. "Gruber," he called softly. "Hold up a minute."

A grunt was the only response, but Wendy saw Gruber's shadow halt in the darkness beneath a tree.

"You okay?" Yuma asked her.

"I'm fine," she said softly. "Just fine." Except for a feeling that her perception of things was about to be irrevocably altered. Except for a suspicion that she would never again be the same person she'd been once she walked out of these woods later tonight. Her dad had been right, she thought now with a sick feeling in the pit of her stomach. She didn't have the experience or wisdom to deal with this.

"You shivered," Yuma said. "Are you cold? Or afraid?"

"Both," she admitted. "I'm okay. Really. Let's go."

But he didn't move immediately. He was looking down at her, and since her face was turned up to the moonlight, she was sure he could read every nuance of her expression. She wondered what he saw there. His own face was in shadow, unreadable. "I won't let anything happen to you," he said.

"I know that, Yuma," she answered through a throat grown suddenly tight. "I wouldn't be here otherwise."

She heard him draw a sharp breath and wondered what she had said to startle him so. But before she could question him, he turned. "Let's go," he said roughly. "Artie's waiting."

The first sign that they had reached their destination was the orange glow of firelight. It was a welcome sight in the dark forest, a beacon that drew them in.

When they reached the small clearing, Wendy froze. This was it, she realized. The bottom rung on a long ladder of despair. Shacks had been built of old boards and tarps. A couple of motorcycles were drawn up beneath a sagging lean-to. A table had been hammered together from rough logs, and around it were scattered tree-stump chairs and a solitary, rusty lawn chair. From a rope clothesline hung a couple of threadbare towels, some Jockey shorts and T-shirts.

And nowhere was there another soul in sight.

Then she heard a soft rustling sound. Swinging around, she saw eyes gleaming in the dark and gasped. Yuma's arm closed tightly around her waist and hauled her snugly up against his side.

"Shh," he said. "Shh. They heard us coming and they're checking us out."

Slowly she became aware that other eyes watched from the very edge of the firelight. They were surrounded.

"It's Yuma, all right," said a voice in the darkness. "Who the hell is the woman, Gruber?"

"A nurse," Yuma said. "You know damn well I wouldn't know what to do for Artie."

"Not a doctor?"

"She's a nurse. Period."

The eyes moved closer, and now Wendy saw the gleaming barrels of guns leveled at her and Yuma. Instinctively, she edged even closer to the hard side of the man who was her only protection.

"Come off it, Vance," Yuma said irritably. "Are we gonna help Artie or not?"

Another few moments passed in tense silence, and then Vance stepped into the light. "Yeah, we're gonna help Artie. He's in the shack."

Yuma turned Wendy to face him. "You stay right here. Don't move an inch. I'll try to get that grenade away from him, but don't come any closer until I do."

"Yuma..."

He shook his head, silencing her. "Gruber? Cowboy? Make sure she doesn't come any closer. If the sheriff's daughter gets blown up, he's going to be all over you guys like flies on rotting meat."

A snicker came out of the dark, but suddenly Gruber was there, nodding. "You got it, man." And beside him stood another armed man in tattered camouflage.

Yuma helped Wendy out of her backpack, then dropped his own to the ground beside hers. "Artie won't hurt me," he told her quietly. "I'm just going to try talking to him. You stay here until I get him calmed."

She wanted to stop him. It was apparent in every line of her face. She was scared to death for him. Her eyes searched his face wildly for a moment, but then she bit her lip and simply nodded.

She stood with Gruber and Cowboy and watched Yuma cross the campsite and disappear into the ramshackle hut.

"Damn Quaker," Cowboy muttered. "Always rushing in like a damn fool, sticking his neck out. Always trying to save some *other* damn fool."

Wendy looked at the man called Cowboy and saw someone else beyond him nod agreement. Then she looked back at the hut and waited, everything inside her frozen in an agony of dreadful anticipation.

Inside the hut a couple of oil lamps burned, casting yellowish illumination across the cot where Artie lay. The man was clearly in severe pain, with sweat beading his brow despite the night's chill. A crude splint had been manufactured for his leg out of old boards, then tied in place with rags. A blood-soaked wad of cloth lay on his shin.

"Artie." Yuma waited for the man's gaze to focus on him. When at last it did, Artie forced a smile.

"Yuma, man! What're you doing here?"

"Trying to talk some sense into you, I guess." He stepped closer and saw that Artie was holding the grenade to his chest. The pin had been removed, but Artie's grip kept the lever depressed so it wouldn't explode. But if he let go of that lever.... "If you fall asleep, man, you're going to be one hell of a mess."

"Yeah. I keep thinking about that." Artie gave a humorless chuckle. "It'd sure be a quick solution."

"Maybe. But, hell, Artie, you ought to know you don't always die when you should. Then you get left walking around with parts missing and pains you never had before." Unconsciously, he rubbed his own aching leg, the decades-old reminder of the copter crash and subsequent prison camp abuse.

"Ain't that the truth," Artie said grimly. "Damn booby trap shoulda killed me."

"Well, this broken leg might. Why don't you let me get you some help? I brought a nurse up with me. Maybe she can do something."

"She'll just want to take me to some hospital, and I ain't never again gonna let some damn butcher put his hands on me. Never!"

Sighing, Yuma pulled up a stool and sat, taking care not to get so close that Artie might get nervous. "You afraid of having a cast put on?"

"I'm afraid they'll take the damn leg off! Like they took all that other stuff last time. Damn it, I ain't even a man anymore!" He half sat in his agitation, then fell back on the cot, groaning. "Damn butchers," he said through his teeth.

"There's more to a man than that," Yuma said quietly.

"Damn wife didn't think so."

"So she was stupid. Doesn't mean you have to believe her."

Artie gave a dry, raspy chuckle at that. "It's time to die, Yuma. That's all. It's time. There just ain't any point in it. Hasn't been any point in years. Now this. Might as well finish it."

"But are you sure this would finish it?"

Artie turned his head and glared straight at him. "Now don't start giving me that damn Quaker crap."

"What Quaker crap? Even Hamlet wasn't sure death was the end."

A few seconds later Artie dropped his head back on the dirty pillow. "Yeah. Okay, so maybe it wouldn't finish it. But it sure as hell can't be any worse!"

"Wish I could guarantee that."

Artie laughed again, that same dry, raspy chuckle. "Damn it, Yuma, you're good. What about this nurse? What do you expect her to do?"

"Take a look at you and tell you what your options are, that's all. You can refuse treatment even after she looks at you. But *she* can tell you what you're facing. And maybe it's not time to die."

Artie looked away briefly. "It's a bad break, Yuma," he finally said, his voice little more than a whisper. "Really bad."

"You'd probably be surprised how well they could fix it. Come on, man. Give me the grenade and let her look at it. Just let her look."

"She can look while I hold the grenade."

For a heartbeat Yuma didn't answer. When he did, his voice, soft until now, was threaded with steel. "No, Artie, she can't. You can kill yourself, and you can kill me, but no way on God's earth am I going to risk *her.*"

Chapter 3

"I can't stand this." Wendy barely whispered the words, but Cowboy and Gruber both looked at her.

"Waiting is always tough," Cowboy said after a moment. "Don't worry, lady. Artie won't hurt Yuma."

"But if he's in shock, he could be combative, aggressive..." She looked at Cowboy. "Has he been bleeding?"

"Not a lot, but probably slow and steady for a couple of hours."

"Then he *could* go into shock. At any moment. I've got to get in there."

"Wait just one minute," Gruber said, grabbing her arm. "Yuma said—"

"I know what Yuma said. I know the man has a grenade. I also know they're both apt to get killed if Artie goes into shock. He could lose control of that grenade."

She could feel the uneasiness of the men beside her as they weighed what she said. Neither of them, she realized, wanted to see anyone get hurt. For some reason that surprised her. Perhaps because they looked so hard, so rough around the edges and uncaring. Stereotyping, she thought. I'm stereotyping.

And suddenly she looked around her with new eyes and saw not men who couldn't cope, but men who had been wounded so badly they still hadn't recovered. Invisible injuries might not bleed, but they could be every bit as devastating, and much harder to heal.

"Artie needs help," she heard herself say, then took a step toward the shack. Cowboy grabbed her arm and halted her.

"You go in there and startle Artie and you might get a lot of people killed." He stared down at her, his gaze intense and slightly wild, as if he were controlling himself by a massive exercise of will. Suddenly he looked past her, and she instinctively turned to see what had grabbed his attention.

Yuma was stepping out of the shack, a grenade in his hand. "Vance? Artie said you have the pin for this?"

"Yeah, got it right here." Vance crossed the site and bent toward Yuma, reinserting the pin, rendering the grenade once again harmless.

"Okay, Wendy," Yuma said, lifting his head to look across the fire at her. "Artie says you can look at his leg. He's still not consenting to treatment."

She bent to lift the backpacks, but Cowboy and Gruber beat her to it. They followed her across the clearing, carrying all the equipment.

They didn't enter the shack with her and Yuma, though. Only Vance joined them, and he stayed well back, like a guard, though whom he was guarding wasn't clear.

Wendy hesitated, giving Artie time to look her over. He spoke first.

"The sheriff's daughter, huh?"

"Wendy Tate," she replied, nodding. "Can I look at your leg?"

Artie waved a hand. "It ain't pretty, lady. Bone's sticking out and looks like snapped matchwood. Damn butchers'll probably want to cut it off."

Wendy neither agreed nor disagreed. Approaching the cot, she knelt beside the injured man and touched his cheeks and forehead, finding sweat but not the clamminess of advancing shock. His pulse was rapid but strong, so he was still withstanding the effects of the blood loss.

"I need to take your blood pressure," she told him as she turned to his injured leg and pressed her fingertips to his ankle to find the distal pulse. It was there, so his circulation wasn't impaired.

Then she lifted the bloody wad and looked at the lacerated skin of his shin where the bone poked right out, exposed. Just like snapped matchwood, as he'd said. The surrounding area was swollen dark with bruising. Gently, she laid the rag back over the wound, to keep the air out.

"Here." Yuma had dug the blood pressure cuff out of one of the packs, along with a stethoscope. He handed it to her.

"Everybody be quiet for a minute," she said, and pumped the cuff up. When she was satisfied, she removed the stethoscope from her ears and loosened the blood pressure cuff on Artie's arm, but left it in place.

"Okay," she said, looking the man straight in the eye. "From the size of the bruise in your leg, you've lost a liter of blood into the bruise itself, never mind how much more you may have lost to external bleeding. You're hovering on the edge of shock, and it won't take much to throw you over. A little more blood loss could sure do it. Then you'd probably go into cardiovascular collapse and die. Your heart's already beating too hard, trying to keep up with the reduced blood volume."

Artie nodded. "The leg?"

"I think you know about the leg. You've still got a strong pulse in the ankle, so you don't have to worry about losing your lower leg to gangrene, okay? But you're damn well going to get infected. You need to go to a hospital."

"No."

Wendy sat back on her heels and looked at him, trying to decide what was the best approach to take. Some people you needed to sweet-talk. Some people you needed to yell at. Some people you needed to get downright nasty with.

"If you don't go to a hospital," she said presently, "you're going to die. There's no question of that at all."

"So maybe it's time to die." He thrust out his chin a little.

"Maybe it is." She tilted her head. "Of course, there are a lot of different ways to die, Artie. You could die in the next hour or so from shock. That'd probably be the easiest way to go. You could get a really bad infection of some kind, something that would kill you in a few days. And then, of course, you could always take weeks to die from it. Some people just don't die easy, Artie. They take days. Weeks. And you *could* still get gangrene and die by inches if you don't get treated. I hear that's one of the most painful ways to go."

Artie swore. "You don't pull any punches, do you?"

"Why should I? You talk about dying like it's an entertaining thing to try some evening when there's nothing else to do. I'm a nurse. I've seen a lot of people die, and I'm telling you, most of 'em didn't find it a fun experience!"

He glared at her, baring his teeth and lifting his head and looking for all the world like he wanted to take a piece out of her. "I've seen 'em die, too, missy. By the dozens! Cut into little pieces. Burned alive. Blown up. Gut shot! No, it ain't pretty! But it's *final!*"

She leaned forward, glaring right back. "If—*if* we get you to the hospital and onto intravenous antibiotics as soon as possible, you'll probably be walking again in a few weeks. But every minute we waste increases the likelihood of osteomyelitis—bone infection—and that's hell to treat. You need a good surgeon who'll put your leg back as good as new!"

"Surgeon! Butcher, you mean! They cut a man up and throw away pieces like they don't count...like nothing counts...." He turned his face away from her suddenly and fell silent, breathing heavily.

He was trying not to cry, Wendy realized with an unexpected, abrupt wrenching in her heart. He was trying not to cry. This man was at the end of his rope emotionally, mentally, physically. Maybe death did sound easy.

Slowly, taking care not to startle him, she reached for his hand and held it tightly. "I'll stay with you, Artie. I swear nobody will cut off your leg. I'll be right there, and I won't let them. And if they say that's the only way, I promise I'll make them wake you up and let you decide. I promise."

It seemed like forever, but finally he turned his head and looked at her. "Why should you?"

"Because it's a little thing to do if it'll get you into treatment. Because I hate like hell to lose a patient."

"I'm not your patient." But he didn't look quite so fierce.

"Not *yet,*" Wendy agreed.

After a moment, Artie sighed. "Oh, hell, all right. But I won't let 'em cut it off."

"Then neither will I."

Oxygen, an I.V., back board, basket stretcher, padding in between the splints to prevent movement of the leg in any way. She put her own splinting over what the vets themselves had done because she didn't want to risk jarring the bone, possibly interrupting circulation. It was slow, painstaking work, careful, cautious work, and Artie was out of it through the whole thing, because as soon as she got him on the I.V., Wendy injected morphine.

They had plenty of willing hands, though, to help them carry Artie and the equipment out of there to the ambulance. Wendy wondered just how many vets were actually hiding in these mountains; in no time at all a dozen men had appeared to lend a helping hand, to take turns carrying Artie and the equipment.

It was a silent, strange procession through the woods back to the logging road. No one talked, no one joked or even swore. Wendy could almost imagine that it must have been like this in the past, during the war, when they carried a wounded comrade through hostile territory. And she wondered how many of them were reliving that right now.

Because they were so silent, little more than dark, dangerous-looking shadows in the night, she would never know. Back at the ambulance, they loaded Artie gently, jarring him not at all.

And then she and Yuma and Artie were headed back down the logging road. Back to the real world.

Looking at the back of Yuma's head as he drove, while she sat in the rear and kept watch over Artie, Wendy found herself wondering about that. Wondering if Yuma ever *did* really get back to the real world. Or if he carried the lost silence of those men in his own soul no matter where he went.

The hospital lights were startling after the long drive in the darkness. Artie, under the influence of the morphine, had dozed almost the entire way. But the lights disturbed him, and as soon as he saw the hospital and the orderlies in white uniforms, he tensed up again.

"Easy," Wendy said soothingly. "I'll be there. So will Yuma. We'll take care of you, Artie."

"I shoulda seen that damn booby trap!" Artie cried out. "I shoulda seen it! It got Murf. I saw him. God, he was just hamburger!"

Yuma climbed out of the driver's seat and came into the back so he could lean close to Artie.

"Hey, man," he said. "It's over. It's over. You're okay now. You're okay."

Wendy kept the waiting orderlies back while Yuma quietly talked Artie into the present. It took a while, and as Wendy listened she began to understand the true depth of Artie's wounds. And Yuma's. God, she thought, it must be so hard for him to sit there and talk Artie down like that. So hard to be reminded of what he lived with himself, so hard to hang on to his own calm and reason.

But he managed. His voice never lost its soothing cadence, his patience never faltered. Finally they were able to move Artie into the emergency room.

Yuma stayed with Artie while his clothes were cut off, and Wendy collared Dr. MacArdle in the corridor to explain about Artie.

"I understand what you're saying, Wendy," he said when she finally ran down, "but I'm not the person you'll have to deal with. We need to stabilize him and then ship him to a bigger hospital. He needs an orthopedic surgeon, not me."

"There's no way he'll agree to that! It was hard enough to get him this far!"

"Then I guess we have a real problem."

Suddenly Yuma came out of the cubicle and grabbed both Wendy and MacArdle by their arms. "Artie's got a grenade. Don't ask me how the hell he managed it, but when the nurse went to remove his shirt, he pulled it out of a pocket."

"I thought he gave it to you!" Wendy said.

"It appears he had more than one." He urged them toward the exit. "Clear out of here. Tell everyone else to get out. Call the sheriff and tell him what's coming down. We're definitely going to need the area cleared. In the meantime, I'll try to talk Artie out of this."

MacArdle moved immediately to take care of it, shooing a few more people out of the building ahead of him. Wendy stayed, stubbornly clinging to Yuma's arm.

"What happened?" she asked. "What set him off?"

"Who the hell knows? Half the time he thinks he's in Nam. Damn it, now he's really screwed!" Turning, he slammed his free hand savagely against the wall. "Damn it! Let go of me, Wendy. Just get your sweet little butt out of here."

"I can't. You can't possibly expect me to let you—"

Suddenly she was off her feet and falling across his shoulder with an "Oof!" as her diaphragm connected hard with muscle. "Don't be a fool, woman," he growled. "There's not a damn thing you can do except keep yourself in one piece!"

Gasping, she tried to pull air into her lungs as Yuma carried her out of the emergency room and into the parking lot beyond. Furious, she hammered his back with her fists and tried to find enough air to speak. To shout.

He ignored her. The harder she tried to get away, the tighter his hold grew, until his fingers were biting painfully into her thigh. Then, suddenly, she was airborne again and falling backward into ready arms.

"Keep her here," Yuma growled. He turned and stalked back to the emergency entrance.

Stunned, Wendy stared after him and then looked at the two orderlies who were holding her by her arms. "Let me go," she said.

They shook their heads and continued to hold her.

As she calmed down, though, she was forced to admit Yuma was right. She didn't know how to handle a man with a grenade. Had no idea how to talk to him or calm him. Had no experience with such things. All she could do was add another factor to a complicated equation.

And the only reason she hadn't wanted to let Yuma face it alone was because of her feelings for him. It had been a gut reaction, not to let him go into danger alone. It had been a purely irrational, purely protective instinct.

The first deputies arrived, their flashers casting lurid colors around the parking lot. Nate wasn't far behind. The first thing he did was assure himself that Wendy was all right and that everyone had been moved away from the danger zone.

And then the waiting began.

"Why don't you go home, baby?"

Wendy tugged her denim jacket closer and looked up at her dad, shaking her head. "I can't. Yuma's in there. I'd just worry myself sick."

Nate sighed. "I thought you said you were over him."

"Come on, Dad, I'd worry myself sick over any friend of mine."

"Yeah." He snorted softly. "I'm kind of upset with him myself. He never should have taken you out to the woods when he knew this guy had a grenade."

Wendy turned and faced him. "Wait a minute. Am I or am I not a grown woman? Am I or am I not the chief emergency medical officer in this county? Are you telling me that Yuma shouldn't let me do my job? And why should he do that? Because I'm your daughter?"

"He carried you out of that hospital." Nate's scowl was enough to make most men quail.

"And he never let me get anywhere near Artie while he had that grenade." It was killing her that there was nothing she could do. Yuma must be talked just about hoarse by now...if this hadn't reawakened his own nightmares.

"Gage is on his way back from Denver," Nate remarked. "Maybe he'll be able to talk this guy down. He's had hostage-negotiation training."

"I didn't know that. But Yuma isn't a hostage, Dad."

"No, but the whole damn hospital *is*."

Hours had passed. Endless, terrifying hours while Wendy counted minutes and wondered if Yuma would ever walk out of there. If this night had accomplished nothing else, she found herself thinking bitterly, it had shown her just how far she still had to go to get over Yuma.

And she *had* to get over him. Tonight had really brought that home to her. After seeing Artie, she was beginning to develop an appreciation of what Yuma had been through and of the delicate psychological balances he must have learned to maintain in order to rise above it. Her dad was right—she didn't have the experience or wisdom to deal with it, and therefore she might seriously hurt him. Never before had she understood just how easy that would be.

There was movement in the emergency room, a shadow visible through the doors. *Yuma*. Wendy recognized his lanky silhouette in her heart. She straightened, holding her breath. Beside her, her father stiffened. The swinging door opened, and the figure stepped out.

"Nate?" Yuma called.

"I'm right here, buddy."

"Artie wants me to take him back up into the mountains."

"But what about his leg?" Wendy called out. Immediately her father's hand clamped her arm in a vise-like grip.

"Shh!" he said sharply. "Don't get in the middle of this."

"Artie's not too worried about his leg," Yuma said. "He doesn't seem to be worried about too much except getting out of here. I told him I'd take him. Problem is, I can't carry him out of here by myself, especially with his leg the way it is. If I hurt him too much, he might let go of that grenade."

"So what do you need?" Nate asked.

"I told Artie I'd get somebody I really trust in here to help."

Suddenly Wendy understood. She drew a hissing breath. Oh, God, this was so dangerous! Instinctively, she started to move forward, but her father's grip restrained her.

"Who do you want?" Nate asked.

"Micah."

Wendy's head swiveled, and she searched the crowd of law-enforcement people for the huge Cherokee deputy. It wasn't hard to find him—he towered over nearly everyone else. And she knew why Yuma wanted him. Micah had spent more than twenty years in the Special Forces. If anyone could safely get that grenade away from Artie, Micah would be the one.

"Here I am, man," Micah said. He stepped forward out of the crowd so that he was clearly visible. "How do you want to do this?"

"No gun, Micah. No weapons. Leave whatever you have out there, and then come in here. He wants me to search you."

"You got it." Micah unbuckled his gun belt and passed it to another deputy.

Wendy watched, wondering how Yuma had managed to gain so much of Artie's trust, and wondering how bad he was going to feel about this deception. Pretty rotten, she guessed—if he survived. Her fingernails dug into her palms as she watched Micah walk slowly toward the emergency entrance, and she began to pray feverishly.

"Smart move," Nate murmured approvingly. "Smart move." He ordered his deputies to move farther back and lie down.

Minutes dragged by in nerve-stretching silence. Finally, a lifetime later, Micah and Yuma reappeared, and this time they were pushing Artie on a gurney. They maneuvered him up to the rear doors of the ambulance and opened them up. Micah leaned over Artie.

"Okay, man," they all heard Micah say. "I'm going to lift you now. That means I gotta grab."

"Okay."

He grabbed then, all right. His arm moved as swiftly as a striking snake and grabbed the grenade right out of Artie's hand. Yuma snatched the grenade from Micah and began to run across the parking lot, away from the gathered police, while Micah forcibly held Artie down, making sure the man couldn't give them any more surprises.

"Oh, God, no..." The words passed Wendy's lips as little more than a taut whisper while her eyes followed Yuma's vanishing shadow as he ran unevenly toward the open acres behind the hospital. "Oh, please, God..."

When the grenade went off, no one moved.

The roars and whines of helicopter engines and rotors, the loud concussions of explosives, had damaged Yuma's hearing years ago. He figured the grenade had just wiped out a few more frequencies.

His ears were still ringing when Wendy fell to her knees beside him.

"Yuma? Yuma?"

She sounded muffled, as if she were speaking under water.

"I'm okay," he said. His own voice sounded as if his ears were stuffed with cotton. "Okay." He rolled onto his back and looked up at her. The full moon was nearing the western horizon, and it cast a silvery glow over one side of her face. He wanted... Oh, God, he thought miserably, he wanted to just reach out and pull her into his arms. It had been so damn long since he had held anybody. So damn long since anybody had held him. "Artie?"

"I imagine they're putting him in restraints right now. Are you sure you're all right?"

"I'm fine." A crowd was gathering. Time to get up. He hated crowds. "I'm just fine. Let's go see about Artie."

He felt a momentary dizziness as he shoved himself to his feet, then suddenly realized that he hadn't had a flashback. If anything should have precipitated one, that grenade going off should have done it. But it hadn't. A deep internal tension, one he had lived with for a quarter of a century, eased just a little.

Emergency-room staff had come racing to his aid, but when he stood up, they congratulated him. As they walked back to the hospital, he had to endure some backslapping from medical personnel and deputies he'd worked with over the years.

In the midst of the confusion and the almost celebratory atmosphere, he glanced at Wendy and found her watching him gravely. That look reached him somehow. "What?" he said.

She shook her head.

He looked away and stomped around the corner of the building, heading for Artie. She'd seen what it was about, he thought angrily. She'd seen Artie, and by extrapolating, she knew just how screwed up Billy Joe Yuma had been. Probably still was. Well, that was one less reason he would have to cite.

Except that she hadn't been coming on to him the past couple weeks. Not at all. She'd been friendly, but no more than she would be to anybody. She hadn't wiggled, hadn't teased and hadn't shown him an inch of skin, not like she had that long-ago summer. She'd given up on him, he realized. And this evening had merely added another brick to the wall he'd wanted between them. That was good.

Wasn't it?

They had Artie in restraints, all right. His wrists and his one good leg were tied to the gurney. Two more straps crossed his chest and hips. Dr. MacArdle was leaning over him, talking earnestly, while Artie glared furiously.

"The longer you keep us from treating you, Artie," MacArdle was saying, "the likelier it gets that you *will* need amputation. The danger of infection is increasing with every minute. I want to give you morphine and start you on an intravenous antibiotic. Then I want Yuma to fly you out to a hospital where they can fix your leg so you can walk again."

"The minute I get the chopper running," Yuma agreed. He limped up to the gurney and just stood there. Artie saw him almost immediately.

"You tricked me, man."

"Yeah. I couldn't let you do it, Artie."

"Why not?" Artie demanded, and there was no mistaking the anguish in his voice. "Why the hell not? What the hell is the point to it, man? Tell me, damn it! What the hell is the point?"

What the hell is the point?

Yuma was still wondering hours later as he lay on his back in a dingy motel room trying to get enough sleep so that he could safely fly himself and Wendy home once Artie's leg was set. Wendy was keeping her promise not to leave the man's side, and Artie, out of it on morphine, had thanked her at least forty times. The orthopedic surgeon hadn't been thrilled, but, he *had* been understanding, and the last Yuma had seen of Wendy, she'd been wearing fresh green scrubs and heading into the surgical anteroom with Artie.

"Get some sleep, damn it," she'd said over her shoulder to Yuma. "Tell the gray lady in the waiting room where I should look for you later."

He was past arguing. He needed, desperately, to be alone. He hadn't always been that way, but since Nam there were times when the mere presence of other people seemed to cause his nerves to jangle, to make his skin feel almost raw.

It didn't happen very often anymore, but it was happening now.

The cool darkness of the motel room soothed him. Air-conditioning pumped away the warmth of the August afternoon and drowned the sound of passing traffic. He'd walked close to some of his worst memories last night, he realized. Awfully close.

Memories of hiding out in those same woods, of walking endless miles across rough terrain, driven by a formless anxiety that wouldn't let him hold still. Memories of nightmare visitations set off by things as innocuous as a rumble of thunder over the mountains. The present fractured by the past. Emotional earthquakes that cracked internal dams and thrust up buried corpses to lie rotting in the unforgiving glare of the mind's eye.

He remembered plenty of times when death had looked like a viable alternative and the only thing that had stayed him had been his upbringing. His mother's gentle face as she told him again and again that nothing—*nothing*—justified violence. A lot of guys in his boat didn't have that to stop them. An awful lot of them tried to kill themselves. Some, like Artie, got stopped. Most succeeded.

And Yuma wasn't at all sure that they weren't the lucky ones.

The gray lady told Wendy that Yuma had gone to a motel within walking distance, so she hoofed it, needing the fresh air and sunshine after a night and a day during which she had felt as if she were caught up in another reality. The darkness of last night's trek into the woods, the hours spent in the parking lot, the predawn flight with Artie had all combined to leave her feeling dislocated. A few hours of sleep would probably straighten that out, she told herself. She would be back to normal in no time.

It was Yuma she was worried about. Something about the look on his face last night after he'd taken care of the grenade had told her how close to the bone the whole night had come for him. It must, she thought, be terrible not to be able to trust your own mind.

It wasn't much of a motel. The desk clerk, obviously never having heard about guest privacy, and not caring, gave her Yuma's room number without a moment's hesitation. It was down at the far end of the row of rooms, and she stood there a minute wondering if she should wake him. But if she didn't, he wouldn't know where to find her whenever he was ready to fly back. Sighing, she leaned wearily against the wall and knocked on the door.

He hadn't been sleeping. She knew it by how fast he opened the door. He stood there, blinking in the bright light, his flight suit unzipped nearly to his waist, revealing a chest matted with dark hair. "Artie?" he said.

"He's doing just great. They pinned his leg, and the surgeon said the prognosis is excellent." Except, of course, for the little matter of the grenade and whether he was going to be charged with a dozen crimes.

Yuma reached out, snagging her wrist gently and drawing her into the darkened, cool room. "You look beat," he said. "Hot and tired. Just stretch out while I go rustle you up a cold drink. Have you eaten anything?"

"A candy bar a couple of hours ago. I'm okay."

But he didn't listen. Leaving her on the room's one double bed, he went out to find something for her. There was a hamburger joint around the corner. He figured her lip would curl over all the grease—for two weeks he'd watched her eat yogurt, fruit and rabbit food—but he didn't give a damn. She needed a solid meal and a sugar fix. No doubt about it.

When he returned with his greasy treasure, she was sitting up, propped against the pillows. She'd ditched her shoes and socks and had her ankles crossed, and something about the sight of those small bare feet hit him hard. Small, bare, dainty, pink. Smooth skin. Damn, she had pretty feet.

And he didn't want to notice that.

She arched a brow at the sight of the bags he was carrying. "A cardiac lunch, I see."

"I think the bags have soaked up most of the grease."

She laughed then, a small, weary sound. "Hand it over, Yuma. It smells too good to be believed."

She didn't even turn down the french fries. She ate her own and some of his, as well. Finally, she flopped back on the pillows with a sigh and pronounced herself stuffed.

"When do you want to head back?" she asked.

"Not until later."

Something in his tone snagged her attention, and she opened her eyes to look up at him. They'd turned on the reading lamp to eat by, and now it highlighted his ravaged face, accentuating the deep gouges life had left on him.

"This has been terrible for you, hasn't it?" she asked softly.

His gaze pinned her. "Why do you say that?"

She heard defensiveness in his tone, read it in his stiffening posture. "Because going through all this with Artie must have felt like having the scab torn off a wound that won't heal."

He wanted to deny it. Instead he shrugged a shoulder and looked away. He didn't want to think about it, didn't want to talk about it. What he wanted to do was forget it. Picking up their trash, he dumped it into the wastebasket and then sat on the edge of the bed with his back to Wendy.

"Take a nap," he said gruffly. "We'll leave in a few hours."

Wendy stared at his broad back and ached with a wish that she had the right to reach out and comfort him. Just because he would never admit it, that didn't mean he never needed comfort. Everyone needed it sometimes, even gruff, tough, macho men who had to look away when their emotions were touched.

"Okay," she agreed, because she could do nothing else. "I'll nap if you will."

A double bed provided barely enough room for two people. That awareness made him hesitate, but finally he stretched out on his back beside her. He had zipped up his flight suit before he went out, and he left it zipped up now, even though it wasn't comfortable and he felt too warm.

Too hot.

"Sleep," he growled, sounding almost nasty.

"Yes, sir!" she snapped back, and turned onto her side, giving him the cold shoulder.

He was, he thought a while later, going to lie there and go quietly out of his mind. Not from memories this time. No, this time he was going to go out of his mind because of right now. Because of the woman lying beside him. Because of the soft scent of her wafting around him, arousing memories and feelings and needs he wanted to keep buried. Because he couldn't get his mind off the sheer womanly softness of her.

During his years as a POW he had learned to use his mind as a tool to stay sane. He had been able to imagine himself elsewhere with such strength and clarity that he was sometimes shocked to remember where he really was. In his mind, he had sailed around the world, had voyaged to the moon, had submarined to the ocean's depths. He knew how far his mind could carry him from reality.

But right now his skills failed him, probably because his body, his instincts and his heart all wanted to be right here. Wanted to roll over and draw Wendy close. Wanted to take all the things she had once so eagerly offered. All the things he had no right to take. Would never have a right to take. Hell, he was poison to a woman. Unconsciously, he sighed.

Wendy rolled over and looked at him. "Yuma?"

"Hmm?" Damn it, why didn't she just sleep?

"Are you okay?"

He hadn't been okay in twenty-five years. The thought crossed his mind, and suddenly he laughed mirthlessly. "Sure I'm okay," he said. "I'm always okay. What makes you think I'm not?" As soon as he asked, he wished he hadn't, because she might actually answer.

And she did answer. "It's just . . . you're so sad."

Sad? "Me?"

She propped her head up on her hand and looked straight at him. The girl who six years ago had thrown herself at him while being hardly able to meet his eye now looked right at him. She had changed quite a bit, he realized yet again.

"You," she insisted. "Any fool with eyes can see it. I know it's none of my business, and I know you wish I'd just go away and leave you alone—"

"So why don't you?" he interrupted with a growing sense of desperation. He didn't want this woman—or anyone, for that matter—inside his head. "Why don't you just shut up and go to sleep, damn it!"

Silent and still, she stared at him for a long moment. Then she said quietly, "Okay," and lay back on her pillow and closed her eyes. But not before he saw her lip quiver. Not before he saw her eyes begin to glisten. Not before he saw the effect of his anger.

"Look," he said. "I'm sorry. I'm just tired."

She didn't answer. This time her chin quivered, and he had a sudden sense of how hard she was having to struggle to maintain her self-control. She hadn't slept in maybe thirty hours, she'd faced grenades and angry men, had stood beside a man who might have killed her and had argued with him, and now she was being yelled at by him for no better reason than that *he* was tired and edgy, too.

Poison. He was poison, all right.

"Wendy? Really, babe, I'm sorry."

"Forget it." Her chin quivered again, and she started to roll away. That chin, and her movement away, undid him. Forgetting every lick of common sense he'd ever had, he caught her and drew her right up against his chest. Wrapped her in his arms and offered comfort as he had not offered comfort to anyone since he had realized that no one could comfort him.

He was going to bitterly regret this, but right now he didn't give a damn.

"I'm sorry," he said again. "Try to sleep. I promise to be nicer when you wake up."

She unleashed a deep sigh and then tilted her head back, opening her eyes to look straight at him. Lifting a hand, she touched gentle fingertips to his cheek.

That touch pierced his soul. No one, absolutely no one, had touched him with gentleness or caring since Carla had walked out. No one. All the walls he had built to protect himself and others began to tremble and shake before the overwhelming force of her caring.

"Don't," he said hoarsely. "Wendy, don't."

She continued to look at him, her eyes reflecting a deep sorrow. "Don't what?" she asked, her voice little more than a breath.

"Don't care. Damn it, don't care! I can't handle it."

She drew her hand back and bit her lip. For a while she studied the front of his flight suit as if a story were written there. And then she sighed again. "I'm trying not to," she told him quietly. "Really, I'm trying not to. The last thing I want to do is make you feel any worse."

And that, he realized, was another sign of how much she had changed in six years. Back then, she had been firmly convinced that she could be his salvation and had never realized that she might cause him pain. During the last six years she had become an adult. He wondered if he would ever manage to do that himself.

"Look," Wendy said. "We can be friends. Just quit worrying about every damn thing, Yuma. You're not responsible for me, okay? You'll never be responsible for me. I'm attracted to you. I probably always will be. That's not your problem, and I promise to keep it to myself." She looked up at him then, a sort of sad, rueful, wry smile on her face. "It'll wear off. Especially if you keep snapping at me."

He felt a smile stretching his own face, and a kind of relief seemed to settle through him all the way to his toes. She wasn't pinning her hopes on kissing a frog and living happily ever after. She'd left the fairy tales behind and was looking reality straight in the eye. It was okay.

And in that moment, realizing that it was okay, he forgot himself and made one of the biggest mistakes of his life—and he'd made a few humdingers. Allowing himself to believe her assurances that she was her own problem, allowing himself to believe that she really *had* left behind her fairy-tale notions, he gave in to the urge to kiss her.

Oh, God, thought Wendy as his face moved closer. Oh, God! He couldn't really mean to... But he did. His mouth settled over hers gently, telling her that, despite everything he said, she mattered. Telling her that he was uncertain of his welcome, uncertain of her, uncertain of himself.

Oh, God, she thought again, as she realized that at long last one of her smaller dreams was coming true. How many times had she wished to feel his arms around her? How many times had she wondered what it would be like to be kissed by him? How many times had she wished he would.

Now he was. She felt his entire length against her as he drew her even closer, felt the accelerating beat of his heart beneath her palm as suddenly, miraculously, he touched the tip of his tongue to her lips.

He wanted to deepen the kiss. The realization sent a spiraling shaft of longing straight through her center. He wanted a real kiss. A lover's kiss.

Yuma hadn't kissed a woman since Carla. Hadn't wanted to kiss a woman since Carla. It was a quirk of his that he considered a kiss too intimate to share with just anyone. His physical relationships over the years had been just that, arrangements to assuage biological needs for himself and his partners, but they had never been truly intimate.

Not in the way this kiss was. Not in the way any kiss was for Yuma. And that was his humdinger mistake. He gave Wendy what he had given no one since Carla and took from her what no one but Carla had ever given him—intimacy.

And even as he slipped his tongue past the soft velvet of her lips, past the smooth edges of her teeth, even as he found the shy warmth of her own eager tongue, alarm bells were ringing wildly in his mind. This moment of intimacy was going to be branded on his very cells. From now unto eternity, he was going to know exactly what he was denying himself.

But that didn't stop him. A thirsty man too long in the desert might drink himself to death. Yuma felt no wiser now as he found Wendy's sweet heat, her even sweeter response. He had been alone and lonely too long, lost in a dark nightmare created in a faraway land. He had lived in a prison cell of the mind and spirit and suffered the tortures of the damned inside his own head. Wendy was a touch of sunlight and warmth, a human touch. A humane touch. A womanly, soft, caring touch. He might curse himself for the rest of his days, but he could not refuse himself this one taste of light and life and warmth.

Damn, she was soft. She curled into him, melted into him, as if she felt not the slightest fear or hesitation. As if she belonged there.

And that was what shook Yuma back to reality. That heedless, mindless surrender to him. Heat pooled in his groin, every cell in his body wanted to pursue this path to the sweet, sweet culmination, but his mind woke suddenly to the danger of what he was doing.

He had sworn he would never again hurt another human being, yet here he was, on the brink of inflicting a terrible hurt. A terrible betrayal.

The realization stilled everything inside him, swamped all the light and warmth in cold and ice. In an instant he was off the bed and on his feet, heading for the door.

"I'm going out to the airfield to check on the chopper," he said, not looking back. "We'll leave around six. Have the desk call you a cab."

Then he was gone, leaving an aching, empty silence behind him.

Chapter 4

Wendy flew back beside Yuma in the co-pilot's seat, with headphones on so that she could hear all radio conversation. So that she could have talked to him despite the deafening hammer of the engines and pounding of the rotors. Neither of them said a word.

She had come back to get over him, Wendy reminded herself. Instead, all she seemed to be doing was developing a worse addiction. The memory of Yuma's hard, muscular frame pressed against her, the memory of his strong arms surrounding her, his hot mouth pillaging hers, was going to haunt her dreams for a long, long time.

She had tried, often enough, to transfer her interest to another man. In college and at the hospitals where she had trained and worked, there had been an ample supply of unattached young men. Not one of them had managed to curl her toes. Not one of them had ever put the kind of magic in a kiss that Yuma had a couple of short hours ago.

Watching the dry August countryside slip by beneath them, she gave glum thought to her predicament. To her feelings.

It was as if, she found herself thinking, she had been made for this troubled man who sat in the pilot's seat beside her. As if the very first time she had set eyes on him she had recognized him in her soul.

A silly, stupid romantic fantasy, one she had tried to escape by going to school in California. Soul mates? Hah. It sounded crazy even to her own ears.

But how else could she explain that instantaneous sense of connection she had felt for Yuma? How else could she explain what a sixteen-year-old girl had seen in a red-eyed, hung-over drunk in a jail cell?

Seeing Yuma that long-ago Sunday morning had been looking at her destiny. She had felt it then, and she felt it now, even as she fought it. Craziness. Sheer craziness. It couldn't possibly be sane or rational to feel that way about a man who kept trying to show her that he was poison. About a man who had run from her as hard and fast as he could and then had turned on her, cutting her to ribbons with scathing words and scorn.

"We used to have red crosses painted on the noses of the Medevac choppers in Nam."

The sound of Yuma's voice crackling over the headset startled her, and she turned to look at him. He kept his attention forward, sunglasses covering his eyes. She couldn't read a thing on his ravaged face.

"You did?" she said, finally, into the microphone that was attached to the headset.

"Yep. Charlie used to use them for target practice."

Shocked, it was a moment before she could respond. "But weren't you unarmed?"

"No door guns. My co-pilot always carried a sidearm. I never carried anything. We'd fly in as low as we could go to avoid SAMs and radar, and then pick up a lot of ground fire. Used to be quite a turkey shoot."

"But...but that was a violation of the Geneva Convention, to shoot at you!"

"The Geneva Convention amounts to a hill of beans in war, babe." He glanced her way, his eyes completely concealed behind the dark lenses of his sunglasses. "We used to carry boxes of ammo in to the troops. One of the guys called it 'preventive medicine.'" He banked the helicopter a little to the left and then straightened them out. Beneath them a dirt road flashed past, replaced by grass and sage.

Wendy hardly noticed. What he had told her revealed a great deal, she realized. Yuma was a Quaker, a conscientious objector who had gone to war as a Medevac pilot, had gone to *save* lives. Instead he had been shot at and had carried ammunition behind the ineffective, desecrated shield of a red cross. If she lived to be a hundred, she would probably never grasp the depth and breadth of the spiritual violation he had suffered.

"Oh, God," she whispered as the full import of it drove home. "Oh, God." The whisper was lost in the louder sounds of the helicopter.

Suddenly her hands were knotted over her stomach and her eyes were closed against the pain of understanding. Her dad had tried to warn her, but she hadn't even had enough experience to imagine such things. Even now, her insides twisting in horror, she barely grasped the enormity of the burden this man carried.

And that was only the beginning. That didn't even touch on his years as a POW and the mistreatment he had suffered. It didn't cover the shattering months of risking his neck, of living in anticipation of being shot and killed. It didn't touch upon what it must have been like to make it safely back each time only to know that he would have to go out again the next day to take the same risks all over again. Didn't touch upon the horrifying memories he must have of the shattered bodies he had airlifted out of the jungles. Of the friends he must have lost. Of the terrors he must have known.

And it certainly didn't touch on the nightmares of the years since.

With her eyes closed, she clearly heard the anguish in Artie's voice as he had demanded of Yuma, "What the hell is the point?"

Maybe that was the only question that mattered, Wendy thought. With the echo of Artie's anguish and the understanding of Yuma's suffering fresh in her mind, there didn't seem to be any adequate answer.

Nate was waiting for them at the hangar when Yuma set the helicopter gently down.

"I wonder what he wants," Wendy muttered into her microphone, then heard Yuma's snort of laughter in response.

"He's your dad, babe. He wants to be sure I got you home in one undamaged piece."

"He hasn't been sure of that from minute to minute for the last six years. I don't see why it should suddenly have become important."

She went ahead to greet her father while Yuma stayed to tie down the chopper. Nate opened his arms and pulled her into a bear hug.

"Everything okay?" he asked.

"Yeah. Artie's leg is going to be okay."

He leaned back and made her look up at him. "I meant between you and Yuma."

Wendy felt color stain her cheeks and hoped her father couldn't see it. "What do you expect? Yuma's even more convinced than you are that he's bad for me, and I told you I was over him, anyway."

Nate rolled his eyes. Having dealt with daughters for twenty-four years, he wasn't easily misled. "Why do I find that so hard to believe?"

"You don't have to believe it. And you don't have anything to worry about." Not when Yuma could kiss her the way he had, then roll away and stomp out. She'd been on enough dates to know that most men never walked away from a willing female, and it was hard to get rid of them even when you *weren't* willing. "Yuma doesn't *want* me, Dad."

The words came out in a tight whisper, and Nate's whole expression changed as he looked down at his eldest daughter. It was a moment before he cleared his throat and spoke. "When you were little, I used to be able to kiss it better. I wish that still worked."

"Me too, Dad. Me too." Flinging her arms around him, she hugged him tight and let him rock her side to side the way he always had when she stumbled and got hurt. He was a big bear of a man, and he always made her feel safe, so very safe, but her hurts were no longer so easily mended.

Yuma hung back until they separated, then limped his way across the apron to join them. His leg was bothering him this afternoon, and since this was just Nate and Wendy, he didn't bother trying to hide the limp.

"I thought you'd want to know about this," Nate told him after they exchanged greetings. "There's a school-board meeting tonight about the teacher-salary increase. Anyhow, what I'm hearing is that some folks are going to change the agenda because of the little incident we had last night at the hospital. Thought you might want to be there to speak up for your friends."

Yuma looked away a moment and compressed his lips. "Yeah. Sure. One man goes bonkers, and a bunch of good citizens decide to go after a couple dozen others. Makes great sense."

"I never said it made sense, son." Reaching into his pocket, Nate pulled out a roll of antacids and popped a couple into his mouth. "Damn diet's going to be the death of me. Look, I'll speak on the subject myself if it comes up. I don't want any vigilante justice in my county, and I've got no patience with folks who stir up trouble just for the sake of it. You don't need to come. Just thought you might want to know."

"So I can warn my friends in the hills? So I can tell 'em that now not only are they being accused of thefts they didn't commit, but now they're being blamed for Artie's problems?"

Nate sighed and turned to the side, watching the slow change of color in the mountains as the sun sank lower.

"Yuma," he said finally, "you don't remember the aftermath of the My Lai massacre because you were a POW at the time, but I came home from a tour while Calley's court-martial was going on. I got spat on. I got socked in the jaw in the Denver airport. Now, most folks didn't pull that kind of crap, but enough did that I gave a couple minutes' thought to changing out of my uniform."

"Did you?" Wendy asked finally when he stayed silent. She had never heard this before, and she ached for her father.

"No." Nate shook his head. "I was never ashamed of that uniform, and I never did a damn thing to shame it. What Calley and others like him did...well, not all of us were like that. And those who were have paid for it in their own consciences in ways beyond imagining. But it was war. It didn't make sense, and it didn't have any rules."

He turned and looked at Yuma. "The same mentality that causes wars can make men act stupidly when they feel threatened. Folks around here are feeling threatened. When folks feel threatened, they create My Lais. Am I clear?"

Yuma nodded, his face grim.

"Now, it occurred to me that you're pretty well-known in these parts. Folks know you were one of those guys, and they've seen how you pulled yourself back up. Most of 'em respect how you've gotten it back together. I don't think most of them know how you work with those guys, though. Don't realize that you're up there nearly every week with clothes and food and medicines."

"Nate, I won't—"

"I know you won't toot your own horn, son. I know you won't tell these folks that. But you can tell 'em that you know these guys and you know they aren't a threat to the public health and welfare. Maybe, just seeing you, they'll calm down."

Yuma stared at him for a long time, then smiled mirthlessly. "You could've saved the speech, Tater. You knew sure as hell I'd be there."

Nate smiled faintly. "Never hurts to get the fighter psyched for the battle." He looked at Wendy. "Your mom's expecting you for dinner tonight. Figured you'd be too tired to want to cook." He glanced over at Yuma, "You're welcome, too."

Spend any more time with Wendy Tate? Yuma had his limits, and right now he was getting close to them. "No. Thanks, Nate, but no. I'd be rotten company with this meeting looming."

"Well, it might turn out to be nothing."

It might, Yuma thought as he watched Nate and Wendy walk toward their cars. It might. And Santa Claus might be real, too.

Yuma was one of the first people to arrive at the high school for the board meeting. People thought Quakers were a quiet, passive bunch, but folks who thought that didn't know Quakers. Social conscience was inbred, and no true Quaker ever remained silent in the face of injustice. Whether or not he had been a vet, Yuma would have felt conscience-bound to raise his voice in defense of anyone who was unjustly accused. If the good folks of Conard County wanted to point fingers at the innocent, he would be there to place himself in the way of trouble.

He found a front-row seat and settled down to wait, trying not to think back over the long road that had led him here. His own parents had been vocal and visible protesters of the Vietnam conflict. They had understood Yuma's need to go as a noncombatant in the hope of saving lives, but they had never understood how he could have let his conscience and his mission be perverted by permitting ammunition to be loaded on his helicopter. Nor could he ever explain to them what it had been like to go out and pick up all those bloody, mutilated, still-breathing bodies and know that others just like them were still out there with no protection except bullets. You saw enough of that, you carried ammo.

And then tried to live with the violation of your deepest beliefs.

His parents couldn't understand the anger in him, the anger that had grown day by day, hour by hour, out there in that terrible war. The helpless, hopeless rage that had made him want to take up a gun and help. The violent, savage dreams that had grown in him during his own captivity, dreams that had stolen past the guard of his conscious mind while he slept, dreams of cutting the throats of his tormentors. Dreams of torturing them as they tortured him. Dreams of bloody, mindless vengeance.

No, when he had returned, his parents had looked at him and had seen that he was tainted with violence, and that his conscience was violated. They hadn't rejected him or even condemned him, but he couldn't live with the knowledge of their disappointment.

Carla hadn't been disappointed in him, but Carla hadn't been a Quaker. She had been just a nice, ordinary girl-next-door who had wept with joy upon his return and then divorced him a few years later because she couldn't stand his coldness and his rages. Because she felt as if he had cut her out of his life in some essential way. Which he had, he guessed. He'd cut out everything except his own pain.

Sometimes he wondered if he still wallowed in it occasionally. Maybe he did. But the fact remained that he couldn't get rid of it by ignoring it. He'd tried that, too. That didn't keep time from fracturing, casting him back into a past he would just as soon forget.

Or worse, it didn't keep the confusion from coming over him, the mixing of past and present in a way that he knew was wrong, that terrified him because he couldn't sort it out even though he knew it was mixed up.

Time had healed him enough that he didn't often have flashbacks anymore, and he had learned to recognize the danger signs, so that he could usually manage to evade one when it threatened.

Like today in the chopper. The edgy, ready-to-fight feeling had started to come over him, and he'd found himself getting confused. He was flying in Nam. But he knew he *wasn't* flying in Nam. So he'd talked to Wendy, had found a lifeline in the present to hang on to until the danger of slippage was past. He'd gotten real good at that.

The auditorium was filling rapidly now. Turning, he caught sight of Maude Bleaker. She nodded at him, probably as friendly as she ever got, but he figured she was going to be the first one hollering to have the vets driven out of the mountains.

And there were the Ironhearts, Gideon and Sara, Sara still in her deputy's uniform. Behind them came Micah and Faith Parish, with their infant daughter. Micah, too, wore his uniform, and Yuma suddenly realized that the Conard County Sheriff's Office was making a quiet but visible statement about law and order. By the time the meeting was called to order, there were nearly a dozen uniformed deputies and their families in evidence.

And there was Nate with Marge and all six of their daughters. Marge, Yuma thought, not for the first time, was a beautiful woman at forty-five. She was a few pounds plumper than she had been years back, but those pounds didn't make her any less attractive. She had laugh lines around her eyes, gray in her flaming hair and fire in her heart. Yuma had envied Nate more than once.

Tonight, though, she looked strained. Tired. And Nate, he realized suddenly, looked troubled. What the hell was going on? When they seated themselves, they sat with their girls between them, Wendy next to her dad and twelve-year-old Krissie next to Marge.

Considering that Nate expected trouble tonight, Yuma was surprised that he'd even brought his youngest daughter. And then he understood. Nate was reminding everyone present that he had as much to lose as any man in the county if there was danger.

Deeply moved, Yuma quickly turned his attention back to the stage, where the school-board members were taking their places.

The meeting was called to order. Several teacher representatives spoke in favor of the cost-of-living increase in salaries. The board heard a report on the financial impact of the raises, and then the motion was passed with little audience reaction. A few other subjects were discussed briefly, with almost no dispute.

Yuma was surprised when it was Elwyn Carruthers, the chairman of the board, who brought up the question of last night's events.

"A school-board meeting is a public forum," he said by way of excuse, "and it's the only organized public meeting planned in the county for several more weeks. I therefore move we discuss the incident last night at the hospital. The public safety was recklessly endangered by a man with a grenade, a man who should never have been brought into our community when he was known to be dangerous. What's more, there are plenty more like him up in the mountains. We need to address this question now."

Maude Bleaker, naturally, rose to the occasion. "I'm sure not all those men are a threat," she said, with a hard look at Yuma, "but any who are, ought to be found, brought down and put in the hospitals or jail, where they belong!"

The empty chair next to Yuma creaked. Startled, he turned and saw Wendy taking the place beside him. She didn't even look at him, merely sat down, crossed her legs and laid her hand on his arm in support.

Nate rose. "Maude, with all due respect, you can't go around locking people up unless they've done something wrong. It just isn't legal. But apart from that, what makes you think *any* of these men are a threat? As far as I know they stay up in the hills because they want to be left alone, not because they want to commit murder and mayhem."

"Then what are they doing coming down to steal things from the ranches?" demanded a rancher from the back.

"Are you sure they are?" Nate asked mildly. "Could be anybody."

The meeting erupted then with counterclaims about the thefts, who might be stealing and what the sheriff needed to do about it. The business with the grenade had some people upset, but surprisingly few were worried that all the vets posed that kind of threat. Mostly they were uneasy and wanted the thievery stopped. Yuma listened, registered the anger and fear in the deep, dark places of his soul, and felt himself slipping.

He hated crowds, but he hated shouting crowds worse. The irritability in him grew, the ready-to-fight feeling. Turning in his seat, he wrapped his hand tightly around Wendy's and looked at her, seeking an anchor in a tipping universe. Saigon. Not Saigon. Shouting people. Wounded cries. Not wounded. Back and forth he see-sawed, clinging to Wendy's hand.

"Talk," he said gruffly. "Talk to me."

She looked at him, surprised, looked at their linked hands, then looked at the barely controlled savagery of his expression. "After we get out of here," she said, "let's go make out."

Astonishment trickled through him, driving the seasick feeling away. He squeezed his eyes shut, and a reluctant, short laugh escaped him as the world righted itself. "Talk about shock therapy."

She tightened her hand around his. "I made a point of studying PTSD," she said quietly. "You okay now?"

"Yeah." He opened his green eyes, stared intently into hers for a long moment, then released her. Slowly he rose to his feet.

He didn't say anything immediately. Around him arguments raged, but gradually silence spread in a widening pool as folks realized that one of the vets under discussion was in their midst and waiting to speak. And finally every eye in the room was fixed on him.

"Friends," he said quietly, "if I could have a few minutes of your time?"

Heads all around nodded, and the people who were on their feet sat, giving him the floor. There wasn't a soul here who didn't remember Yuma as he had been and who didn't respect what he'd made of himself since.

It was hard to stand up before them, knowing they knew his past, but it was something conscience required. They were all good people, he reminded himself. All of them. They just didn't understand.

"You all know that I spent time up in those mountains. You all know that from time to time I'd just up and disappear up there and be gone weeks, maybe months. Then I'd come back and find a job and try again. In all that time, none of you ever asked me why I went up there, why I didn't just stay here. Maybe if I tell you about that, you won't be so concerned about my friends."

He looked around and saw he had their attention. "I went," he said slowly, "because it was the only place I could feel safe. I went because when I walked down the streets of Conard City I'd get confused and afraid, because I kept thinking I was in Vietnam. I went because a sudden noise or a baby's cry was more than I could take. I went to be safe. And all I ever wanted when I was up there was to be left alone.

"My friends are no different, they just have it all the time instead of some of the time. They're up there guarding against attacks that won't come, living in terror of battles that are over. They exist in fear, because war stole their sense of security and left them feeling powerless. They just want to be left alone. That's all they're asking. Just to be left alone."

He looked around the room once more. Then, without another word or even a backward glance, he walked out, a tall rangy man with a limp. And behind him, the room remained silent.

The night air was chilly with the breath of arriving autumn, and the sky was obscured by the clouds of an incoming cold front. Yuma hesitated by the door of his old pickup, drawing deep breaths of cleansing air and letting the quiet and emptiness of the parking lot soothe the rawness of his nerves.

"Yuma?"

He swung around at the sound of Wendy's voice. Evidently his penance wasn't over for the evening. And he owed her. He sure as hell owed her for what she'd done. "Thanks for helping out in there," he said.

She shrugged a shoulder. "It wasn't anything. Can I hitch a ride with you? I can't sit still for any more of that crap."

"Are they at it again?"

"Just as soon as the door closed behind you."

"Hell."

She shoved her hands into her pockets. "Well, they're a little more sympathetic than they were before you spoke. Dad's handling it. I don't think there'll be any more trouble."

"Until something else happens."

She looked down at the ground, then back at him. "So, can I hitch?"

"What happened to your car?"

"Dropped it off at my place. You know Dad. No way was he going to let me drive home alone after dark."

In spite of himself, Yuma laughed. That was Nate, all right. "Yeah, you can hitch."

"Thanks."

He walked around to unlock her door for her first. She'd traded the jumpsuits she wore to work for a skintight pair of old jeans and a fuzzy red sweater. Being a man, he couldn't help but notice the soft fullness of her breasts beneath the sweater, or the way her jeans molded her gentle curves. Being a man, he couldn't help responding to her, either. But then, his desire for Wendy Tate had never been in question.

He closed the door, walked around to the driver's side and wondered if it was getting to be time to go visit a lady friend in Sheridan. She was always glad to see him, rare as his visits were. It was an easy, uncomplicated, undemanding relationship, the only kind he was capable of.

It was a stopgap, and he knew it. What he needed was a hell of a lot more than any casual, uncomplicated relationship could give him. What he needed was—

More than he could ever have.

At her house, he pulled into the driveway. "Let me walk you to the door," he said.

She gave him a humorous look. "Yuma, this is Conard City. I can walk ten feet without being in danger of rape or mugging."

He shook his head and climbed out, anyway. He'd been raised with a certain standard that, outdated as it was, he couldn't shake. He certainly couldn't shake it around Wendy, who brought out every chivalrous instinct that still survived in him. He climbed out and walked around, and since she had been brought up to politely wait, she did.

At the door, he took her key and unlocked it for her. She watched his face as he performed the simple task, and when he shoved her door open and turned away, saying good-night, she stopped him.

"Yuma? Are you all right?"

"I'm fine." But he wasn't. No, he wasn't fine, hadn't been fine in a quarter century, and what he wanted more than anything in the world was to go inside, to leave the nightmare out in the cold dark and head into the warmth.

Wendy caught his hand. "Come in. I'll make some coffee."

"I don't think—"

"Just shut up," she said impatiently. "Coffee. You can handle a damn cup of coffee, can't you? And quit trying to protect me! I'm sick to death of everybody trying to protect me from every little thing!"

She stormed into the house, leaving the door open behind her. Yuma stared after her, amused and bemused all at the same time; then he followed her in and closed the door behind them.

"Coffee sounds great," he said as he followed her into the kitchen.

"I've got some coffee cake, too, if you want." She spoke as if she hadn't just given him a piece of her mind, then turned to find him smiling. Really smiling, in a way that was rare for Billy Joe Yuma.

"Sounds good." He pulled out a chair at her little dinette and sat, watching her move around the kitchen.

There was something about the way a woman moved, he thought. Something about the way her legs were attached at the hip that made her sway gently, like a willow in the breeze. It was graceful, and it was sexy, and he couldn't tear his eyes from her.

No, no, no. He told himself that again and again, but it didn't keep him from reaching out when she came to the table. When she set the cups down, he reached out and, without a word, without a sound, snagged her gently by the waist and drew her over until she stood between his spread legs. Then, fighting himself every step of the way, he wrapped his arms tightly around her and pressed his face to the valley between her breasts.

Oh, God, he thought with the despair of a man going down for the third time. Oh, God, she smelled sweet, and in the warm soft valley her own scent was the only fragrance, the most enticing perfume ever created.

For a heartbeat, perhaps two, time stood still. Then Wendy raised her hands and cradled his head to her, her fingers finding their way into his silky dark hair. She said nothing, simply held him close and tight and let him know that whatever he needed from her was his for the asking.

That trust, that totally undeserved trust, was all that stopped him. He couldn't betray her. He just couldn't do it. Nor could he betray Nate, his friend. But the emptiness in him was huge, and he couldn't make himself pull back from the warmth of her yet. Not yet.

But finally he let her go.

She took her place across the table from him. For long moments, neither of them looked at one another. Finally Wendy cleared her throat.

"That speech you gave tonight—it must have been difficult for you."

"Which part? The business about being afraid?" He turned his head and looked at her. "Why should it be hard to admit that? I'm the world's number-one coward, and everybody knows it."

Wendy's head snapped up, and she gaped at him. "What are you talking about?"

He shrugged. This was something else he'd had to face a long time ago, one of his ten million reasons for not getting involved with Wendy or any other woman. He might as well tell her, he thought. Do something to banish that fragile hope he'd glimpsed in her too-warm, too-soft, too-gentle eyes.

"Well, start with the fact that I hid in the bottle for more than a decade. Or how about the way sometimes I just can't handle it. Can't handle it, so I have to run and hide. Sometimes...sometimes I get the shakes so bad I can't even stand up." He nearly glared at her, hating his own failures, and hating feeling honor-bound to expose them. "Sometimes it almost takes more guts than I've got to step through a door and face the rest of the world. Enough?"

For a moment Wendy said nothing. Her eyes never wavered from his face, though, and any hope he'd had that she would be shocked died. She wasn't shocked, and her expression never changed.

"When I was in L.A.," she said quietly, "I volunteered at the VA hospital. There was one man who couldn't come out of his room. He just couldn't do it. It was the only place in the world where he felt safe. So I used to spend hours in there reading to him, talking to him. I didn't think he was a coward. I didn't think his suffering was any different from that of the paraplegic up the hall who'd been shot in the spine. Or any less real than the guy who lost both his legs and one arm. Or any less terrible than the man who'd been shot in the head and couldn't remember anything from one minute to the next. Maybe they don't give Purple Hearts for PTSD, but they sure as hell ought to."

He opened his mouth to reply, but nothing would come out. His throat locked against emotions so intense that there was simply, absolutely, no way they could emerge. Nothing he could possibly say to express them. He didn't know, he realized suddenly, if he could handle her understanding. Sympathy could be dismissed. Compassion was unwanted. Understanding was something no one had ever given him, except another vet.

Until now. Until Wendy. Why couldn't she make it easy on him and be disgusted? Why couldn't she just look at him the way Carla finally had and say, "Yuma, you're crazy."

Carla had said that. She'd looked him right in the eye while she sobbed her heart out and told him he was crazy, that he wasn't fighting it, that she wasn't coming back until he learned to control himself.

The thought vanished as Wendy suddenly materialized in his lap, sitting on his thighs, wrapping her arms around his shoulders, pressing her cheek to his.

"It's okay," she whispered raggedly. "Whatever it is, Billy Joe, it's past now. It's past. It's okay. It's okay...."

But some things were never past, he thought as he helplessly wrapped his arms around her and held her close. Some things never went away. But they could be held at bay for a little while, and Wendy's caring touch, the weight of her on his lap, pushed the memories back, battened down the aching awareness of all his losses.

For this moment, just this little bit of time, he could feel normal. Glad to be alive. Glad to hold a woman on his lap and feel *her* hold *him*.

It was a dangerous, seductive enchantment that she wove around him, this feeling that he could forget for just a little while. This feeling that he could be an ordinary man.

Dangerous, he thought again, and he turned his head until his face pressed into the side of her neck, until the satin of her skin was pressed to his longing lips. Seductive. Enchanting.

Irresistible.

Chapter 5

"Oh, God."

He heard Wendy whisper the words on a caught breath as his lips brushed against her soft, sweet neck. He felt her arms tighten convulsively around him. She wanted him. Oh, sweet mother, she wanted him, and he knew a man's fierce triumph. She wasn't just saying it, as she had six years ago, with innocence gleaming in her brown eyes. Now she was telling him with her quickened breath, her tightened arms, that she felt exactly what he was feeling.

Too young. Nate's daughter. The warnings sounded in his head, but it was already too late, because she was stretching her neck, begging for another caress in that sensitive place, and the invitation was so appealing, so bewitching, that his warning voices were drowned in the hammering of his heart. Her weight on his lap was the sweetest torment in the world, pressing against his engorging sex.

Right. It was right. Oh, God, had anything ever felt so right? The world was slipping away, escaping his grasp. The ever-present uneasiness at the back of his mind was buried in sweet sensations, sweet hopes, sweet yearnings.

Gently, gently, he brushed his lips back and forth against her neck and felt the delicate shivers run through her. Again and again her breath caught, and she pressed closer and closer, but she said nothing, as if afraid of shattering the spell.

She tasted so sweet, he thought, opening his mouth and sending his tongue on a tantalizing foray. Almost like fresh, clean rain. And she smelled so good. Her gentle fragrance filled his nostrils as he nuzzled just behind her ear and felt her nails dig into his back.

Oh yes! So little to give her, but she came so alive, unable to hold still as he kissed that tender spot behind her ear, then traced the delicate shell with his tongue.

"Yuma," she whispered almost soundlessly, and tried to twist closer. "Oh, Yuma..."

"Easy," he whispered, some remnant of sense rearing its ugly head. "Easy. Just this. Just this little bit...." He plunged his tongue into her ear, meaning only to give her exquisite pleasure, meaning to stop there, as if they were high schoolers who dared go no further.

But she gasped and twisted like a cat, and the next thing he knew she was straddling him, pressed to him, riding him as she sought his mouth with hers. He grabbed her hips, meaning to stop her, but his body betrayed him, rising to meet her, causing him to groan out loud and throw his head back. Again. Again. Oh damn, fully clothed, like kids in a back seat...

This was Nate's daughter!

The thought jarred him just as she suddenly froze. An instant later she was off his lap and across the kitchen, her back to him.

"I'm sorry," she whispered hoarsely. "I swore I wouldn't... I'm sorry. I shouldn't have... I don't know what... Oh, God, I'm sorry."

He could have absolved her. He *should* have absolved her. She, after all, had only meant to comfort him. He had been the one to turn it into something more.

But there was more at stake here than her momentary embarrassment. There was her future. His friendship with Nate. His ultimate need to do the best thing for her. So he lied.

"Sorry for what?" he said, his voice harsh with anger and suppressed feeling. Because he sure as hell was angry again—at himself, at life, at the unfairness of it. "It was just a little sex." He watched her back stiffen. "Just don't mistake it, Wendy. That's *all* it was. All it could ever be with me. You turn me on like hell on fire, but there's nothing more to it." Turning, he left, refusing to look back.

Behind him, Wendy stood staring at her reflection in the night-darkened window above the sink. Slowly she wrapped her arms around herself and began to shake. She'd done it again, thrown herself at him, and once again she had been rejected.

Her heart was breaking, aching. She wanted Billy Joe Yuma so badly that she thought she would die from the yearning. Not the sexual yearning, though she felt that strongly, but the emotional yearning. She needed his arms around her. She needed him to be there. She needed so badly for him to be part of her life. She needed just to be close to him, even if he never wanted a thing at all from her. She needed his confidence, his trust, his affection.

And mostly, in the most incredible, overwhelming and inexplicable way, she needed to give him all that was in her heart. All the love, all the understanding, all the support. She needed wildly, insanely, to make him whole.

Sometimes she thought she would die from the need to give to him. She wouldn't, of course, but her plan to come back and get over him had backfired in a big way. Working with him daily had only deepened her feelings for him. There was so much to admire about Billy Joe Yuma.

Now this.

She shivered again, and a huge silent tear rolled down her cheek. How clear did he have to make it? Did she need to be hit over the head? He didn't want her, except sexually. He hadn't wanted her six years ago, and he didn't now.

All her aching, breaking heart could do was beat painfully and try to go on. And hope that somehow, some way, she could get over him.

Each morning, Yuma had to find a reason to get out of bed. That was just the way it was. Something essential in him had been broken a long time ago, something crucial that kept other people going without really thinking about it. He had to think about it. Every morning he had to come up with a reason for getting out of bed and facing a new day.

It wasn't as tough as it had been years ago, but this morning was tougher than it had been in a while, because the first thing he remembered was how he had treated Wendy last night. Just a minor crime against his conscience, he told himself. The bigger one would have been accepting what she offered.

But now he had to face her, feeling about two inches tall. Not the kind of thing that made a man eager to confront another day.

But he climbed out of bed, anyway, because the alternative was unthinkable.

The morning light was still tinged with pink when he arrived at the airport. Wendy was already there; her Jeep Wagoneer was parked out front, along with a strange pickup. Damn, he would have liked to have a few minutes to get his feet under him before he faced her, but it looked as if he was out of luck. He wondered if she would be spitting mad or icy cold. She sure couldn't be indifferent.

Whatever she was, it was immediately apparent that he wasn't going to know for at least a little while. She was sitting behind her desk when he entered, and there were two other men in the room, Alvin Teague and Les Forman. He knew them both from his drinking days, and knew them to be troublemakers.

He looked from them to Wendy, and he didn't like the look on her face. It was a closed, tense look, as if these men had been giving her a hard time and she wasn't quite sure what to do about it. Instinctively, he moved to stand near her, a protective stance that, he thought with miserable anger, was useless. He didn't know how to fight well. Fighting had been forbidden and was against his conscience. But if he had to defend Wendy...

"Got a problem, friends?" he asked Teague and Forman.

"We just wanted to talk to you, but little Missy Tate wasn't saying if you'd be in."

Yuma glanced at her, but she was watching the two men uneasily. "She didn't know when I'd be here. What's up?"

"It's about these friends of yours in the hills," Teague said.

Yuma stiffened, not liking the man's tone at all. It was almost a sneer. "What about them?"

"We don't take kindly to thieves around here, Yuma," Teague said. "Folks have been putting up too long with little things disappearing."

Yuma shook his head. "I think I've heard this before. And nobody knows who's responsible for the thefts."

"Well, we all got a pretty damn good idea," Forman said. "Only one bunch of folks in the world around here got any reason to steal anything."

"That's right," Teague chimed in. "Only one bunch. And now they're taking things like money and tools, and even Mrs. Johnley's wedding ring turned up missing the other day."

"The sheriff is investigating," Yuma said, careful to keep his voice level, never taking his gaze from the two men.

" 'The sheriff is investigating,' " Teague mocked. "Well, we don't need no investigation to know who's the culprits."

Yuma didn't bother to respond to that. He just waited, knowing what was coming.

"You tell your damn crazy friends," Teague said. "You tell 'em if there's any more trouble, some of us are going to take care of it. And some of us is real good at hunting."

Yuma kept silent, meeting Teague stare for stare. What he really wanted to do was pop the man in the nose. After another moment the man spat tobacco juice on the floor at Yuma's feet and then turned to stomp out, with Forman right behind him.

"Oh, God," Wendy whispered shakily when the sound of their engine faded away. "Oh, God. I'm calling Dad."

"He won't be able to do anything," Yuma said, facing her reluctantly. "Not a thing. But he'd better know. Are you okay? Did they bother you?"

"Just some innuendo. A few sexual remarks. Nothing I haven't heard before. I was just...uneasy because I was alone here."

She shouldn't have had to feel that way, Yuma thought as a surge of anger rolled through him. Nobody should have to feel that way. And what if he'd come upon them hurting her? What good would he have been?

Not for the first time in his life he looked down at his hands and wondered how heaven could expect any man to always be a pacifist. "Call your dad," he said gruffly, and turned away. Just another way he would have failed, if it had come to that. Just another great big failure.

Quaker pacifism was not an absolute, nor entirely bound up in doctrine. Yuma's parents had been totally pacifistic, but others weighed circumstances in their decisions as to whether violence was justified. Many Quakers had fought in World War II because they could not in conscience ignore what was happening in the concentration camps.

When a third party was at risk, many a Quaker felt bound to intervene or help. Yuma was one of them, but he had been raised in such a way that he was always uneasy about it. He'd been in a barroom brawl or two when he was drunk out of his mind—just another failure—but if those two men had bothered Wendy, he wasn't sure he would have been able to protect her, no matter how hard he tried. And he would have tried. He might let another man beat him to a pulp without resisting, but he would never stand by while someone else was being harmed.

That was what had gotten him into all that trouble with his conscience in Nam. Now he was feeling it again, the conflict between the principles he'd had driven into him from birth and his own Inner Light, the guide that Quakers acknowledged as coming from the Divine. And when the two were in conflict, how could you be certain which was right?

Enough to drive a man mad, he thought now. Quite enough.

He turned as Wendy hung up the phone and he saw that her hands were still trembling. Damn, she was so young, so naive, so innocent. She should never be exposed to men like Teague and Forman. Never.

And he wanted to cross the room right then and take her into his arms. The yearning in him was strong enough to be almost scary. She made him feel protective, when he knew damn well he was incapable of protecting anything. That he could be as bad for her as those two cruds.

"Dad says he'll look into it," Wendy said. She sounded calm, and her face was a carefully trained mask that revealed nothing. If he hadn't seen her hands tremble, he never would have suspected a thing.

"What did they say to you, Wendy?"

She still wouldn't look directly at him. "Nothing that matters. Nothing that means anything. Nothing you need to know."

That was when he knew. Alvin Teague had been calling Billy Joe Yuma a coward for the last eight years. To some folks, that was what being a conscientious objector meant. To some folks, having PTSD meant you were a chicken who couldn't handle reality, that you weren't a man, because real men didn't suffer from such things. Only wimps and cowards had problems. Teague, never having been to war, was, of course, an expert on such subjects.

And Teague had said something to that effect to Wendy. Combine that with the sexual innuendo she had mentioned, and the picture wasn't pretty. He didn't even want to think about all the ways those two things could have been combined to taunt Wendy. His hands clenched into fists, and he wondered just what he could do.

But he didn't dare touch her, not even to offer comfort.

"Sonofabitch," he muttered after a moment. "Sonofabitch. Wendy, I—"

Her head snapped up, and she interrupted him without apology. "You know, Yuma, you feel responsible for too damn much. You're not responsible for anything that creep Teague does. I've known him all my life. When I was sixteen, he grabbed me in the alley behind Houlihan's and tried to persuade me to come 'have a little fun' with him. I knew what he was then, and I know what he is now, and if he ever lays a finger on me, I'll do what I did then—give him a knee to the groin he's not likely to forget."

"He grabbed you? When you were just a kid?" Teague would have been well over thirty at the time. "Damn it, Wendy—did you tell your dad? Anyone?"

She shook her head. "I was afraid Dad would kill him. I was afraid because I thought maybe I'd done something to make Teague think..." She trailed off and looked away. "Doesn't matter now. I never told anyone but you, and I trust you to keep it to yourself. Since then, it's all been just talk. Nasty, suggestive remarks. Nothing I can't ignore."

"You'd think he'd know better than to mess with Nate Tate's daughter."

She laughed, a humorless sound. "You keep presuming that Teague *thinks*."

Disturbed, he paced the length of the office. "Look, I don't like this. Teague is looking for trouble. Looking hard enough that he came all the way out here to initiate it. It's no big deal if he wants to threaten the guys in the hills. I'll just tell 'em to move deeper... and anyway, they're experienced combat vets. They can handle Teague and his friends just fine, if it comes to that."

"So?" She watched him moving swiftly back and forth.

"What bugs me is that they're drawing you into this."

"Now, look..."

"No, you look." He turned and nearly glared at her. "Teague's been trying to get under my skin for years now, ever since I hung my hat in Conard County. We've duked it out a couple of times when I was too drunk to remember my principles, but nothing's ever been settled between us."

Wendy's brow furrowed a little as she listened, and her brown eyes sparked with something very like anger. "I had no idea he had it in for you."

"No reason why you should. You don't hang around in bars. The point is, he's still itching to get me."

"But *why?*"

Yuma stared at her for a moment, noting with one corner of his mind that she was no longer avoiding looking at him. Then he spread his hands. "Why? Who the hell knows? Maybe he's just got a moral objection to conscientious objectors."

"But you performed alternative service. Dangerous alternative service. He can hardly believe you're a coward."

"But he does. Or claims to."

Wendy chewed her lip for a moment. "Well, I'll bet it's because he knows your principles keep you from popping his nose... at least when you're sober. The bully principle. Pick on the guy who can't—or won't—fight back."

"Maybe." It was as good an explanation as any, but it didn't really matter. He had a bigger concern on his mind. "Wendy, let's get back to the real issue here—you."

"Me?" Her eyes widened as she looked up at him.

"The man wants to get under my skin, Wendy. He's been trying real hard for years. Do you suppose he finally figured out he could use you to get there?"

Her face turned an uncomfortable, brilliant shade of red, and she quickly looked away.

"What did he say, Wendy?" The ideas that occurred to him were enough to make his stomach roil and his adrenaline start pumping. She didn't answer. "Wendy, what did he say? Or am I going to have to talk to your father about this?"

"No! Don't you dare say a word to Dad. He's got enough on his mind—" She broke off and rose to her feet. "Keep him out of this, Yuma. I mean it."

"Then quit keeping *me* out of it. What did he say?"

She glared at him, but when he didn't give an inch, when his green eyes never flickered and his jaw stayed set, she knew he wasn't going to give up. She looked away and swallowed hard. She'd seen a lot and learned a lot in the big city and as a nurse, but some things were still difficult to speak of.

"He said he was going to beat you to a pulp and make you, uh, watch...you know."

"Make me watch him rape you." He said the words levelly, never betraying how they struck at him.

"He didn't put it quite so nicely," she admitted. "Teague never does." She still refused to look at him. "Anyhow, I just acted unimpressed, and I don't want Dad to hear about it, because he can't do a damn thing legally about threats. It'll just get him upset...and if he *did* do something about Teague, he might get into serious trouble. So just let it lie, okay?"

The rage that ripped through him had been unequaled since his days as a POW. Not since then had he felt so close to murder, or so capable of it. He needed to smash something, yell something, *do* something to vent the fury; but he stood there and forced himself to master it, forced himself to be in control. Because what a man didn't control controlled him.

"From here on," he finally said quietly, "you go nowhere alone. I'll follow you home, I'll follow you to work, and in between you make sure you're not alone."

"Don't be ridiculous, Yuma! That man's a bully and a big mouth, but he'd never—"

"He did once before," he reminded her. "In an alley behind Houlihan's. I'm not kidding, Wendy. He might really hurt you to get at me."

She shook her head, not in disagreement exactly, but in disgust. "I can't live the rest of my life in an armed camp."

"Just until this cools down, honey. Just for a little while." He would beg if she wanted, because suddenly he was scared for her, a fear that felt like ice in his veins. Teague hated him for some reason, and he didn't for one minute believe Teague was above using someone else to score. And then there was Wendy's rejection of the man eight years ago. No, Teague could get two birds with one stone this time. And Yuma was very afraid he might have figured that out.

"All right," Wendy said quietly. "Okay. Be my shadow. But damn it, Yuma, I don't know how either one of us is going to stand this."

Neither did he, but he was no stranger to hell on earth. He would survive.

They took the chopper out on a call during the midafternoon. An eight-year-old boy had fallen from a barn loft and was unconscious and bleeding from his ears. Wendy flew up with Yuma, along with EMTs Bud Grissom and June Hawley. The boy's neurologic signs were deteriorating, so they stopped at County Hospital just long enough to stabilize him for the flight to the trauma center.

It was midnight before the helicopter set down again on the landing pad in Conard County. Wendy, feeling too keyed-up to even think of bed, shooed the EMTs on their way and told them that she would handle the cleanup. There wasn't that much to do, anyway; they'd taken care of the worst of it during the flight back. Mainly she just needed to restock some things.

When she looked up from slipping a sterile tray into place, she saw Yuma standing there like a watchdog. There was little he could do to help—pilots were not allowed to be medical personnel.

"Go on home," she said. "I'll be done in just a minute."

"I'm not going anywhere until I see you safely home."

She'd forgotten. In the course of the day, she had clean forgotten about Teague. "Look, Yuma, there's no reason to think he'd come out here tonight looking for either one of us."

"There's no reason to have thought he'd show up this morning, either."

Wendy stifled a sigh and turned back to her task. She should have known that coming home would put her in this position, but after six years on her own, all this caring and concern she was getting from her family and Yuma felt stifling. "Okay," she said, thinking to throw him and maybe get him to back off. "If you're really worried, move into my guest room. Then you don't have to worry about Teague coming in the middle of the night."

"Okay."

She froze, then turned slowly to face him. Squatting as she was inside the lighted helicopter, to her he was hardly more than a tall shadow with glittering eyes in the darkness outside. "Come on, Yuma."

"Come on *what?*"

"Just how the hell would I explain that to my dad? Don't be ridiculous. You're carrying this too far."

Remembering the look in Teague's eyes, he knew he was not. His hands curled into fists at his sides. "Tell him I'm renting the room. He knows better than to think I'd take advantage of you."

"So do I," she muttered under her breath. He heard it, though; she could tell by the way he stiffened. "And what about the place you're really renting?"

"Mrs. Connaghy doesn't care whether I'm there or not, so long as the rent is paid. She's a remarkably un-nosy woman."

Remarkably deaf and nearly blind, Wendy thought, turning to stuff a dressing pack into its cubbyhole. "Dad wouldn't believe it for a second."

"Then maybe he'll believe the truth."

She rounded on him, still squatting, and nearly lost her balance. He was there instantly, steadying her. "I told you, I don't want him to know about that. Damn it, Yuma, he's as protective of us girls as a mama bear. He'd *kill* anyone who hurt any of us, and he wouldn't be worrying about his badge or the law. I've spent years protecting him from the truth at times. We *all* have. He's never heard a word about guys who got too fresh or any of the other things that just naturally happen in life, because he wouldn't take it lying down. Not when it comes to us. He'd say something. Or *do* something. If you tell him one word about this, so help me I'll—I'll—" She couldn't think of anything terrible enough and spluttered in frustration.

He chuckled. It was a soft sound, not at all mocking, and he touched her chin gently with his fingertips. "Wendy-bear, you *do* take after your daddy. So tell him I'm renting the damn room because there's a problem at my other place. Only temporarily."

"I don't like to lie, Yuma." Her voice had grown breathless, though, and her gaze seemed to have become attached to his mouth. Such a firm, well-shaped, thin-lipped, masculine mouth. A mouth that could be both hard and soft, as she now knew.

"Then don't tell him anything about it. How will he know?" His own voice dropped a little, and he wanted in the worst way to touch her lower lip with his thumb.

"A strange truck parked out front?" Was that breathless, hushed voice really hers? Oh, God, she couldn't let him do that to her again, could she?

"I'll ride with you. We just won't say anything. Wendy, I..." His brain was turning to mush, and he had just enough sense to realize it before his needs overruled his sense. He turned quickly away. "We'll stop by my place and get a few things I'll need. I'll stay out of your way as much as possible, Wendy, but don't ask me to act as if Teague never threatened you. Because he did. And I feel responsible."

"But you *aren't!*"

"Don't try to argue with a Quaker's conscience." He gave her a grim smile over his shoulder. "It doesn't sway easily."

* * *

Hardly able to believe she was doing it, Wendy drove Yuma to his apartment, a room above a garage, and waited while he gathered some clothes and shaving tackle.

Being a normal woman, she looked around and didn't like what she saw. It was clean, fairly neat, but devoid of any sign that it was a home. Naturally. Yuma wouldn't ever think of decorating. This was just the place where he showered and slept, nothing more.

But the absence even of photographs said something. Books teetered on a table, all of them reference works on history and psychology. There wasn't a novel in sight.

He emerged from his bedroom in short order with a duffel in his hand. "That's it," he said. "Let's go."

She had rented a duplex with a second bedroom because she had expected friends from L.A. to visit occasionally, and because she knew her sisters would enjoy coming over to spend the night sometimes. Now Yuma was filling that small room and looking too big for the twin bed and too masculine for the cheap pink curtains.

He dropped his duffel on the bed without any comment and followed her as she showed him the small bathroom and the linen closet where he could find fresh towels, and told him to help himself to the contents of the refrigerator.

"But I am *not* doing all the cooking," she told him, hands on her hips.

He smiled for the first time in hours. "I'll do it."

"You cook?" Somehow that surprised her.

"Darlin', a man who's lived alone for the better part of fifteen years had damn well better know how to open a can and broil a steak."

"Oh, what an exciting menu." She pretended to groan. Truth was, having him here was making her edgier than a cat on a hot stove. She kept thinking of last night, wishing it would happen again and feeling humiliated that it had happened at all. Some things left you too exposed. Too vulnerable. And over and over again she kept making herself vulnerable to Billy Joe Yuma.

"Well." She cleared her throat. "I'm going to bed now. See you in the morning."

"Good night."

Good night. Hah! Twenty minutes later she was curled up on her side, eyes tightly closed, determined to sleep. But she didn't feel sleepy. How *could* she feel sleepy, when she could hear him stirring in the next bedroom settling in?

Her dad would kill her if he found out about this. Nate Tate was as old-fashioned as they came when it concerned his daughters, and he wouldn't care that Yuma was sleeping in the guest room. She should have insisted that Yuma forget it. She should have forbidden him to set foot in the house.

Except that she never for a minute doubted that he would have called her dad and told him about Teague. And while Nate Tate might not have done anything illegal, he would certainly have had a talk with Teague before the night was out. And then what? There might be trouble. Or Teague might just await another opportunity. Or he might take it out on Yuma....

Her head spinning almost dizzily with speculations and extrapolations, she finally drifted into a light sleep. It had been a long, long day.

Sometime during the night, she awoke in a state of heart-pounding terror. Someone was moving in the hallway outside the bedroom. She sat up at once, clutching the blanket to her chest, remembering all the things her father had taught her about dealing with such a situation.

And then she remembered that Yuma was in the house. He probably couldn't sleep. But she hesitated, remembering Teague and Forman, and wondering if they might have broken in.

Then she heard the refrigerator door open, heard the kitchen chair scrape back from the table. Yuma.

Common sense dictated that she lie down again and go back to sleep. Every other urge she had made her climb out of bed and pull on her velour robe over her pajamas so she could check on him.

He was sitting at the table with a glass of milk, wearing nothing but old jeans. She hadn't even realized he owned a pair. For a minute she hesitated on the threshold, taking in the breadth of his tanned, muscular back, his strong arms, the enticing little shadow where his jeans gaped at his lower back. Boy, did she want to touch him.

She cleared her throat. "You okay?"

"Yeah." He straightened immediately, but he didn't look at her.

"Can't sleep?"

Suddenly he turned, and the face he showed her was a grimace. "Babe, go duck. I'm in no mood for friendly conversation. There's a monkey on my back driving me crazy tonight."

She didn't move. "Flashback?"

He turned away. "Missy Nurse thinks she knows so damn much! No, not a flashback. Just plain old ordinary memories. Now get out of here."

She sniffed. "This is my house, damn you. I'm not going anywhere."

Not by the merest twitch of a muscle did he respond. He sat there hunched over that glass of milk as if it were the only reality in the universe. After a moment she crossed the room to start the coffeemaker. From the look of it, it was going to be another long night.

Fifteen minutes later she joined him at the table with two hot mugs of fresh coffee. At first it appeared he was going to ignore the coffee and her both, but then he said, "Thanks."

"Sure." Lifting her mug, she pretended disinterest, as if she were there for a cup of coffee and nothing else. Sometimes all you could do was be there.

Minutes ticked slowly away. Wendy took another sip of the coffee she didn't really want. Yuma continued to stare into the milk as if it were a crystal ball.

But then, abruptly, he lifted his head and looked at her with hollow eyes. "I'm divorced, you know."

Hesitantly, she nodded. "Dad, um, mentioned that once, I think."

"She couldn't stand me anymore. You know, Wendy, if there was one person in the world who ever honestly loved me, Carla was the one...and she couldn't stand me anymore."

His words pierced her like spears on more than one level. He believed that no one but Carla had ever honestly loved him, which she could have argued quite hotly, and that hurt. But it hurt worse to think of the pain he must have suffered at Carla's abandonment and rejection. Instinctively she wanted to reach out, but she hesitated. Let him take his own time, do it his own way. That he was confiding in her at all was a major step all by itself.

"PTSD does more than give you nightmares and flashbacks, more than just make you confused at times," he said after a while. "It makes you...insecure, I guess is a good word. Makes you feel totally unsafe. Part of the compensation is withdrawal. You distance yourself from things that used to be really important."

When he didn't continue, she prompted him. "You distanced yourself?"

He shrugged one shoulder. "That's one way of putting it. I quit caring, is another way. Or I thought I did. I wouldn't let her in anymore. Wouldn't talk. Had these terrible rages whenever I felt anything at all. Sometimes I was able to control the anger, keep it inside, but other times...well, I never hit her, but she probably wondered when I would."

Again she restrained herself from reaching out. Active listening, she reminded herself. Active listening. "Did you worry about that, too?"

He glanced sharply at her. "Yeah," he said after a moment. "I did. All the time. When you get mad enough to lose control, you worry about things like that. I still thank God she didn't get pregnant. What it would have done to kids..." He shook his head.

"There was..." Again he shook his head a little, as if trying to clear it. "There was a Fourth of July celebration when the fireworks suddenly turned into tracers, like in a firefight, and I knew they weren't, but they were.... I went over the edge a little, started seeing bloody bodies on all those blankets instead of people watching the show, and I guess...I screamed for medics...got combative...a couple of other vets knew what was coming down and tried to control me, but..." He shook his head again. "It was the last straw for Carla, I guess. Until then it had been private. She was the only one who ever saw me hiding in the bushes or under the bed. This was...in front of everyone. And like she said at the time, it wasn't even as if I still loved her anymore—" His voice broke, and he looked swiftly away.

"But you did," Wendy said softly. "But you did."

"Yeah," he said thickly, after a bit. "I did. And it took losing her to remind me."

"Not a chance of fixing it?"

"Are you kidding? The hurt was too deep. I just...looked at her...the way she was crying.... God, I knew just how badly I'd hurt her." He looked away, swallowing hard. "I knew."

"So you let her go?"

"What was I going to do? Keep her prisoner?" He swung his head around and glared at her. "You don't know what it's like, Wendy. You can't have any possible idea how badly I hurt her. You can't imagine how badly I could hurt *you.*"

She caught her breath and closed her eyes briefly. Then she looked right back at him, her gaze level and unflinching. "I know very well just how badly you can hurt me. You've done it more than once."

She shoved her chair back from the table and turned to stalk out of the kitchen, as angry and as hurt as she had felt in a long time. He acted as if she were a cipher, as if nothing he said had any impact on her at all, and it infuriated her and wounded her even more.

He caught her at the door. There was none of his innate gentleness in him as he swung her around and trapped her against the wall with his body.

"I can hurt you worse than you ever dreamed, lady," he said harshly. His green eyes were hard, glittering, holding that wild look she remembered from so long ago. The look of a trapped, hurt animal. The look of a wolf that would gnaw off its own leg just to escape.

For long moments Wendy hardly dared breathe. For once her training was scant help. This man was teetering on some kind of emotional edge, and she wasn't sure he even knew where he was. Or who she was. Finally his name escaped her on an almost inaudible sigh. "Yuma . . . ?"

His eyes closed, and he threw back his head. An instant later he slammed his mouth down over hers and drove his tongue into her as if he wanted to dive right inside and hide.

For an instant shock held her rigid, then instinct took over. Her arms rose and wound around his neck; her head tipped to the side to give him better access; her entire body melted and conformed to his. She wanted him. Oh, God, she wanted him, wanted him . . . wanted him. . . .

He swore softly on a breath between kisses, then dove into her mouth again, his tongue stroking hers hotly, demandingly. He was hell-bent on conquest, and she could feel it in the way he pillaged her mouth. In the way his hard hips suddenly ground against hers, transmitting an ancient message of hunger and need.

Sparklers of desire danced along her nerve endings and met at her center, right where he thrust against her, to turn into wildfire. She throbbed, she ached, she yearned and she wanted to take him now. Right now. Without finesse, without foreplay, without any romantic interlude, she wanted to lie down beneath this man and take him into her body.

"Oh, baby," he said roughly, "I can hurt you. Believe me, I can hurt you."

"Hurt me so good," she heard herself whisper. "So good."

Suddenly he yanked back from her and turned away, leaving her sagging against the wall, dazed and humiliated.

"Get out of here," he said harshly. "Damn it, Wendy, get your butt out of here now!"

Hurting, shaking, wounded, she got out of there. Now.

Chapter 6

"You want to tell me what the hell he's doing living at your house?"

Wendy looked up into her father's angry face and knew that he wasn't going to be easy to satisfy. Nate had showed up early on a Saturday morning for coffee, unannounced, and Wendy had answered his knock just as Yuma came out of the bathroom with a towel around his neck. Nate had taken one look, stepped through the door and closed it, and now was glaring at them both.

"He's staying in the guest room, Dad," Wendy said, feeling desperate. "And before you say another word, kindly remember that I'm twenty-four years old!"

"You kindly remember that I'm your father." He glared past her at Yuma. "What's going on? *You* tell me."

Yuma lifted his hands and gripped the ends of the towel that hung around his neck. "I wanted to tell you all along. Your daughter's as protective of you as you are of her, man. Come on, let's have some coffee. It ain't the way it looks."

Nate grumbled something and pulled antacids from his pocket. "This had better be good."

"You're losing weight fast, Dad," Wendy said as she led the way to the kitchen.

"Quit trying to change the subject, missy. My health isn't under discussion here."

Wendy, coffeepot in hand, turned suddenly, her temper flaring. "And *my* health is? Let's get a few things straight here, shall we? I'm a self-supporting, independent, fully grown woman of twenty-four. I've seen things in the past six years that fall into the classification of war atrocities. I've handled men who were a bigger threat than Conard County has ever seen. I've dated cops, I've dated doctors, and I even dated one con artist. I'm still whole and healthy, and I think I've earned the right to make my own decisions." Angrily, she poured coffee into a mug and slammed it down in front of him.

"Furthermore, if I want to share my house with Yuma—if I want to share my *bed* with him—that's nobody's business but ours! Period!"

Nate turned on Yuma. "Talk," he growled.

"Yuma, no!" Wendy protested.

He gave her a lopsided smile. "I don't think this is a good time to assert your independence, babe. Your dad needs to know the truth. I've thought so from the start, and I'm going to tell him."

Wendy plopped onto a chair and folded her arms. Annoyance made her eyes sparkle and her lips compress. "If he gets into trouble because of you, Yuma, I'll never forgive you."

"Me?" Nate glanced at her, some of the anger fading from his expression. "What's going on here?"

Yuma finished pouring the coffee, and all three of them sat facing each other at the dinette.

"Teague and Forman came out a couple of days ago and made some threats about my friends in the hills. Before I arrived on the scene, they evidently made some threats against Wendy, too. Sexual threats."

Nate was out of his chair like a launched rocket. He swore a few words Wendy had never heard him use before and circumnavigated the kitchen as if movement were all that kept him from exploding.

Seeing her father's extreme agitation, Wendy glared at Yuma and got almost mad enough to hit him when he smiled back.

"You two are so alike," he said to her. "It's incredible. Come on, Tater, calm down. You know you can't do anything until Teague and Forman slip. I'm sleeping here just to be sure Wendy's never alone. That's all. Check the guest room if you doubt it."

Nate paced for another minute or so, but finally he returned to his seat at the table. "I've been looking to get that sumbitch Teague on something bigger than drunk and disorderly for years." He turned to his daughter. "What else has he done to you? And don't try to tell me this is the first time he's bothered you. I know the creep better than that."

Wendy shifted uneasily, knowing from long experience that her father wouldn't accept a brush-off. "He used to think he was in love with me. That's all."

"*In love with you?* How come I never heard anything about this?"

Wendy shrugged nonchalantly. At least, she hoped she looked nonchalant. "It hardly seemed like interesting dinner conversation." She was uneasily aware of Yuma's gaze on her, aware of his disapproval because she wasn't telling it all. But he didn't betray her trust by telling Nate the rest of it. "I mean, it wasn't the first time some guy pestered me a little. And it wasn't the last."

"Teague's not just any guy." Nate scowled at her, then turned to Yuma. "Why didn't you tell me?"

"Wendy was afraid of what you might do. Afraid you'd feel so protective that you'd forget law and order." He almost smiled at how thunderstruck Nate looked.

"Well, you *are* overprotective, Dad," Wendy said quickly.

"Not so overprotective that I won't turn you over my knee, missy! I *am* the law and order in this county, and have been for twenty years. Not once, not even one little time, did

I step over the line. I can't believe you thought such a thing about me. I'll get Teague, but I'll get him *legally.*"

"Yes, Dad."

He wasn't impressed and continued to scowl at her. "Did he lay hands on you? Ever?"

"Years ago," Yuma said before Wendy could answer. He ignored her glare. "That's why I figure he might not just be blowing hot air."

Nate nodded. "Okay. You stay here. But try to keep it from your mother, Wendy. Something's troubling her lately."

"What?"

"I don't know. When she's good and ready she'll tell me. In the meantime, I don't want her disturbed any more."

Wendy shook her head. "May I remind you that *I'm* the one who didn't want *you* disturbed?"

Her father just snorted. "I'm used to being disturbed. Goes with having six daughters, never mind being sheriff. What did Teague say he was going to do about your friends?" he asked, turning to Yuma.

"Hunt 'em."

"Stupid idiot," Nate muttered. "They'll make mincemeat out of him if he tries."

"Probably. I'm going to go up today and warn 'em to pull deeper into the mountains, though. They don't want trouble. They don't *need* it."

"Can't you stop Teague from going after them?" Wendy asked her father.

"I can't stop a man from going up into the mountains, if that's what you mean. And I can't stop him from going up there with a rifle. Or even an arsenal, as long as they're all legal weapons. Nope, Teague's going to have to do something. Really do something."

For long moments there was silence around the table as the three of them contemplated the price of adhering to the law. Finally Nate shook his head.

"At least I know what direction to keep an eye out now. And *you,* missy," he added to Wendy. "I want you to stick to Yuma here like a burr. Teague's a born coward. I don't think he'll try anything serious unless he catches you alone. Damn, I wish I knew what was eating the guy's guts."

Wendy shifted uneasily. At once her father, reading her like an open book after twenty-four years, looked at her. "What aren't you telling me?" he said.

Wendy looked uneasily at him and then at Yuma. She didn't want to say this, but she figured she was going to have to. She had suddenly remembered it, and it seemed as if it might explain a lot. And if it explained anything at all, both men had a right to know—her father because he might have to deal with it, and Yuma because he might have been dealing with it all along.

"Back right after I graduated from high school, Teague kept pestering me to go out with him. I kept saying no. He told me... that he loved me and wanted to marry me."

Yuma and Nate exchanged glances as they connected that with the fact that Wendy had been chasing Yuma that same summer. Finally Nate prompted her. "And you said...?"

Wendy looked down. "I told him I loved Yuma and wasn't interested in him. He said something about Yuma being a coward because he was a conscientious objector."

"And you said...?" Nate prodded again when his daughter didn't answer.

Finally she answered, her voice muffled. "I got mad. I told him he wasn't half the man Billy Joe Yuma was, and that he never would be."

I told him he wasn't half the man Billy Joe Yuma was....

Yuma sighed as he jolted his pickup down a logging road so old that it was little more than a series of potholes. Well, that sure as hell explained why Teague had had it in for him for years. There had been a while there, right after Wendy left for college, when Yuma had felt that Teague had been out-and-out hunting him. Gradually it had lessened, getting so there was a problem only if they happened to show up in the same place, which didn't happen often, once Yuma quit drinking.

Of course, that didn't explain why Teague had given him trouble even before Wendy, but it sure explained the escalation afterward.

Part of the reason Yuma had moved to Conard County all those years ago was because a big chunk of handling PTSD was to avoid stressors. The quiet pace of life here had made it possible for him to hold a job...most of the time. To stay sober...most of the time. Occasionally everything had closed in on him and he'd had to run to the hills to get away from it, but it had been better here by far than in Denver, where he'd been living.

Teague had sure done his part to destroy the peace Yuma had found, and now he was at it again. Anxiety was riding at the back of Yuma's mind, like a monkey on his back, a premonition of doom. He knew that feeling. It was PTSD. All those years of sitting on the edge, waiting for the next bullet, the next grenade, the next blow from his jailers, had taught him to always be on edge. Some lessons, it seemed, couldn't be unlearned.

But worse than anxiety was the hard edge of pain that never went away. A purely emotional pain, it rode him, tore him, clawed him, nearly every minute of every day. At first he had distanced himself from his feelings because he couldn't handle the constant anguish, and that had been part of the reason that Carla had left. He was either indifferent or angry, with no middle ground.

Carla's leaving had ripped away his defenses. Indifference and anger had no longer been enough to hide his pain from him. Then had come the bouts of heavy drinking. In and out of the VA hospital. Finally up to Conard County to escape all the pressures and reminders, the sudden events that cast him back in time, the sudden sounds or smells that precipitated confusion and flashbacks. Hell, once the sight of a Vietnamese woman and her child walking down the street had sent him into a flashback he'd only come out of two days later, back in the VA hospital.

Up here, those precipitators were rarer. Most of the time he had been able to handle himself. And finally he had even managed to get on the wagon and stay.

He hadn't had a really bad flashback in six years now. Hadn't had one of those where he was actually back in Nam, back in the camp. He still occasionally had moments of confusion, when he knew things weren't right, that his mind was getting mixed up, but mostly he could control it with deep breathing and relaxation.

So things were just hunky-dory, right?

Except for Teague.

When he reached the end of the logging road, he just settled down to wait. They would know he was here soon enough and would come out to help unload the truck. He'd brought blankets and canned goods and a couple of pairs of winter boots. As soon as he got paid again, he would bring more.

The first hints of autumn were here, in air that was chilly in contrast to the warmth of the sun. A woodpecker hammered industriously away, the tap-tap echoing through the tall timber. As he sat silently, a huge elk stepped out of the trees and paused, tilting his antlered head back as he tested the breeze.

Yuma nearly stopped breathing, caught in the blessed beauty of the moment. Then, even before he needed to draw his next breath, the elk caught wind of something and vanished with amazing swiftness into the shadows beneath the trees.

Moments later Cowboy stepped out into the road. Yuma shoved open the door of his truck and climbed out. Cowboy nodded to him. "The others are coming, 'cept Hotshot. He's having a bad day."

Hotshot was a former fighter pilot who had been shot down and taken prisoner for nearly five years. Eight years ago he'd given up trying to handle the real world and had gravitated to the safety of the mountains.

"How bad?" Yuma asked.

"Hell, he's on Saigon time. What's the deal with Artie?"

"He's in the hospital. They saved his leg, and he'll be good as new. Did you hear what happened when we got him down to town?"

"The grenade thing? Yeah."

Somehow, even though they appeared to be cut off entirely, these men heard everything. There were plenty of other people who wandered in these mountains apart from the vets—some survivalists, a few lone wolves. There would always be people who didn't fit into the outside world and found sanctuary here.

"Are they gonna charge him?" Cowboy wanted to know.

"Nothing's been done about it yet. I suspect the sheriff would rather just forget about it. Artie doesn't belong in jail. But the grenade thing might be causing trouble for the rest of you."

Cowboy cocked his hips to one side and settled his fists on them as he looked past Yuma. "So now we're a public threat of some kind?" He shook his head and swore. Thirteen months as part of a two-man sniper team in North Vietnam had taken a toll on him. He had finally been invalided out by a fragmentation grenade.

"Folks get a little bent out of shape over things like grenades. But the real problem is a couple of troublemakers named Teague and Forman. They've got it in for me, and they're making threats about you guys. It might be wise for you to pull back deeper into the woods."

Even as he spoke, Vance appeared out of the trees. Right behind him came Crazy and Boggs, a pair of marines who had done their tours in Nam together and trusted each other as they were never able to trust anyone or anything else.

"The truck's loaded with stuff," Yuma said. "I'll help you carry it back to camp."

He had packed everything for ease of transport in backpacks and balanced cartons. The five of them were able to manage the entire load that way and were soon walking deep into the forest.

The peace here was absolute. The occasional call of a bird, the woodpecker's industrious rapping, the infrequent buzz of an insect, all of these were part of the peace and left it undisturbed. The jarring things, the stressors, were almost absent. It was possible to come here, and with reasonable precautions, feel safe most of the time.

But if these men were hunted—if Teague really carried out his threat—their safety would be destroyed, and Yuma wasn't at all sure how they would handle it. Probably treat it as an enemy incursion, he thought as he tramped along behind Vance. Stage an ambush. Teague wouldn't stand a chance, and somebody would wind up going to prison.

He had to find some way to prevent a confrontation. Some way to convince these guys that this was a wise time to sift back into the deeper shadows of the mountains, to move up higher and farther from civilization. Teague would run out of steam eventually and think up some other way to cause trouble. Some easier way of stirring things up.

But if the confrontation wasn't avoided, he hated to think what might happen to some of these men. PTSD held worse terrors than flashbacks. It could fill a man with endless anxiety, with formless terror. It could make his nights sleepless, make him so restless he couldn't hold still, could drive him to end his misery with a gun or a length of rope.

The emotional suffering defied description. Yuma became uneasy just thinking about it, because the old feelings, generally quiescent these days, would stir and remind him that for years he had been the prisoner of a devouring beast that consumed him alive in ceaseless torment. Would remind him that it could attack again, could spring out of nowhere if he let down his guard, if he got too tense, if he remembered too much.

The edginess at the back of his head, which never quite let go, would grow, and he would know that despair was hiding right around a mental corner.

So he kept busy, kept his distance from people and let no one close, except other vets.

And Wendy Tate, damn her. Somehow she was getting closer, and he was damn sure she wasn't even trying. Six years ago, if he had moved in with her, she would have been prancing the halls in shortie pajamas, or forgetting to close the bathroom door all the way....

Remembering, he shook his head. She had been something else. But now she was a mature woman, and that maturity impressed him. She wasn't attempting in any way to take advantage of the current arrangement. At work she stuck to business unless *he* started a more personal conversation. She was efficient, decisive, competent, bright and nice to be around. And something about her soothed his nerves, which were never far from jangling.

Out of nowhere came a memory from his childhood, of an old man next door who had been a veteran of the trenches in France. His hands had shaken all the time, and any loud noise made him jump like a rabbit. The kids in the neighborhood had tormented him for a while, until their parents had caught on and put a stop to it.

But what he also remembered was how they had whispered about the old man's "shell shock." As if it were something to be ashamed of, not the normal outcome of intolerable suffering. Vietnam veterans had come home to the same attitude, the same silence, the same feeling that they should be okay if they were real men. Not for years did anyone address the fact that there *was* an aftermath.

Not that having a name for it made the hell any easier to take.

They reached the camp, and as soon as he had helped stow the items he had brought, he went to look for Hotshot. When Hotshot went on Saigon time, he usually hid in a glade a half mile from the camp, where rushing water screened all other noises. He would be hyperalert, though, and on guard, so when Yuma reached the edge of the clearing, he simply stood there and waited, knowing that sooner or later Hotshot would identify him. Anything else, though, would be dangerous, because he might be mistaken for a foe, rather than a friend.

Ten, maybe fifteen, minutes passed before Hotshot stepped out of the brush into the clearing and faced him. He was a man in his late forties, graying visibly and dressed in ragged jungle camouflage. In one arm he cradled an AR-15. Hotshot, like most military pilots, had gone through a survival training course and could subsist on beetles and bark if need be. It looked as if he might have been doing just that.

Finally the pilot motioned to a log, and Yuma joined him, the two men sitting side by side, taking care not to look at each other. For a long time, silence reigned. Finally, Yuma spoke.

"How bad is it?"

"Well, I recognized you, man."

One corner of Yuma's mouth lifted. "Yeah, you did. What year is it?"

"Who gives a damn? One's the same as another."

"Mm."

Another long silence.

"Need anything, man?" Yuma asked.

"Naw. Well, a woman would be nice. You ever want a woman, Yuma?"

"Am I a man?"

Hotshot laughed shortly. "Don't necessarily mean you want a woman. I don't mean just any woman, man. A special woman. You know. That special kind of…belonging."

Yuma closed his eyes for a minute, and all he could see was Wendy's face. "Yeah, man. I want a woman. Just like that. Special. But I'm poison."

"Me too."

They sat there contemplating that fact for a while, neither especially needing to say what was understood inside.

"I get to thinking sometimes," Hotshot said presently, "about why I can't be like everybody else. I mean, what did I ever do? Why shouldn't I have a wife, kids, a home? Why can't I have that *place?* All my own. Where I belong."

Yuma tightened his mouth and averted his face. "I know, man," he said, his voice a little husky. "I know."

"It doesn't seem like so damn much to want. You know? But then I think about this, about going on Saigon time the way I do sometimes, and I don't know if I could ask anybody to put up with it."

"Maybe...maybe somebody could handle it." He tried not to think of Carla, who couldn't, and Wendy, who had once thought she could but didn't have the experience to know. But he didn't want to tell Hotshot it could never happen. There were women out there who hung on through thick and thin, women who understood. He'd seen them. Met them. He just personally didn't feel he had the right to ask anyone to do it.

But maybe most importantly was that he didn't feel anyone really would want to do it. Wendy, for example. How long would she stick it out? That question alone was enough to terrify him into not even trying. He couldn't...he really couldn't survive another abandonment.

Sitting there in the chilly air with the sun warming his back and neck, he faced the real truth of his isolation. He might be poison, but his fear of forming an attachment was purely on his own behalf. Being utterly alone was at least safe, however miserable it might be.

He glanced at Hotshot, who was staring off into the trees. "You were married, weren't you?"

"She divorced me while I was in the camp. Can't say I blame her."

They all said that, that they didn't blame the wives who divorced them while they were POWs. Every one of them claimed to understand. Claimed that she had every right to get on with her life and find happiness. Generous sentiments. Truth was, deep inside, they all felt abandoned and resentful. All of them. And plenty who had come home to find wives still waiting had watched it all go down the tubes, anyway.

You might come home in one piece, but it didn't mean you came home whole. Big difference.

"So," Yuma said, "you need to stay out here awhile yet?"

"Yeah. I'm edgy. Jangly. The guys get on my nerves."

"Need anything?"

"Naw. I'm a survivor."

Sorry epitaph, Yuma thought. A sorry epitaph indeed. "You hear about Artie and the grenade down at the hospital?"

"Yeah."

"Well, in case you don't talk to the others soon, there's a couple of guys who are threatening to come up here and give you all a hard time over it. Keep a weather eye out."

For a long time Hotshot just sat unmoving, staring off into the gently stirring trees. Finally, though, he turned and looked at Yuma with flat, expressionless eyes.

"Like I said, man, it doesn't matter whether it's one year or another. Always somebody looking to start a fight. Always some reason to watch your back."

Yeah, thought Yuma. Yeah. It sure as hell felt that way.

It was nearly dark when Wendy came out to the office to pick Yuma up. She was being handed off like a baton in a race. All day she'd been with her family. First her dad, who hung a porch swing for her, and then her mom and sisters, who had been making pies for the church bake sale. Now she was under orders to drive straight to the office and pick up Yuma, who had returned from his trip to the mountains. Nobody had needed emergency services today, so she hadn't needed to come out here for any other reason.

Funny, she thought as she pulled up to the big hangar, how quick her dad was to trust Yuma with her safety. Six years ago, immature and self-centered as she had been, she'd been aware of her father's torn feelings over her pursuit of Yuma.

Nate Tate loved his daughter, but Yuma was his friend, his very good friend. Nate had told Wendy once of all the times that Yuma had piloted the Huey that had airlifted the casualties from Nate's unit. And since Nate had been the platoon sergeant, he'd felt all of those casualties as if they were his sons. Nate Tate was that kind of guy.

He had nothing but respect for Yuma and the risks Yuma had taken, and a lot of affection and concern for the man as well. So he had been torn, feeling protective of both his daughter and his friend, not wanting either of them to be hurt, knowing they both might well be. Short of locking Wendy up for the entire summer, there had been little he could do to intervene, though. He couldn't warn Yuma away, because Yuma was already trying to stay away. He could only lecture Wendy, who would calmly listen, nod and agree, and then go off after Yuma again.

In the end, he'd had to rely on Yuma. And Yuma had lived up to her father's trust, Wendy thought now as she parked near the office door. Billy Joe Yuma had protected Wendy from himself as assiduously as if she had been his own daughter. Another man, she had come to realize later, might have had fewer scruples. Another man might have left her truly wounded and wrecked, rather than just hurting her pride.

Evidently Nate felt his daughter was as safe with Yuma as she could be. Otherwise he would not have ordered her gruffly to go get the guy on her way home so she wouldn't be alone at her house.

Yuma came out as soon as he saw her pull up. He locked the building behind him, even though Brad and Sylvia were on duty, and then climbed into the Wagoneer with her. His beeper was prominent on his hip. Wendy's was clipped to her breast pocket.

"Your friends doing okay?" she asked him as she pulled away from the hangar.

"Yeah."

"Are they going to move their camp?"

"I don't know. Teague and Forman aren't really a serious threat, from their perspective. They could handle a damned invasion, let alone a couple of hotshot hunters who think hunting men is no different than hunting deer."

"That could be bad." She felt him glance at her.

"That's what worries me," he admitted after a moment. "If they hurt those two, even in self-defense, the situation will get worse, not better. I hope I made them see that."

At a stop sign, she turned to look at him. "What would they do without you, Billy Joe?"

He didn't look at her. "Nobody calls me Billy Joe."

"Why not?"

"I prefer to be called Yuma." He'd decided that at the age of fourteen, because Billy Joe sounded like a little kid's name. Other kids had teased him. Now the name felt like some kind of secret he didn't care to share. Worse, when Wendy used it, it made him feel as if she shared all his secrets.

She didn't reply to him; in fact, she didn't say another word until they reached her duplex. Once inside, though, she suggested they order a pizza and eat it on the back porch on her new swing.

"Sure. Okay." He pulled out his wallet, prepared to pay for the meal, but she reached out and stopped his hand, covering it with her own.

"No, Billy Joe," she said firmly. "This is *my* treat."

This time he didn't argue about the name. After the briefest hesitation, he nodded and went to shower off the day's dirt and sweat.

The pie was delivered just as he was coming out of his room in fresh jeans and a gray sweatshirt. He hung back so the delivery boy wouldn't see him and emerged only when he heard the door close.

Wendy smiled. "Come on. The porch swing is great. It'll be a little chilly out there, though." She had put on a sweater over her blouse.

He shrugged a shoulder. "It'll be nice."

It was. The duplex had a privacy-fenced backyard. An old garden had gone to seed and turned brown, and the grass needed trimming, but it was private and peaceful, and the only sounds were muffled ones from neighboring houses.

"I'm looking forward to the snow," Wendy said lazily. "I've missed it something awful. I want to get my skis on and just go for miles and miles.... Do you ski?"

"Cross-country? Sure." Not for miles and miles, though. His leg always kicked up too bad.

"Maybe we can go sometime."

His every instinct went on red alert. This was getting too cozy, he thought. Too close. It was too easy to slip into a relationship in little ways. Sure, we'll go skiing. Sure, we'll have dinner. Sure, we'll go to that movie....

Time to put the distance back.

"No, probably not."

The refusal was blunt and unapologetic, and though he didn't look at her as he said it, he could feel her shrink back a little. And that was when he realized he was doing it more to protect himself than to protect her. The realization filled him with terrible guilt. He started to turn toward her, to speak, but she forestalled him.

"Listen to me, Yuma," she said flatly. "I'm a lot older now, and I know a lot more about how the human mind works. You can push me away, you can shove and kick and scream and be as nasty and ornery as you want, but I'm not going to go away. I'm not going to stop caring. I'm your friend, whether you want it or not."

Something in him snapped then, something that had been pulled too tight and too thin for too long. Reaching out, he seized her by the shoulders and drew her toward him. A slice of pizza fell from her hand into the box at their feet. Neither of them noticed. Without a word, he lifted her onto his lap and wrapped both arms around her, tight and hard as steel bands.

"Friend? What if I want more?" he asked in a gritty voice. "Will you stop caring then? Will you go away then?" Deep inside, half of him hoped she would flee and half of him hoped she would stay. He was torn in two, was Billy Joe Yuma, and bleeding on the inside over something as simple as not being able to have what he had always wanted.

Nothing new, even. Just the old, old story, made fresh and painful by Wendy Tate and her incredibly trusting naiveté.

She never even spoke. Instead, tilting her head, she pressed her lips to his throat and snuggled closer, just as if he had taken her into a lover's embrace rather than one of threat and confinement.

Something in him stilled. Like the hush just before dawn, when even the air becomes motionless and the world holds its breath in anticipation. The quietude that filled him was stunning, enrapturing. He was caught in a timeless moment of peace such as he hadn't known since childhood. Not since a simpler world with a simpler faith and an absolute trust had been ripped from him by war's fury.

Her breath was warm against his neck, entrancing. *Real.* Her weight on his lap felt as if it had always belonged there. The soft tickle of her short hair against his chin and cheek was meant to be.

His arms, reacting instinctively, shifted their grip to one of embrace. He cradled her then, held her nestled to his chest, her head beneath his chin. She reached out a hand in response and kneaded his upper arm gently, soothingly.

Oh, man, it was a feeling like sunshine on a cold, cloudy day. Warm, penetrating. Relaxing. Tensions that had been with him for years seemed to slip away, until inwardly he began to feel soft. Open. Easy.

So easy.

And somehow, so easily, he turned his head and she turned hers and their mouths met in the gentlest of touches. A kiss meant to comfort, not arouse. A kiss meant to share caring and warmth and concern. A kiss unlike any kiss he had ever received.

"Oh, Yuma," she whispered against his lips. "Oh, Billy Joe, why are you so hard on yourself?"

He hardly understood her. He wasn't being hard on himself right now, he thought. No way. He was soaking up her warmth and vitality like a desiccated tree. She was filling him with a goodness he had thought he would never feel again. Filling him with life when he had been half-dead.

He shifted her a little, bending her gently back against his arm so that he could deepen the kiss. So long...so very damn long...

She opened to him eagerly, taking him deep so fast that his head began to spin. Her tongue mated with his hungrily, teasing and taunting and promising in a way that made him completely and totally forget he was kissing the young, inexperienced daughter of his closest friend.

In a way that made him aware only of her womanliness and all the promises she might fulfill. The pulsing rhythm of the kiss was filling him, and he could tell it was filling her, as well, causing her to move slightly against him, causing her to arch a little in an attempt to get closer.

He found the hem of her sweater, yanked the tail of her shirt from her jeans and found the smooth, warm skin of her midriff. Oh, God, he thought. Satin. Living satin, hot to his touch. The sensation against his callused palm was hypnotic, arousing, undeniable. He could no more give up the sensations coursing through him than he could have given up breathing.

"Oh, man," he whispered roughly, tearing his mouth from hers to fight for air. "Oh, man..." His hand slipped upward, driven by instincts and needs older than mankind. He felt Wendy grow still, heard her catch and hold her breath in anticipation.

Whatever conscious control he might have had was buried in a red haze of longing so intense that he was sure he had never felt this way before. Slowly his hand inched upward and at last found its goal—a small, exquisite breast. She wore no bra, and the realization streaked through him like lightning at the same instant that the sheer wonder of the feel of her nearly sent him over the edge.

Her hands reached up, clutching his shoulders as she gasped and pressed herself deeper into his touch.

"Oh, man," he whispered roughly again, as he realized she was not only *letting* him touch her, she was encouraging him to touch her. It had been long, so long, since a woman had genuinely *wanted* his touch. So long.

Suddenly impatient, he pushed her sweater and blouse up, and in the little bit of light granted to the night by the stars, he looked at her. Wide-eyed, she held her breath and waited, as if expecting judgment.

A long, long breath escaped him, and he reached out a finger to touch her nipple with a gentleness he had nearly forgotten. "Small," he whispered. "Small and sweet. Just what I like." It was true; he had never liked large breasts, had never understood the attraction. "I'll bet you taste just as sweet."

She inhaled sharply, and her mouth stayed open. Finally she whispered raggedly, "Taste me, Billy Joe."

Oh, man! Wildfire streaked through him, driving the last of his sense to the devil. This woman lying across his lap wanted him, and he would have had to be more than a saint to say no. Slowly, oh, so slowly, savoring every single second of anticipation, he leaned down toward her, closer and closer, loving the way her nipples puckered as if reaching up for his mouth. Loving the way they were eager for his kiss.

And then both their damn pagers tweeted, rupturing the night, rupturing the mood.

In an instant Wendy was off his lap, tugging down her sweater and blouse, heading for the door. "I'll call in," she said. "You'll probably want to get your boots on."

"Yeah. Right." But it was a long, long moment before he could even bring himself to move.

Chapter 7

There had been a two-car head-on collision, three miles out of town on the state highway. One of the drivers had been drunk. Both ambulances were already on the scene, along with sheriff's vehicles and a fire truck. The driver of one vehicle had a crushed chest, and it was for him the Med-evac flight had been called.

Yuma stayed at the controls of the helicopter. The pilot was not trained as a medic specifically so that he could not become involved in or preoccupied with patient care. He was there to fly and fly only.

Plenty of times in Nam, he'd hardly let his wheels touch the ground, had just hovered at ground level as the litter bearers ran up. This time he settled down on the pavement and kept the rotors turning as Wendy and Brad went to take care of the victim. He was pretty sure they were going to have to head directly to the trauma center; Sylvia wouldn't have hollered for them otherwise.

Less then ten minutes passed before Brad and a fireman came hurrying up with the stretcher, Wendy right beside them, steadying IVs and bending over the patient.

"Trauma center," she said as she climbed aboard.

Just as soon as they had the stretcher locked into place, he lifted off and throttled up to top speed.

He radioed the trauma center to tell them that they were coming, then let Wendy take over to describe the man's injuries. It wasn't a pretty picture, and he felt himself shaking his head as he listened. Chest wounds... well, he'd transported a lot of them, and an awful lot of them never made it as far as a doctor.

"I've got to intubate," he heard Wendy say. Guy's chest must be filling with blood, he thought. Lungs could collapse then.

"Hold it as steady as you can, Yuma," she asked through the microphone.

"You got it, lady." It was a calm, clear night, and keeping them steady wasn't a big problem. He thought of her back there with Brad, the two of them fighting to save this guy's life. Calm. Capable. Competent. That was how she sounded. That was what she was.

And it had to take a toll on anyone as caring as Wendy.

He set them down gently on the helipad and waited while the patient was transported inside, thinking about all the different kinds of trauma there were in the world. There was this guy with his crushed chest. There was Artie with his emasculation and PTSD. And there was Wendy, who surely bore scars from some of the things she must have seen.

He'd met a doctor once, a talented surgeon, who could no longer perform surgery because he had lost a patient on the table. He had cared too much. Maybe that was the problem. Caring.

And if you didn't care, if you kept a distance, those things couldn't hurt you anymore. Hadn't he been practicing that philosophy for years now?

But Wendy... she cared. He heard it in every word she spoke. Her heart was open, vulnerable. Exposed. Even a few minutes ago, sounding so calm as she inserted a tube into that guy's chest, she was caring.

He didn't wait long. The trauma team, having been alerted, had taken over the patient's care even as they were racing him into the building. Wendy and Brad stayed just long enough to provide whatever information they had.

Wendy climbed aboard, sitting in the co-pilot's seat. Brad stayed in back, beginning the tedious cleanup procedure. When Yuma had them airborne, he looked over at her and saw that her mouth was tightly compressed, that her hands were clenched into tight fists.

"Wendy?" He spoke into his microphone, saw her stiffen a little as his voice came over the headset. "Tell me about it."

She shook her head. "Nothing unusual. He probably won't make it. He certainly won't if they tell him that his four-year-old son went through the windshield and was decapitated."

Yuma swore savagely.

"Why don't people use their seat belts, Yuma? Why didn't that man put his little boy in a seat belt?"

He didn't even try to respond. How could you respond to a question like that? What could anyone possibly say in the aftermath? Reaching out with a gloved hand, he gripped her forearm and squeezed tightly. Over the headset he heard the unmistakable sound of a raggedly drawn breath.

Sometimes he wanted to demand from God an answer to such questions. Sometimes he actually did. So far, it seemed even heaven couldn't answer for the stupid, thoughtless, careless things people did, for the senseless tragedies that just happened.

When they got back to the base, Brad refused Wendy's help with the mop-up, insisting that he would get it done quicker by himself. He, too, saw the look in her eyes, a look of haunted anguish.

"Come on, lady," Yuma said gently. "I'll buy you a beer."

It wasn't until he was driving them back to her duplex in her Wagoneer that she even responded. "You don't drink."

"No, but it won't kill me to watch you have one."

"I don't like to drink."

"Then how are you going to get to sleep?"

She sighed and let her head fall back against the headrest. "I'll probably cry, Billy Joe. I'll cry until I fall asleep."

She said it wearily, as if she had done it many times before. The image pierced him. He could just imagine her all curled up on her bed, sobbing her eyes out, with no comfort to be found anywhere.

He knew about not being able to find comfort. He'd sure as hell never found any. Sometimes he even cried, it got so bad...and he knew how bad that kind of hurt was. He glanced again and again at Wendy. She needed more tonight than the dark solitude of her bedroom. The question was, was he capable of giving it to her? Or was he damaged past the point of being able to give enough of himself?

At home, he tried to get her to eat something. She merely shook her head and started pulling off her bloody jumpsuit as she walked down the hall, as if even ordinary modesty was past her comprehension in her current state. He saw smooth, creamy shoulders, the delicate line of her spine, and then the door closed behind her.

He listened to the shower come on and waited. The water pounded, but there was no other sound. No other sound at all. Minutes passed. Five. Then ten. Then fifteen. Not a sound. Wendy never dawdled in the shower. She was in and out in five minutes.

Twenty minutes. There couldn't possibly be any hot water left.

His heart clenched as if a giant fist had grabbed it. Ignoring every instinct for self-preservation, he reached for the knob and opened the door.

The room was full of steam. Evidently there *was* still some hot water. But no sound from the enclosure. Cautiously, he pulled back the curtain and peeked in, not wanting to scare her, scared to death *for* her, uncertain if he was making a big mistake.

One look and he felt as if his heart had been ripped wide open.

She was huddled under the spray, leaning against the wall and sobbing silently in great gulps. She didn't see him. She was past seeing anyone or anything.

Reaching in, he turned off the water. Without a word, he grabbed a towel, wrapped her in it and lifted her out of the tub. She wasn't even startled. She simply sagged against him and sobbed those terrible, silent gulps.

"Come on, baby, let's get you dry."

Another time he probably would have lost it. She had a great body, lean and healthy from hard work and exercise. Another time he would have gone out of his mind over those small breasts, that narrow waist and flat tummy, those jogger's legs. He sure would have lost it over the honey-colored curls at the juncture of her thighs and the sweet curve of her rump.

But tonight, right now, while some corner of his mind catalogued those things, his heart was aching too hard for her. He knew how badly she hurt, because he had hurt that badly himself.

And suddenly he was terrified. What if...what if Wendy became traumatized, as he had been? What if she lived the rest of her life with nightmare images of the kind that haunted him? He knew she wouldn't have the POW experience, which had certainly helped make his own case worse, but it didn't take all of that to scar the mind.

He helped her into her bedroom and found her bathrobe. Like a child, she lifted her arms and let him put it on her. And still she was drawing those ragged, uncontrollable sobs. He took her to the kitchen, set her down at the table and pulled out the beer that was at the back of the fridge.

"Drink it," he said.

"I hate it," she said brokenly. "That's for Dad...."

"Drink it."

But it was a few minutes before she even had sufficient control of her breathing to swallow. And in between swallows, she gave little hiccuping sobs.

"I'll be okay," she said finally, dragging her sleeve across her eyes.

"Who says you have to be okay?"

That seemed to shock her somehow. Her head jerked a little. After a few more little catches in her breathing, she asked, "What... do you mean?"

"You don't have to be okay. That's what I mean. Man, we came back from that damn war thinking we were wimps if we couldn't handle it. Well, who the hell said you have to handle it? Who said you have to be okay when you see what you've seen tonight? Who says you have to be calm and apologize for crying when it hurts so bad? Who said you *can't* cry?"

Wendy heard more in that question than a reference to her own tears. "Did you think you couldn't cry, Billy Joe?"

"Hell, I cried," he said gruffly. "I sure as hell cried. But I was ashamed of it. It was years before I finally realized that you were weird only if you *didn't* cry."

He looked away, angry at himself. They weren't here to talk about him. No way.

But his inadvertent revelations had the effect of dragging Wendy out of her own grief. They were sitting at right angles, and she reached out to touch his arm. "I imagine it took a while to realize that."

After a moment, he answered. "Only babies had a problem. It was years before anybody even mentioned PTSD out loud. Hell, Patton slapped a man for having combat fatigue. Real men don't do those things. Real men eat it up, you know. Ask any marine. Like Crazy or Boggs, two of the guys up in the hills. Hell, they'll tell you that stuff just doesn't touch you. Not a real man."

He turned suddenly. "Cry as much as you need to, Wendy. You only make it worse by pretending it doesn't exist. It *should* hurt. Damn it, it's *supposed* to hurt. If it ever stops hurting us, we won't be human anymore."

For a long, long time she simply looked at him from tear-filled eyes. Then she closed them, and two big tears rolled down her cheeks. "It builds up," she said finally, in a husky whisper. "You keep stuffing it away into some dark corner of your mind, telling yourself you can't deal with it right now, that you'll deal with it later, that you've got too much to do... whatever. But it finally comes out anyway. And when there's a child..." Her voice trailed off, and she compressed her lips, fighting more tears. "When there's a child," she whispered finally, "it hurts worst of all."

"Yeah." It was all he could say.

"There really isn't any rhyme or reason to it, is there? I mean, there's no reason why that man didn't put the seat belt on his little boy. He just didn't think. He never thought they'd get into an accident. It never entered his head that he was killing his little boy. But it will now. If he lives. How can anyone live with something like that?"

"I don't know, baby. I don't know."

"Don't call me baby."

"Why not?" He managed a faint smile. "I like it. I haven't called anyone baby in a long, long time."

"Your wife?"

His smile faded. "No. I never called her that." He looked away briefly. "I think the last girl I called baby was my date for the homecoming game. She was this bouncy little red-head with a huge grin and lots of cute freckles. I thought the sun rose and set on her. For a few weeks, anyway. Then she got the eye from a football player, and he held more appeal than a bookworm like me."

"You were a bookworm?" Somehow that seemed inconceivable.

"I had a very religious upbringing. That didn't leave room for a lot of other things. And learning was encouraged. But I probably would have buried myself in books, anyway. I like to read. Anyway, she was my last baby."

"A high school kid. I don't find that very flattering."

"You should. You have all that freshness, and you make me feel fresher just being around you."

Grief gripped her again, drawing a ragged breath past her lips. She averted her face. "Sorry."

"I told you not to be sorry. Let it come out however it needs to."

What he wanted to do was haul her onto his lap and tell her that everything would be okay. Easy to say, stupid to promise. Some things didn't get any better. This wouldn't get better, it would just fade with time. Maybe. He knew too well that some things never faded with time, they kept rearing up like gory ghosts, reviving themselves to new life.

Finally, though, Wendy let go a long, shaky sigh. "I guess I'll go to bed."

"Okay. Holler if you need me."

She didn't say anything until she reached the doorway. Then she paused and looked back over her shoulder, meeting his green eyes with her soft, swollen brown ones.

"I've needed you for six solid years, Billy Joe Yuma, and you haven't come running yet."

She might as well have punched him in the gut.

A string of curse words kept running through his mind like a broken record. He didn't sleep, but when he got like this, anxiety riding the back of his head like one of the Four Horsemen of the Apocalypse, promising serious trouble if he lost control, sleep was the last thing he seemed to need.

He was on the edge again, a place he hadn't been in a while. A place he hadn't been, really, since he gave up drinking. Somehow he had pretty much learned to control his PTSD, keep it at a level where he could handle it and still function.

Something—Wendy probably—was knocking him seriously off kilter. He hadn't let himself hurt so much for another person in an awfully long time. Now he hurt so bad for her that he could hardly stand it.

And then that remark... Damn, why did she have to say that? So clear, so plain, so unmistakable. Hadn't Nate said she was over him? Hadn't she said so herself, that she would always find him attractive, but...

Attractive. God, she found him attractive. And remembering the way she had responded to him on the porch swing, he believed it. She had made him *feel* attractive, and he couldn't remember the last time he'd felt like that. She wanted him. He wanted her. Hell, there was no sense hiding from the truth.

But she was Nate's daughter. He would just ruin her life. Just rip her to shreds with his moods, his withdrawals, his rages, his craziness. Nobody could stick it out for long. Improved as he was, he wasn't yet whole.

He would never *be* whole, either. Even as practice improved his control, even as time eased many of the tormenting memories, he knew he would be damaged forever. And damaged just plain wasn't good enough for Wendy Tate.

Wendy stood at the window of the closed back door and looked out into the backyard. Yuma was out there, standing in a brisk, chilly breeze, his head thrown back, his hands on his hips, looking for all the world like a man enjoying the beauty of the day. She knew better. He hadn't moved a muscle in more than twenty minutes.

She was supposed to be on her way to church. Failure to show up in the family pew this morning would be sure to earn her a visit just as soon as the service was over. Reaching an abrupt decision, she reached for the phone and punched in her parents' number.

"Mom? Hi. Just wanted to tell you I'm not coming to church this morning.... No, it was just bad last night. I couldn't sleep for thinking of the accident, so I'll try to catch up this morning.... Okay.... No, I'm fine, really. Talk to you later."

Then she resumed her watch.

As usual, Yuma was clad in a sage-green flight suit. She suspected that anything at all that mattered to him in the world was probably tucked into one of those multitudinous pockets. Ready to go at a minute's notice, the same way he had moved over here, with nothing but shaving tackle and an armload of flight suits and underwear. Nothing to tie him down.

Nothing anybody could steal that mattered.

The thought caught her like a punch in the chest.

Nothing that mattered.

In that moment she saw Yuma's loneliness and solitariness with a force that shook her. He was transient because he trusted nothing to stay. Because he expected to lose everything at any moment. So he didn't let anything matter that he couldn't carry in his pocket. Anything else was too big a risk.

And like most victims of PTSD, he never felt safe. Never. That one fellow at the VA hospital couldn't leave the security of his room. Yuma faced the world more readily, but he made his own security by needing nothing. Needing no one.

She swore, a soft sound in the silent kitchen. She looked down at her blue wool suit and shiny pumps, then out at the lonely man in her backyard. The breeze was knocking dying leaves off the poplar out back, and there was something so forlorn about the scene, and the man in it, that for a moment she couldn't even breathe.

And then she was out the door, crossing the dying lawn, hardly feeling the bite of the wind.

"Billy Joe. Billy Joe?"

He turned in time to see her running toward him. He never even paused to think, just opened his arms and caught her.

"Don't," she said, hanging on as tightly as she could. "Don't."

"Don't what?" he asked, unconsciously pulling her closer.

"Don't leave. Don't even think about it."

He looked down at her, unaware of how hungrily she soaked up the look of him, the feel of him. The reality of him. "I'm not leaving."

"You were thinking about it." Her fingers dug into his upper arms. "Billy Joe, promise me. Promise me."

He shook his head. "Promise you what, Wendy?"

"That you won't kill yourself."

He drew a sudden deep breath. "I wasn't..."

"You were." Desperation made her voice sharp. "I could feel it. You were. You *have* thought about it. Plenty of times. Don't bother pretending with me. I know how badly PTSD hurts. I know how many guys turn a gun on themselves! I saw it, Billy Joe. I saw it *happen*. Now promise me you won't! Promise!"

Suddenly he was gripping her upper arms, holding her away from him, almost glaring down into her face. "You *saw* it happen?"

"Damn it, I'm a trauma nurse! What do you think I've been doing for the last six years? Living in a convent? I worked in a major city hospital. Night after night I saw guys like your friends in the hills, guys who could never go home. Guys who tried to hide in drugs and ended up overdosing. Guys who finally couldn't stand it anymore and ate a gun. Guys who never really got back from that damn war! I saw it, Yuma! And one night, I saw a guy do it! Somebody called 911 because this guy was suicidal. They restrained him and brought him in, but he grabbed a gun from a cop who was looking the other way and—and—" She shook her head. "Nobody could talk him out of it. He just stood there and shook his head and said, 'Man, it hurts too damn much.' Then he pulled the trigger."

"Oh, sweet God," he whispered. He yanked her against him, holding her so tightly that he could feel the straining of her ribs as she gulped in air. "Wendy, oh, baby, I swear I wasn't. I've thought about it in the past, but not for a long time now. I never would, anyway, because it's against my convictions. *I never would.* I promise you."

"You—you looked so lonely out here. So alone," she said brokenly. "So lost. I couldn't— It reminded me—"

"Shh . . . shh . . . Aw, honey . . ." Some long-guarded wall inside him began to crumble, and he fought for a moment to shore it up. But her anguish was so clear that it reached him, anyway, making a mockery of all his defenses.

Last night, he thought. Last night had unleashed all the things she had kept deeply buried. The death of that little boy had opened the sarcophagus in which she had been burying all the painful things, and one by one they were coming out. Now this. God, he'd had no idea, not the merest inkling, that she had been facing things like this while she was away.

Something inside him shifted as he looked at Wendy Tate with new eyes. She was so far removed from the heedless child she had been six years ago that he realized quite suddenly that she was a stranger to him. She was not the person he had thought she was these past weeks. Not at all.

She was a woman, full-grown. A woman suffering from delayed stress because she cared so much.

"Come on," he said. "Let's go inside." Gently he urged her toward the house. "Actually, I was just out here, well, worshiping. There's no Meeting House here for me to go to, so I generally find a quiet spot for... contemplating the Divine. Quakers look inward, unless we feel moved to witness. That's all I was doing, babe. I swear."

A stray tear wandered down her cheek as she managed a nod. "Sorry. I—"

"Don't be sorry. There's not one thing to be sorry for, Wendy."

"It's just that you didn't move for so long. It...reminded me..."

"Yeah. I know how that goes. I know all about that."

In the living room, he settled them on the battered couch and pulled her into his arms, holding her comfortingly against his chest. "You're beginning to sound like a wounded warrior yourself," he remarked.

She made a small sound. "I guess. A couple of times before it got to me a little, but nothing like this. Nothing like this."

"Too many things all at once," he said. "Two little boys in a row and...other things." Him. He knew he was part of it. As were Teague and Artie and, indirectly, all the vets up in the mountains. The situation evoked a lot of memories for her, and the added stress of Teague's threats could only help precipitate it.

"Well, I'm all right now." She tried to say it with conviction, but the words came out sounding lost and doubtful. Yuma merely tightened his arms and held her where she was.

"You were going to church?" he asked.

"I changed my mind."

"It might help."

She shook her head, then slowly looked up at him. "I'm in no mood to try to fool my mother into thinking I'm okay. She'd take one look at me and know something was wrong, and she wouldn't give up until she found out what it was."

"What would she find out?"

Wendy sighed deeply and looked away. "That I'm feeling all messed up. I guess I'll go change into jeans and work in the yard. I need to be busy."

"There was another robbery last night," Nate said.

Wendy sat across from him at the dinette, her short hair tousled by the wind, the knees of her jeans stained from the garden dirt. Yuma sat between them, every bit as dusty since he had been helping her with the yard work.

"What happened?" Wendy asked.

"Somebody broke into the Cardiff home while they were in town last night. Stole Joe Cardiff's hunting gear and three rifles." He looked up from his coffee at his daughter. "You should have been in church this morning. All those good souls were talking like a lynch mob."

"Guess who they want to lynch," Yuma said heavily.

Nate nodded. "Of course. Who else is there to point the finger at? And it's easy to think those guys in the mountains would want the rifles and the hunting clothes. Oh, the thieves also took Cardiff's reloading equipment."

Yuma swore. Wendy glanced worriedly at him and didn't like the despairing anger she saw on his face. She wanted to reach out, but she couldn't, not in front of her dad. "Do you think anyone's going to do anything?" she asked instead.

Nate shook his head. "Not yet. Not just yet. But tempers are rising, and I expect when Teague hears about this, he'll do some additional stirring of the pot."

"There's got to be something we can do!" Both men looked at her, but neither of them said anything. "Are you telling me there isn't?"

Nate sighed. "Wendy, you can't hang people for talking. Not in the U.S. of A. I know we've discussed this before." He gave her a crooked smile. "The first time was when you were four and wanted me to arrest Jimmy Stedman for calling you a dumb sissy."

She felt her cheeks flush a little and was aware of Yuma's sudden amusement. "But this is different. Teague is making threats."

"You can ask Judge Williams to give you a peace bond," Nate said. "If he makes any more threats against you, she'll fine him."

"Dad..."

He shook his head. "That's the extent of it, doll. Not worth the trouble."

Frustration brought her to her feet. She went to the kitchen window and folded her arms beneath her breasts, wrestling with a sense of outrage. "You're young yet, Wendy," she could imagine her mother saying. "You've got to realize, life isn't fair. Never has been and never will be." And of course that was true. But somehow Wendy could never quite get past the feeling that life *ought* to be fair.

"Walk me out to my car, Yuma," Nate said.

Wendy glanced over long enough to say goodbye, but she recognized her father's wish for a private word with Yuma. She knew better than to try to argue. Nate Tate could be utterly unyielding when he chose.

Yuma followed Nate out the front door. When Nate signalled him to get in the Blazer, he climbed in on the passenger side.

"Okay, son," the sheriff said when they were closed inside the vehicle and couldn't be overheard. "What the hell is going on with you two?"

"Wendy had a rough night last night at that accident. Then she got hit with some delayed stress over some stuff she saw in L.A."

"What stuff?"

"Emergency-room stuff." He didn't feel he could say much more without betraying her confidence...if you could betray a woman's confidence to her father. "Apparently your little girl has been growing up the rough way."

Nate swore and drummed his fingers on the steering wheel. "I figured when she decided to be a trauma nurse that she was going to be seeing some pretty bad things. The kinds of things I'd always tried to protect her from."

"Well, she's seen them. Atrocities, she calls them."

Nate swore again. "I'm going to tell you something, Yuma. Six years ago, I would have killed you if you laid a finger on her."

Yuma couldn't help it. A soft laugh escaped him. "I kind of figured that, Tater. Only a fool would have missed it."

Nate turned and looked straight at him. "She became a trauma nurse because of you, man. She told her mother that she wanted to understand some of what had torn you up. That she didn't see how else she could understand where you'd been. And, of course, I inadvertently encouraged her by talking you up, how you saved so many lives . . . how not very many people have that kind of guts."

A sensation of shock ran through Yuma, at once hot and cold. She'd gone into trauma work because of *him?*

"I thought it would wear off," Nate continued. "I really thought she'd meet some doctor or something and get married and settle down to having kids. I figured it wouldn't take much to change her mind about emergency medicine. I figured she couldn't handle it and would get into something a little easier. I underestimated her."

For long moments there was only silence in the cab. Nate frowned out the window and Yuma tried to absorb what he'd just been told.

"I wasn't ever going to tell you this," Nate said finally. "I wasn't ever going to do anything to encourage you. You're still too old for her, still too screwed up...but hell, man, I'm pretty damn sure you'd kill yourself before you'd ever really hurt her."

Yuma didn't bother to confirm the obvious. He wouldn't kill himself, but he *would* move to China to avoid hurting her. "So?"

"So...I'll stay out of it. She's done some growing up, and I figure...well, she's a lot older than Marge and I were when we got hitched. She's old enough to decide this one for herself. Whatever happens between you two, I'm out of it."

Yuma was stunned. He couldn't remember the last time anyone had offered him the kind of trust Nate was offering now...except for Wendy. Wendy just kept right on believing the good in him. And now Nate Tate was saying essentially the same thing.

"Look, Nate—"

Nate interrupted him, shaking his head. "Forget it, son. If she hasn't changed her mind in six years, she's not likely to. Sometimes a parent just has to know when to step back and let it happen...even if it's going to hurt. If you're in her system, nothing I can do or say is going to change that. So..." He shrugged.

Then he turned and looked straight at Yuma once again. "I also think you're better than you think. You've come a lot farther than you admit. That monkey might still be riding your back, but it's not controlling you anymore."

A sudden surge of strong feeling forced Yuma to look away. "I wish I were half as sure as you seem to be. What brought this on?"

"Marge. She reminded me of a few things." Nate shook his head again. "Funny how different it looks when it's your kid instead of you." He sighed. "Frankly, son, I've had a taste lately of what it's like to want something so bad you can't stand it and not be able to get it. I'm not going to be the cause of making anybody else feel that way."

Yuma almost asked, then stopped himself. Nate had already been uncharacteristically open, and it was unlikely he would answer questions. He never had in Yuma's memory. "I'm poison, Nate. She'll figure it out eventually. I'll blow up over some stupid thing, or I'll pull away inside.... She'll change her mind. Just give her a little time to see what I'm really like."

Nate faced him. "You really believe that."

Yuma nodded. "I know myself. Maybe I haven't had a flashback in six years, but the monkey's there. It still has an effect. It'll show sooner or later, and she'll run like hell. So don't worry about it. Maybe you'll bow out, and I thank you for your trust, but I have no intention of making the rest of her life miserable by falling in love with her."

Nate swore, an expression he rarely used. "Well, it's your call, son. Always thought you were too damn self-sacrificing for your own good, and I guess I was right. But, buddy, I've seen the way she looks at you. She's been away from home six years now, and it makes it easier for me to see her as an adult woman instead of my daughter. And I'm telling you, when a woman looks at a man like that, he ain't got a chance in hell."

Nate's closing comment was still rolling around in Yuma's head when he went back into the house. He was willing to admit that the attraction between himself and Wendy was incendiary—they'd surely proved that—but he didn't think Nate was right about Wendy still wanting him. No way. She didn't do a damn thing to entice him. Instead, she acted as if they were just friends. Really good friends, but just friends.

Hell, he was forty-four years old. He damn well knew when a woman was strutting her stuff for his benefit, and Wendy wasn't strutting anything at all.

So Nate was wrong about that. What the hell was going on with Nate, anyway? This diet business, comments that would lead somebody to believe there was trouble at home... But Marge Tate worshiped the ground Nate walked on. Anyone with two eyes could see that. They might quarrel at times, but the love was there, solid and strong, something anyone else would envy. Or so he would have said.

"What did Dad want?" Wendy asked as he entered the kitchen.

Yuma smiled. "You know better than that."

Wendy tried to keep a severe expression, but she couldn't help responding to that twinkle in his eye. A slow smile came to her own face. "Guy stuff?"

"Guy stuff."

"I hate it when he does that!"

"Curiosity killed the cat."

Just then the phone rang. Wendy turned and reached for it, half expecting it to be her mother checking up on her. Instead, a man's rough voice said something crude and very explicit.

She slammed the phone down, and at once Yuma was there, gripping her upper arm.

"Wendy? What was it?"

She shook her head. "Obscene phone call." Then, slowly, she raised her eyes to his and saw there the same thought that came to her own mind.

"Teague," he said.

Chapter 8

Yuma would have liked to commit a few acts of violence against Teague for that phone call. As it was, he restrained himself for two reasons. First, they couldn't be sure it was Teague who had called. Secondly, if he read Teague's character correctly, any response would only make things worse as Teague attempted to prove that he wasn't intimidated. Nate agreed with that reasoning, once he heard what was going on.

There were no further calls in the following week, and things around the county stayed quiet. Then there was another break-in and robbery, this time closer to town. The items taken included canned food, rifles and hunting knives. From that moment, the sheriff's office was besieged and talk in the local bars grew ugly. Teague's voice was hardly louder than the rest.

In fact, it soon began to seem that Teague was lying low, as if he sensed that the Conard County Sheriff's Office was paying more than ordinary attention to him. Which it was, Nate admitted to Wendy and Yuma. Expecting some kind of trouble from that quarter, he had told his deputies to keep a sharp eye out.

By the end of yet another week, Wendy complained to Yuma that it felt as if the county were sitting on a powder keg, just waiting for something to happen.

"The last time it felt like this around here," she told him, "was right after John Grant was killed by that escaped con, remember? Everybody was tense like this until they caught him. Expectant. Uneasy. Angry. Ready to blow if something else happened."

"Robbery and murder aren't the same thing, though." Yuma had just come back from another trip into the mountains to see his friends and was sitting at the table, rubbing his bad leg and looking fatigued.

"No, they aren't the same thing," she agreed. "But these folks are feeling violated, and that's every bit as bad. They consider their homes and property sacrosanct, and every one of them is wondering who will be next. Or what'll happen if somebody is home when these guys break in."

Beyond the kitchen window, the autumn night had grown dark. A chilly wind was blowing stiffly enough to rattle the flap on the exhaust fan. Wendy wrapped her arms around herself, as if she suddenly felt cold.

She had gone into trauma medicine because of him. That thought had been whirling around in Yuma's mind since Nate had told him.

Eighteen-year-old girls were one of life's most priceless treasures, Yuma had always thought. They were young, innocent, pure and loving. Full of a need to give, full of confidence that love could make anything right. It had been to protect that incredible purity and innocence in Wendy that he had kept her at a distance.

Now he knew that she had deliberately and willfully sacrificed some of that naïveté and innocence for no better reason than to understand his pain. She had willingly shouldered pain in order to share his.

It hurt. It hurt him in deep places that he tried to keep locked up. That kind of...love, for lack of a better word, was something he didn't deserve. Had never deserved. Yet it had been offered selflessly, and all he had done was reject it. He hadn't given her one little thing in return.

Now, six years later, looking at her and seeing what she had done for him, he saw also that he had wasted it. She no longer sought him out. She no longer looked at him with the helpless, hopeless yearning she had shown so openly six years ago.

She still wanted him, but he had smashed even that on two occasions by his treatment of her. It was hardly any wonder that these days she talked to him and looked at him as if he were just another acquaintance. That for two weeks now she had studiously avoided getting close to him without a piece of furniture somewhere in the middle. "Just sex," he had told her. And Wendy was not the kind of woman to ever want that kind of a relationship.

She deserved a whole hell of a lot more, anyway. She was incredibly generous with everyone—caring, concerned, always ready to give of herself and her time to anyone who needed it. He watched her sweat bullets over each patient, watched her listen to the personal problems of co-workers and friends, watched her volunteer with kids at the church.... Incredibly generous.

But since the day she had demanded his promise not to commit suicide, she had offered him nothing more than her casual friendship. It was as if she had realized she had exposed too much and was seeking to evade further exposures.

Hell, he knew all about that avoidance. It was something he did all the time himself. And it told him that he had traumatized her. She no longer felt safe enough to be vulnerable around him.

He hated himself at that moment more than he had hated himself since he had called Wendy a baby. For an instant his thoughts drifted to that bottle of Jim Beam out at the station, but he brushed it away. That had never solved anything.

"How are your friends doing?" Wendy asked suddenly.

"Okay. They're going to pull back up farther into the mountains. Finally. And they're going to stay on the move until this gets settled. It'll make 'em hard to find."

"So you won't be able to find them, either, until the culprits are caught?"

"Oh, I know where they'll be. Nobody else will, though. I could get to them if I needed to." He shook his head. "Hope I don't need to."

"Me too." She shivered again and rubbed her arms. "It's so drafty in here today. It feels like that wind is blowing right through the windows."

"I'll get some caulking compound on Monday and see about sealing this place up." It seemed like the least he could do.

"Can I do that for you?"

Startled, he looked up and saw that she was watching him knead his thigh. "It's okay. Really." The thought of her hands on his thigh was almost enough to put him through the roof. Whatever other things he might feel about Wendy, there was no doubt in his mind or body that he wanted her like hell on fire.

"What happened to your leg?"

"Hip was broken in the crash."

"Crash?"

It suddenly occurred to him that she didn't know anything about his past. Not really. Nate Tate was so opposed to gossip that it was a wonder he could discuss the weather without feeling guilty. "My chopper was shot down when we were flying in to pick up the wounded. I was the only survivor. My hip was broken."

So he'd lain beneath the jungle growth, curled up in a ball, feeling as if he were solely responsible for the death of his crew, convinced he was going to die.

"The North Vietnamese found me and put me in a POW camp," he continued. "I didn't get much medical care. The army fixed me up pretty good when I got home, but when I walk long distances, I ache for a while afterward. That's all. No big deal."

"Of course it's a big deal," Wendy said, startling him. "Whyever should you pretend it isn't?"

He cocked his head, wondering what was eating her. "It's just a little ache."

Just a little ache. Just a little reminder, she thought, of a kind of hell no one should ever have to know. Suddenly she jumped up from the table and went to start dinner. Minimize, she thought. He minimized everything: his pain, his service, his worth, his goodness...

She pulled a round steak from the fridge and slammed the door. No fancy cooking tonight. She was going to slap the darn thing under the broiler and serve it with steamed spinach.

"It's my turn to cook," Yuma remarked.

"Forget it. You've been hiking in the mountains all day. You can cook tomorrow."

At that moment, their beepers shrilled simultaneously from the top of the fridge.

"Oh hell," Wendy said, and closed her eyes. "Oh hell."

Cardiac arrest. The family knew CPR and kept it going until the chopper arrived. Wendy and Cal were able to revive the patient, but he went into atrial fibrillation three times on the flight to the hospital. It didn't look good.

And Wendy was at the end of her rope, Yuma thought. It was well after midnight when he drove them home in her Wagoneer, but more than ordinary fatigue was shadowing her face.

She looked...lost. Worn-out. Coped out. For the past couple of weeks he had sensed a growing tension in her, a growing wariness and weariness, and tonight he had the distinct impression she was near the edge.

As soon as they stepped into the house, the phone rang. Wendy was closest, and she picked it up automatically, half expecting to hear that they were needed somewhere else.

She slammed the phone down with a force that told Yuma what she had probably heard. He was beside her immediately.

"Wendy? Baby? What did he say?"

"Stop calling me *baby!*" She shrieked the words at him, losing the last vestige of her tattered control. "Don't you *dare* call me baby again! I'm not your baby. I'm not anybody's baby! I am a grown woman, and I'm sick to death of being treated as if I can't take care of myself, as if I don't know my own mind—"

She pulled away from him and stormed halfway across the kitchen before whirling to face him again. "He wanted to know if you were—if you were any good in bed! Because he's got some stuff to—to teach me..." The word died in a gasping, gulping sob. "Only he... he was crude...."

A murderous feeling filled him. "Did you recognize the voice?"

"No...." She turned her back to him and wrapped her arms tightly around herself.

The gesture of rejection, the self-comforting pose, snapped something inside him. Some long-guarded barrier vanished in an instant.

Rage poured through first, a rage he had long felt guilty for even harboring. Rage against a world that was so unjust and cruel. Rage over the things that had happened to him, the way he had been mistreated and abused, not only as a POW, but as a man, as a husband, as a vet.

Rage at Wendy for tempting him with what he could not have. Rage at himself for wanting what he should not take.

Rage that he could never have what he needed so badly.

But rage was merely a shield against something more painful, and as he stood there shaking before the force of his inner whirlwind, he felt the pain sweep past the rage. All the pain of betrayal and loneliness, helplessness and loss. The pain of unworthiness, of failure, of despair.

The anguish of not having lived up to himself.

But somewhere in the midst of the ocean of pain, he felt something else stir. That something carried him across the kitchen, made him turn Wendy into his arms, made him take her into his embrace and rock her gently as if he had the power to heal . . . when he knew he had nothing but a power to wound.

Not a word passed his lips. He simply held her tightly and rocked her gently and let her sob her heart out on his chest.

For a while it seemed her grief was bottomless and would never end, but gradually she quieted, until she was resting limply against him, only an occasional soft sniffle escaping her. Finally she sighed and tried to step back.

But he didn't let go. Instead he tucked a finger beneath her chin and turned her face up so he could see her. Her eyes were swollen and red, her cheeks looked almost chapped, and her nose was a shiny red—and he was sure he had never in his life seen anyone who looked more beautiful.

Her kind of caring was beyond price, he thought. Except for him, she might be happily married, living a happier life with kids—and without all this anguish.

Talk about having your words come back to haunt you. Looking down into her face, he remembered telling her there was no way on earth she could understand his pain. No way on earth she could know where he'd been. That she was a baby, and would always be a baby to him. That—

He cut the thought off, unable to handle any more. The guilt was almost enough to kill him, knowing those tears might never have been on her face except for him.

Trying to do the right thing had once again caused him to do the wrong one. Damn, it was incredible, but he must have some kind of evil genius. Time and time again he hurt someone when he only meant to do right.

"I'm sorry," he said softly to her now. There seemed to be no way he could express the guilt he felt, no way to explain. Those simple words were the only ones he could say.

"For what?"

He shook his head. There was no way humanly possible to explain.

"Damn it," she said, startling him. "When are you going to stop taking responsibility for everything in the world? You have nothing to do with my mood tonight!"

"Don't I?"

"No! I'm just tired. Worn-out."

"Worn-out from work? Then maybe you'd better change careers."

"No, not worn-out from work!"

"What, then?" He might have smiled if he hadn't been hurting so badly. She looked cranky, like an overtired child, and she was frowning at him.

"Just tired from *everything,*" she snapped. "Tired *of* everything. Isn't that allowed?"

"Sure. Tired of having me around? Is that part of it?" Something was goading him, pushing *him* into pushing *her.* A corner of his mind warned him to stop, but he kept right on. "Is it me?"

She opened her mouth as if she were going to snap right back, and then suddenly looked so...hurt. So wounded....

A deep fault ruptured in him, and he teetered on the edge for a timeless moment. And then he slipped over.

Falling, falling, falling. That was how it felt, the same dizzy terrifying feeling he had known when the copter crashed, the same stomach-sinking knowledge that he was helpless in the face of forces beyond his control.

And then he kissed her. He took her mouth with merciless savagery, forgetting every single scruple, inhibition and caution he had ever felt because of her age. He kissed her like a man with one thing on his mind, a man who had been too long without a woman, a man who hated himself for what he was doing, but was helpless to stop.

She should have shoved him away. She should have kicked and screamed and kneed him. She should never have wrapped her arms around his neck and melted into him as if she had finally found her place, as if his savagery answered some need of her own, as if he were the answer to her prayers.

But she did. She leaned into him, breast to chest, belly to belly, sex to sex, as if she had been meant to fit her soft contours precisely to his hard ones. The feeling of her arms winding tightly around his neck, drawing him closer and closer, crept past his last defenses and touched the deep interior places that had been empty for so long.

He no longer cared that she was the daughter of his best friend, that she was hardly more than half his age, that he could only sully her and wound her more. All his scruples, all his principles...everything fled before his need.

His hands, acting on an instinct deeper than thought, slipped down her back to grasp her bottom and tilt her even more intimately into him. His legs spread, widening his stance to bring her closer yet. Every cell in his body awoke with hammering hunger.

And with a little shiver and a little sigh, she let him pull her deeper into his embrace. A deep, muted groan rose in his throat at her response. He kept one hand cupping her rump, holding her as close as he could get her, while his other wandered up her side, seeking the feminine swells of her breasts.

So long...so long...so long since he had last felt anything as sweet as this woman who trembled eagerly in his arms. So very, very long since he had last wanted anything as badly as he wanted Wendy Tate. An eternity since he had last felt this alive...had dared to feel so alive.

His hand found the side of her breast. She moaned softly and then deprived him of breath simply by leaning back to invite his touch.

"Billy Joe," she whispered, making it sound like a love song. "Billy Joe..."

He cupped her and even through the layers of her clothing he felt the peak of her breast already stiff for him. Gently, oh so gently, hardly daring to believe what his senses were telling him, he brushed his thumb back and forth across her swollen nipple and listened with deep satisfaction to her soft groan.

Her hips rocked against him, just an infinitesimal movement, but one he felt to the core of his being. When he felt her legs part, his own was there to immediately slip between them and press until she rode his thigh. And another groan was torn from her as she threw back her head and gave herself up to the feelings he evoked.

"Oh, Billy Joe," she moaned, gripping his shoulders tightly. "Oh, please..."

With shaking fingers, he found the zipper on the front of her jump suit and pulled it down. She didn't wear a bra, didn't need one, and he savored the sight of those small, creamy mounds with their hardened pink tips. *Taste me* she had begged him on the porch swing, and now she was arching her back and lifting herself toward him in unmistakable invitation.

It was an invitation he couldn't refuse. Bending, he touched just the tip of his tongue to her beaded nipple. At once a shudder racked her, and her fingers dug painfully into his shoulders. A moan seemed to rise from her very toes. Damn, she was responsive. Incredibly so. How he savored every shiver, every moan, every sign of her yearning.

Her fingers tightened even more, and he accepted the invitation. Gently, taking great care, he drew her nipple deeply into his mouth and sucked. A low cry escaped her, and the movement of her hips was unmistakable.

She wanted him. She wanted him here, now, this very minute. Her entire body beckoned to him, demanding fulfillment. His own blood was a drumbeat in his ears, and every fiber of his being strained toward finding fulfillment in her.

But just as that final barrier began to crash, he panicked. Some last vestige of common sense warned him that this was no one-night stand, that this woman would expect more, that she had every right to demand more. That if he made love to her, he would be stepping into a long-term relationship.

He couldn't handle that. No way on earth was he ready to handle a relationship.

"Oh my God!" The words escaped him in an anguished whisper. He pulled away abruptly and, without looking back, left the kitchen. He didn't want to see what he was leaving behind. Didn't want to see the hurt and accusation in her eyes. Knew he would die if he saw what he had done. So he walked down the hall to his bedroom and closed the door with quiet finality, and not once did he look back.

"You have to leave."

Yuma lifted his head and looked across the breakfast table at her. She looked like hell this morning—her eyes were sunken, and fatigue whitened her face to chalkiness. He doubted he looked any better. Neither of them had slept.

"I can't," he said. "Not until this thing with Teague is settled."

"I'll get somebody else to shadow me."

"Wendy." His heart beat painfully and he could no longer refuse to acknowledge what he had done. "I won't... touch you again. I swear."

Something inside her snapped. Deep inside her brain, she heard it, an internal crack as a dam broke and the flood poured through.

"No, you certainly *won't* touch me again," she said coldly. "Ever. Six years ago I was a baby. I believed *that* excuse. But what's the excuse now, Yuma? Am I so repulsive that you can't escape fast enough?"

Horrified, it was a moment before he could find speech. He hadn't even dreamed he might be making her feel that way. "Wendy, I... It's not that at all! It's just that I don't have anything to give you—"

"Who the hell asked you to give me a damn thing!" She jumped up from the table and began to pace the length of the kitchen in rapid agitation. "When did I ever *ask* you for a damn thing? When? Just tell me! All I ever remember trying to do was *give* myself to you. Over and over, and you could never run fast enough or far enough to escape me. I thought it was scruples. I really did."

She turned suddenly, glaring down at him. "Now I know better. I'm no naive fool, Billy Joe Yuma. That baby excuse doesn't work anymore. And I refuse to live with a man who finds me repulsive."

"I don't find you repulsive!" He roared the words and leapt to his own feet. "Damn it, woman, I want you more than I've ever wanted anyone!"

"Hah! You expect me to believe that when you run like a scared rabbit the minute things start to heat up?"

For nearly a minute they glared at each other, chests heaving with their anger. When Yuma spoke, it was to grind the words out through clenched teeth.

"*Scared* is the operative word."

It took a while, but little by little the anger drained from her face. "What," she asked finally, "are you scared of?"

He didn't get to answer the question. The phone rang. When Wendy turned toward it, he caught her arm.

"Let me get it," he said roughly. "If it's Teague again, he can spout his filth at me."

Wendy gave a little nod of assent.

It wasn't Teague; it was Nate Tate.

"Yuma, old son," the sheriff said, "I got bad news. Sara Ironheart just called in. It seems Teague and a band of his buddies crossed her property, heading up into the mountains. She said they were loaded for bear."

Yuma swore viciously. "Can you do anything?"

"I'm rounding up some men to go after them. Sara was going to trail them, but she's alone, and I absolutely forbade it. If Gideon were around... But he's not. So she's waiting up there for us to arrive. In the meantime, can you find your friends and warn them what's coming?"

"You bet."

"And, Yuma, try to keep them calm. If they start shooting, I'm going to have to treat 'em just like anybody else, regardless of provocation."

When Yuma hung up and turned, he found Wendy watching him.

"Teague?" she asked.

"Your dad says Teague and his friends have gone up into the mountains. They just crossed the Double Y, and Sara Ironheart called in. Nate wants me to go up and warn my friends, try to keep them cool."

Wendy nodded. "Let me load a backpack. I'm going with you."

"Now, wait a minute."

"No!" She rounded on him, hands on her hips, chin thrust out. "If there's shooting and somebody gets hurt, you're going to need me up there."

He wanted to argue with her and sought desperately for a reason she couldn't ignore. Before he found one, she was speaking again.

"Besides, if you run into Teague and those guys, you wouldn't protect yourself, would you."

It wasn't a question, and he didn't bother to answer.

Wendy shook her head. "I know. I admire you for it, but I'm not going to let you be a dead pacifist. I'll carry a gun, and I'll use if it I need to."

"Wendy, no...."

"Yuma, yes. You'd fight to protect *me,* wouldn't you?"

It was a little scary to realize just how well she knew him. Unable to lie to her, he nodded.

"So you protect me, and I'll protect you." She gave him a wan half smile. "It'll work just as well that way as any other." She half turned toward the door, then paused and looked at him. "Do me the courtesy of accepting that I'm an adult with a right to make my own decisions."

That was all that kept him from calling Nate. The realization that she was indeed an adult with the right to decide. Wendy Tate was no longer a child in any way. That understanding had finally reached the deepest parts of his mind and soul.

Derek Locke would cover for Yuma. Sally Hawthorne, a nurse from the hospital, was qualified to cover for Wendy and agreed to do so.

Four hours later they were driving up into the mountains with backpacks loaded with dried food and medical supplies. Yuma had warned her that it would probably take two days to hike up to where his friends had been planning to be.

Wendy merely shrugged and said, "My sleeping bag is a warm one."

"Your dad's going to kill me," Yuma muttered as he maneuvered the Wagoneer around a deep pothole in the road.

"He has nothing to say about it. When are you and he finally going to admit that?"

"Never, probably," Yuma muttered. "Both of us care too damn much."

He felt Wendy turn and look at him, but he ignored her and kept his attention on the increasingly bad lumber road.

"This isn't the way we came before," Wendy remarked.

"No, they've moved. Way back from any lumber roads. Look, are you really sure you want to do this?"

"It's something I have to do. Period. If somebody gets hurt, you're going to need medical help. End of discussion." But deep inside, she knew it was far more than that. She knew that going up into these mountains was apt to cause Yuma to relive some difficult times, and if he ran into trouble, she wanted to be there for him. Some instinct was propelling her, an instinct far beyond a nurse's desire to help.

Last night... Well, to be perfectly honest, as frustrated and hurt as she felt, she thought she understood what was happening. He was afraid of the hurt he had known when Carla walked out, for one thing. For another, he honestly thought he was no good for her. He had panicked. This morning he had admitted as much when he had said that *scared* was the operative word. And when he had admitted that to her, all her hurt had faded.

She'd known from the start that caring for Billy Joe Yuma wasn't going to be an easy, painless task—although no one seemed to give her credit for realizing that. That entire summer of her eighteenth year, she'd withstood more rejection from him than most people withstood in a lifetime. She had even understood it.

But this sexual thing...well, it had really gotten to her last night. She had felt so open, so exposed, so vulnerable, and he had walked away without a backward glance. Now that she understood what had driven him, though, she couldn't hold it against him. Loving Yuma hurt. It would always hurt. She'd become resigned to that a long time ago. He would never, ever, be an easy man to care for.

They reached the end of the lumber road in the midafternoon. Tree stumps surrounded by new growth left the mountainside looking like a shaved head. Clouds raced low along the peaks to the north but didn't look threatening. The autumn wind had a distinct nip to it here, and Wendy zipped up her down vest.

"It'll be warmer once we get into the thicker trees," Yuma remarked.

Wendy merely nodded. She'd spent a lot of her childhood hiking around in these mountains.

They set out on a diagonal line across the slope, headed higher and farther north. Twenty minutes later they left behind the scarred cleared land and entered the untouched forest. Wendy had been trained from an early age by her father to navigate through these woods with nothing but a compass and topographic maps, but Yuma seemed not to need even those. He gave Wendy the definite feeling that he knew exactly where he was headed, that this terrain was as familiar to him as Main Street in Conard City.

Gradually the terrain became rougher, more forbidding. They had to cross a number of ravines, and while Yuma always seemed to know the best way to go, some of the climbs and descents were very rough.

And as they went, she marked a trail. Her father's training had drilled the importance of that into her. If Yuma were to get injured, she would need to find her own way back.

He carried the shotgun. He wouldn't use it, but he wouldn't let her carry it. That touched her. She imagined its very presence must disturb—even repel—him.

Sometimes, like now, she wondered if she was going to die from needing him. She seemed to be walking around with a permanent ache in her soul, always on the edge of tears from a yearning so intense no word could encompass it. Six years away had gradually managed to dull the ache until she had been able to convince herself she was over Yuma. A few weeks around him had shown her what a farce that was. She would *never* be over him. When she was an old lady of ninety, she would probably still be dreaming dreams of him.

An unconscious sigh escaped her as she followed him along the invisible trail only he could detect. She wanted him. She wanted to put her arms around him and hug him tight until he felt safe. Until he believed he had a right to be loved. Until he forgot that he had ever felt unloved. She wanted to wrap him in the warmth and protection of her feelings for him, wanted to seep into the deepest places of his soul and drive out the dark.

But he had made it plain that he didn't really want her. At this point she wasn't even sure he felt the sexual attraction he claimed to. It was easy, in retrospect, to think she might have hurled herself at him and elicited nothing but a normal male response that had quickly been overwhelmed by distaste.

Wendy's sexual experience was limited. She had never yet met the man she wanted to make love with... other than Yuma. And it wasn't that she hadn't tried. More than once she had found herself in a long-term relationship with a guy she cared for... only to discover she didn't care *that* much. Something had always pulled her back before she got in too deep or went too far.

That something, she thought sourly now, had probably been Billy Joe Yuma. She had never gotten over her feelings, though she had often told herself she had. No, she'd merely put them on the back burner, to judge by the last couple of weeks.

He had said earlier that *scared* was the operative word. Then the phone had rung, interrupting their argument, and now here they were, tramping up the side of the mountain, and she couldn't find a way to bring it up. Men didn't like being scared. Didn't like admitting it or discussing it. And chances were he would never bring it up again himself. Why would he? The words had come out of him this morning only in the heat of argument.

And she suspected that if she brought it up, she might precipitate another argument—a very different kind of argument. At the moment she was in no mood to fight about anything.

"There's a place up ahead where we'll make camp for the night," Yuma said, breaking into her chain of thought. "It's a hollow that's sheltered a little from the wind so it won't be as cold."

"It's going to be cold regardless," Wendy remarked.

"I'm used to it."

She turned her head to look straight at him. He was a little ahead of her and to one side, and she couldn't read anything. Used to it? "Used to the cold?"

"Used to sleeping in it. When I used to come up here to...get away, I didn't always think to bring a sleeping bag. I spent lots of nights with nothing but some pine branches to cover me. I'll be okay."

Nothing but some pine branches. The urge to reach out to him was almost overwhelming. She wanted so badly to wrap him up in her love, to hold everything at bay with her arms. But she knew she couldn't do that. There was no protection from what happened inside a person. There was no way she could erase the scars left by his past. No way at all.

But that didn't prevent her from aching with the wish that she could.

In a bowl that must have been cut from the mountainside millennia ago by a glacier, they made their camp. Because she had wanted to carry the maximum amount of medical supplies, Wendy had forgone her pup tent and a lot of other conveniences. Tonight it would be her down sleeping bag and the chilly wind. Yuma was right—it wasn't as bad here in the hollow, but it still blew, and it carried the ice of approaching winter.

She helped him dig a fire pit and line it with rocks, and shortly they had some dead wood burning. A nearby stream allowed them to refill their canteens and hydrate some dried stew for dinner. Instant hot chocolate rounded off the meal.

And then there was nothing to do but climb into their sleeping bags near the fire and try to stay warm until dawn. One look at Yuma's sleeping bag and it was all Wendy could do to keep her mouth shut. It was nowhere near sufficient for this altitude at this time of year. She couldn't imagine why he didn't have a better one.

"Hell," he said, as he spread it out.

"What's wrong?"

"Grabbed the wrong damn sleeping bag."

She hesitated, biting her lower lip and watching as he shook the bag out and placed it on the far side of the fire. "We can share," she said finally.

His head snapped around as if he'd just been hit. He didn't say anything, just stared at her, his face a grim mask in the flickering firelight.

Wendy managed a shrug and wondered if he could hear how hard her heart was pounding. "We can zip the bags together and put yours underneath for a ground cloth and mine on top. Combining body heat would help a lot, I imagine."

He didn't reply, just continued to stare at her in that strange, grim way.

"It only makes sense," she said, trying to sound firm. "It won't do either of us any good if you can't sleep or if you get hypothermia."

"All right." He came around the fire with the sleeping bag, still with that odd, grim look on his face. They each worked one side and had the bags zipped together in a jiff.

And then came the awkward part. A sleeping bag kept you warmer if you wore fewer clothes. For a moment they both hesitated. Then Yuma took matters in his hands.

"I'll turn my back while you skin out of your jeans."

"Thanks." Her hands shook wildly as she fumbled at the laces of her hiking boots. Once she'd dumped them and her socks, Yuma turned his back. Her fingers ran into some difficulty with the zipper, then gripped the tab and pulled. The sound was unnaturally loud in the silence of the forest. So was the whisper of the denim against her skin as she shimmied out of her jeans.

Then she was inside the sleeping bag, her jacket rolled up for a pillow, her jeans shoved down below her feet to keep them warm and dry for morning. "Okay."

She tried not to watch. In the end, she peeked under her eyelashes and watched, anyway. He left on the sweatshirt he was wearing beneath his flight suit, as had she, so she was deprived of the sight of his strong chest. But when he shoved the coveralls down, she saw his legs for the first time. It was all she could do not to draw a sharp breath. Long, dusted with golden brown hair, they were a runner's powerful, lean legs. And the one that always gave him so much trouble was marred at the thigh and hip by gashing surgical scars. They were pale with age, but the firelight seemed to emphasize them. She felt tears tighten her throat and quickly closed her eyes.

A moment later she felt the breath of chilly air as he lifted his side of the sleeping bag and slipped in beside her. He took a few seconds to settle, and then silence reigned.

And all she could think about was that less than six inches away lay the man of her dreams. She wasn't going to sleep a wink.

"Good night," he said.

She couldn't even find breath to answer.

Chapter 9

The eerie *hoo-hoo* of an owl sounded softly in the darkness. The fire had died to little more than embers. Wendy was closest to it, and she reached out for some of the wood they had left stacked nearby. She placed it carefully into the fire pit, then snuggled back into the sleeping bag to watch dreamily as the fresh fuel slowly caught and burned.

Yuma's body heat was a blessing, keeping her toasty when ordinarily she felt a little chilled, even in a bag that was supposed to keep her comfortable to subzero temperatures. His breathing was deep and even, leading her to believe he slept soundly and well.

So it came as a surprise when he asked, "Cold?"

She turned onto her back so she could look at him. He was lying on his side, and his eyes were wide open. "I just didn't want the fire to go out. I'm not cold."

"I am."

That was when she realized he hadn't been sleeping either, that his thoughts were running along the same scary paths as her own. And something warned her that if she invited him in, tonight he would not turn away. Tonight there would be no beeper, no telephone . . . and whatever scruples he'd wrestled with before had vanished. He was looking at her with an intensity that left her in no doubt that he would take her if she wanted him.

Everything inside her hushed, and she hovered for the merest instant on the precipice. She had wanted this for so long. . . . She drew a deep, shuddery breath. "How cold are you, Billy Joe?"

"Cold to the depths of my soul." He said it levelly, with an honesty that made her eyes prickle.

"Come warm yourself," she whispered. "Come warm yourself with me."

He closed his eyes briefly, as if overwhelmed, and then he edged toward her, closing the small distance that separated them. When his arms wrapped around her, she pressed her face to his sweatshirt-covered chest and yielded a long, heartfelt sigh. This was home. In her mind there was no doubt. *This* was where she belonged.

For several minutes he just held her, his arms snug around her, his face pressed to the top of her head. Then he drew a deep breath, as if gathering himself.

"I don't know," he said hoarsely. "I don't know if I can be what you need. I don't know if I can be what *any* woman needs. I don't know if I have anything more to give than this. I feel so hollow. So empty. There's almost nothing left inside me except pain. And need. God, Wendy, I need you so much."

The tears that had been stinging her eyes began to roll down her cheeks. "I need you, too, Billy Joe. I've been aching with need for you for six long years. Maybe longer." She pressed her face hard against his chest for a moment, seeking to control her tears. Then she leaned back and tipped her face up to look at him. The flickering orange fire glow made him look harsh, strange. "Take whatever you need. It's always belonged to you."

He closed his eyes and held his breath briefly. Then he looked at her again. "Maybe . . . maybe all I need is to hold you."

"Then just hold me." As she spoke, she tangled her legs with his so that they were pressed even closer.

She felt a shiver pass through him, a long slow tremor, and then he pressed her head to his chest again. For a long, long time, neither of them moved or spoke. She could almost feel the internal war he was waging. He was once again fighting the battle between what he wanted and what he felt was right. Wendy wished there was something she could say to settle his mind, but she knew that his mind might never be settled on this issue. He might make love to her this very night and tomorrow despise himself for it. She had no control over such things, but she was wise enough to realize that she could not protect him from himself. No one could do that for another person.

Nor could she tell herself to back off for his sake. Not anymore. The need for him had been part of her for so long, and denied for so long, that she could no longer argue with herself about it. She needed him. He needed her. Tomorrow would be soon enough to deal with the consequences of their actions.

Then she realized that, ever so slightly, one of his legs was moving between hers. Just a gentle, rocking motion, almost undetectable, but enough to make her aware of the texture of the hair on his thigh, enough to send her thoughts spiraling downward to her center. A slow, deep ache began to build, and thoughts of everything but loving Yuma fled from her head.

"Wendy..." He whispered her name in a man's agony just before he tilted her face up and took her mouth in a deep, searing kiss. The moment of decision had passed, and now he was fully committed. There was no more time to waste. Six years had already gone by the wayside.

The thrust of his tongue was no more patient than the rest of him, now that the moment had arrived. He reminded himself to take care, to go slowly, to bring her every step of the way with him, but when she tilted her head back and opened her mouth to take him deeper, something exploded in his brain.

He tore his mouth from hers. "I can't...." He couldn't find air to warn her.

"It's okay," she whispered. "It's okay...." She understood. She was inexperienced, not ignorant. His body was shaking with tremors that told the entire story. A woman's instincts took over, driving everything from her mind but the need to give the man she loved whatever he needed. She sat up and yanked her own sweatshirt and briefs away, then reached for his with impatient hands. He was already pulling at them himself. A breathless laugh escaped her as their hands collided, but he was past laughing. Past breathing. Past doing anything except letting her draw him over her. Between her legs.

She brought him to her, fully conscious of what she was doing, wanting nothing but to give. Later there would be time for more, perhaps, but she knew enough to realize this first time would be a transition for her, not a pleasure. All she wanted from it was to feel him find what he needed deep inside her.

He had just enough presence of mind to test her readiness. She was wet and hot, and the last thought fled from his brain, the last restraint shattered. He plunged into her, ripping her wide and making his place deep inside.

Somewhere in his mind it registered that she cried out, that he had just brutally taken a virgin, but he couldn't stop the chain reaction happening inside him. Her legs lifted, wrapping around his hips and drawing him deeper yet, her arms clasped around his shoulders and hung on tight, and dimly he heard her whisper, "It's okay..."

And then he erupted into her with a force that seemed to blow off the top of his head.

"Wendy..."

"Shh... Hush, Billy Joe. Everything's fine."

He was well acquainted with the miserable sensation of guilt, but what he was feeling now far exceeded anything he had felt in the past. Even as a languorous afterglow made him want to curl up against her and slip away into contented slumber, his mind screamed a protest at what he had just done. There had been no gentleness, no care for her, nothing but uncontrollable lust.

Yet despite that, she held him close and made him feel welcome. Made him feel treasured. His throat grew tight and his eyes burned with feeling. It had been a lifetime since anyone had made him feel precious.

"I'm sorry," he said. He needed to say it.

"I'm not. I'm not sorry at all."

"I hurt you."

"No more than necessary. It's okay, Billy Joe. Just let me know when you're ready to do it again."

Startled, he lifted his head from her shoulder and looked straight down into her face. She was smiling.

"Actually, it didn't hurt as much as I thought it would the first time," she said, touching his stubbly cheek with gentle fingers.

He found himself wondering what he had ever done in his life to deserve this moment. This woman's gentleness. Her caring. His throat tightened again, and he bowed his head to give her a tender kiss.

And almost as if by magic, he felt himself hardening inside her again. He would have said such a feat was impossible at his age, but it was happening, anyway. And he knew Wendy felt it by the way a slow smile stretched her lips.

"Are you trying to tell me something, Billy Joe?" she asked in a husky whisper.

"I think you already heard." The rising of his passion was driving guilt back into the dim recesses of his mind. He couldn't believe he was responding again so quickly, but one look at Wendy's expression told him this would not be a good time to practice restraint.

So instead he turned his attention to making love to her as he should have done from the beginning. She lay naked beneath him, eager for his touches and kisses, a woman who wanted a man to learn her secrets and cherish them.

And she wanted to explore him, too. He saw it in her eyes, felt it in the restless movements of her hands against his chest as he lay propped on his elbows over her.

"Let's play, Billy Joe," she whispered softly.

He laughed then. A real laugh that rose from some nearly forgotten place inside him. He let go of the guilt, the arguments, the fears, and gave himself up to the moment and the joy of this woman's gift.

He levered himself off her so that he lay beside her and could touch her anywhere he chose. The night was cold, so cold that he kept the sleeping bag pulled up to her chin, even though he wanted more than anything to fill himself with the sight of her.

Instead he contented himself with exploring her by touch. Her gaze remained fixed on his at first, as if she needed to see his reaction to her as his hand wandered slowly, gently, tracing her every contour.

He touched the fragile line of her collarbone, delighting in the delicate way she shivered, delighting in the smooth feel of her. Her skin was soft, warm with life. It was a sensation he knew he would never tire of. Bending, he kissed her mouth gently and then watched her eyes flutter closed as his hand trailed lower, toward her breasts.

He touched her with exquisite care, giving her a chance to grow accustomed to the feel of a man's rough hands on her sensitive flesh. Giving her a chance to savor each touch, each stroke, each squeeze. Her mouth fell open, her breath quickened, and when he brushed his thumb across her beading nipple, a small moan escaped her.

"You feel so good to me," he told her, his voice gone gravelly with growing passion. "I wish I had words to say how wonderful. . . ." He trailed off, because he really didn't have the words to express what she made him feel with her eagerness, her willingness, her responsiveness. With her trust.

He couldn't imagine what had possessed her to give herself to him. To save herself for him. For he was sure that was what she had done. No woman her age, with her attractions, could still be a virgin for lack of opportunities. She had refused everyone else, and then, in a single, unhesitating moment, she had given herself to him...as she had once told him again and again that she wanted to.

I've been calling out for you for six long years, she'd said the other night. There was no doubt in his mind now that she had meant it. Nor was now the time to wonder what he was going to do about it, what he owed her because of it. Right now he owed her only one thing, and that was a measure of the pleasure she had just given him so selflessly.

She was stirring restlessly beneath his caressing hands. Sliding downward, he found her breast with his mouth and began to tease her nipple with his tongue. She gasped and arched, her entire body reaching upward for more. He hardly needed her ragged moan to confirm her pleasure as he took her deep into his mouth and sucked. With each pull of his mouth on her, he felt his own insides tighten in pleasure, and when her hands clutched his head and tugged him even closer, he knew a joy he hadn't felt in many, many years.

He had forgotten, he realized, just what pleasure it was to give pleasure to a woman he cared for. It had been half a lifetime since he had done so. Not since Carla had he cared about anyone the way he cared about Wendy. The thought stole into his mind, but he shoved it away. He couldn't afford to care for her. He couldn't afford to admit that he did. For now he would think of nothing except pleasuring her. She was a friend, and that was enough. That was all he could ever ask. All he could ever give.

She moaned and twisted still closer, and her hands moved to his shoulders, pulling, as if she needed him closer. Deeper. Inside.

But he wanted to give her more, so he ignored the demand of her hands. Instead, as he moved to suckle her other breast, he sent his hand on a downward trek, hunting out the delicate place he had so recently violated. He was concerned that she might be sore, but when she felt his hand brush lightly against her curls, a sigh escaped her, and her thighs parted readily.

She whispered his name on a shiver of pleasure he could feel all the way through him. Gently, oh so gently, he slipped his fingers into her moist folds and found the nub that would bring her the greatest pleasure. She gasped at the unexpected sensation, then cried out softly.

"Easy, baby. Easy." He scooted up a little and kissed her lips, keeping his hand where it was. "It's just so new. Just give it a moment and it'll start feeling good...."

Her hands nearly clawed at his back as she whimpered and twisted against his touch, stunned by sensations so exquisite they were nearly torment. Slipping his arm beneath her, he held her as close as he could get her while he brought her to a swift, hot release.

"No," he whispered a little later, when her trembling stopped and she reached for him. "Just sleep, baby. You're too sore for any more right now. Just sleep...."

And she slept in his arms.

It had been a long, long time since a woman had done that. An even longer time since he had wanted one to. While she slept, he stared into the dark beyond the fire and faced a terror he had hoped never to face again.

The first ghostly light of dawn was just beginning to silhouette the towering pines when Wendy came awake. Her back was tucked to Yuma, his naked body pressed warmly to her entire length. His arm rested snugly around her waist, holding her close.

An unaccustomed soreness between her thighs made her sigh, and then she remembered. Memory came to her, bringing a warm rush of color to her cheeks, followed by the fear that this morning he would reject her again.

She knew better than to think that he had made love to her because he loved her. For men, such things were often separate. What had happened in the night had happened because of the long buildup of sexual tension between them, because of their closeness in the dark, because when need grew strong enough, it had to be met.

And now, with the first faint light of dawn, she feared he would have regrets. He had been trying to avoid this for so long, that she could hardly believe he would be glad to have given in. No, he would probably hate himself and go on a big guilt trip. If there was one thing she knew for certain, it was that Billy Joe Yuma went on the world's biggest guilt trips.

Oh, damn, she found herself thinking. She should have had the sense to ease away, to misunderstand, to deflect him before it was too late. Now he would hate himself. Maybe even hate her. She squeezed her eyes shut and tried to battle down a wave of panic.

How many times, she asked herself, had her father warned her not to mess with Yuma? Warned her that the man had found a precarious stability, a delicate compromise between memories, the past and his losses, and that it wouldn't take much to disturb that balance? What if she had shaken that balance? What if she brought back his PTSD? As a nurse, she knew that stress could worsen it, no matter how improved the sufferer might be. It wouldn't take much.

What if she looked into his eyes this morning and saw the look that had been there all those years ago, the look of agony? What if she had driven him back to that merely by not having the strength to protect him from himself?

"If you get any more tense," said his sleepy voice right into her ear, "I'm going to give up all hope of seducing you before breakfast."

The husky rumble of his voice, the suggestive words, poured through her like hot honey. At once all the tension left her and was replaced by a warm languor. As if he felt the shift in her mood, he ran his palm up from her waist to her breast.

"Are you sore?" he asked, the words a mere breath in her ear.

"Just a little." She could hardly find air to speak as his hand evoked ribbons of sensation that ran from her breast to her center. Instinctively, she twisted, trying to press herself harder into his touch.

He felt her eagerness, but he suspected "just a little" was an understatement. "I was rough last night," he murmured. "I didn't know."

"I didn't tell you." Gasping, she twisted again.

"I wish you had. I would've been gentler." And he would have, even if it nearly killed him. He had been nearly uncontrollable, but he had let the last tether snap only because she invited it. Had he guessed her inexperience, he would have taken a nosedive into the icy waters of the nearby stream first.

But he hadn't known, and he hadn't been gentle, and he could only hope that nature was prepared to handle such events, because there wasn't a damn thing he could do now.

"We'll take it slow and easy this morning," he whispered and kissed her cheek. "Slow and oh so easy...."

Gently he drew her onto her back, and then his head disappeared beneath the sleeping bag to trail kisses across her shoulders and down to her breasts. A soft cry escaped her when he drew her nipple into his mouth, and then a louder one when his fingers found her dewy center.

Her cries were the sweetest notes on earth, he thought, as he carried her higher and higher. Around them day began to break, but neither of them noticed. And when he positioned her so that he could give her the most intimate kiss of all, Wendy groaned and arched upward. Never, she thought hazily, never had she imagined anything could feel so good that it was almost painful.

He carried her up and over with the most exquisitely sensual caresses in the world. He held her close while the aftershocks passed, then stroked her gently as the languor held her in thrall. And he never asked a thing for himself.

Gradually the sky lightened more. Then Wendy turned toward him with a smile that warned him it was his turn. And there was no way on earth he could protest. No way on earth he could refuse what she was about to offer. All the needs he had forced himself to bury since Carla left him were suddenly there, extraordinarily powerful after being so long denied.

From behind crumbling defenses came the need for someone to care. The need for someone to honestly give a damn. Wendy had been offering that for a long time, and now, for just these few moments, he was going to forget all his scruples and accept her gift of caring. Later he would live with the guilt. Right now he needed her too much to worry about it.

He opened his arms wide, inviting her closer, silently asking her to help herself to whatever she wanted from him. She moved immediately into his embrace, smiling, kissing him on the lips, at first lightly, then harder, as if she wanted to test each texture, each pressure, each angle, until she found perfection. He had never in his life been kissed in such a fashion, and he gave himself up to it gladly.

Then her tongue swept over his lower lip, and he opened his mouth to receive her. She had learned already just how he liked to be kissed, and her tongue moved eagerly against his.

Then, remembering things she had read, she moved downward, kissing his chin, his throat—how good he smelled there—and moving lower yet until she found one small, pointed male nipple. Gently, she touched it with the tip of her tongue and felt him jerk sharply.

"Is that good?" she asked.

"Oh yeah," he said on a ragged breath. "Oh yeah." A moan escaped him when she settled in to discover just how much he liked it. Tonguing him at first as gently as a cat, then sucking him as he had sucked her, she soon had him moving as restlessly as he had made her move only a short time ago.

Needing to be closer, she struggled a little inside the bag until she straddled him. At once he grasped her hips and drew her down against him so that the most sensitive part of her cradled his throbbing length. Liking the sensation, she rocked gently against him while she moved to his other nipple and teased it to hardness.

"Wendy..." He groaned a soft curse as he pressed himself upward, seeking the place where he needed to be. His hands tightened on her hips, digging in, drawing her tighter, closer, nearer. Together they moved, finding a rhythm, finding pleasure in each other, until both were panting and slick with sweat.

The sleeping bag slipped down, and Yuma saw Wendy above him, her small breasts bobbing with each movement, her head thrown back now, her eyes closed. God, she was beautiful.

"I need you...inside," she whispered brokenly. "Oh, please..."

He was afraid of hurting her and would have finished matters this way, but he couldn't resist her plea. Carefully, he positioned himself beneath her and gently began to ease his way inside. This time there was no resistance, merely soft, hot welcome.

A long, soft moan escaped her as he claimed her fully. For a long, luxurious moment, neither of them moved. Then, gently at first, but with increasing confidence, Wendy began to rock. Finally, needing to feel him deeper and harder, she reared up and threw her head back.

Beautiful, he thought dimly as he watched her move. Beautiful. Reaching out with his hand, he sought her delicate center and tried to add to her pleasure even as she swept him higher and higher in her climb. They reached the pinnacle together this time, their cries piercing the dawn.

She didn't want to move, and Yuma didn't seem to want to let her go. He pulled the sleeping bag up over her and held her on his chest as if she'd been made to fit there. Slowly, soothingly, he ran his palms along her back. From time to time he twisted his head to drop a kiss near her ear.

"We must need to get started," she mumbled.

"Mmm." He didn't want to move. He figured he could do a Rip van Winkle right now without any trouble, as long as Wendy stayed right where she was. But it was a fact that they needed to put in a long day's hike if they were to have any hope of warning his friends. Given time to prepare, Cowboy and Vance and the others would be able to protect themselves. And maybe in the process they could catch Teague and friends in some activity that would put them behind bars.

Wishful thinking, he decided as he reluctantly let Wendy slip away. The good guys might sometimes triumph, but the bad guys didn't necessarily pay.

They cooked powdered eggs over the fire and enjoyed instant coffee after a quick trip to the stream to wash up. Both of them were experienced campers, so it didn't take long for them to pack up and be on their way. A woodpecker began his rat-a-tat search for insects. A hawk shrieked from somewhere above. It was a beautiful, beautiful day.

Yuma kept waiting for guilt to attack him, but somehow this morning it was impossible to feel guilty. Each time he glanced over at Wendy, he felt anew the wonder of what she had given him. He would always remember this morning and the way she had looked in the watery dawn light, lost in the intensity of the moment as she rode him. Damn, she had been beautiful in her passion. And so incredibly, wonderfully natural in her responses. No artifice. No hesitations. No false shyness or modesty. She had thrown herself into the experience as if it were right and good—and in doing so, she had made it both those things.

And this morning he felt as if all of a sudden heaven had decided to smile on him for the first time in years. Somehow he felt as if it would be intolerably ungrateful to regret anything, to feel guilty about anything.

When their way grew smooth enough, he reached out for her hand and clasped it. At once she smiled up at him, and then he couldn't resist pausing to kiss her. She welcomed him eagerly, meeting his tongue with hers in a mating dance. Forgetting herself almost immediately, she lost her balance, and the weight of her pack started to drag her backwards.

Yuma steadied her, and they looked into one another's eyes, laughing, a little breathless. He laughed so seldom,

Wendy thought, reaching up to touch his cheek with gentle longing. He was transformed with it now, smiling, his green eyes dancing. Bending, he dropped kisses on her forehead, the tip of her nose, her chin.

He had forgotten, he thought as they resumed their walk. He had forgotten how simple and beautiful life could be. All the joy had escaped him, leaving him aware of nothing but grimness. But Wendy, simply by giving herself to him, had somehow brought back the joy.

She hadn't asked a damn thing of him, either, he realized suddenly. Not one thing. She hadn't even hinted that she wanted some kind of declaration from him. Hadn't in any way intimated that their lovemaking should be the start of any kind of relationship. Surely, of all people, someone as young and innocent as she was should have had such things in mind. Should have a right to expect such things.

But she hadn't pressed or pressured in any way. All she had done was give whatever he asked and take delight in whatever he offered.

How very rare that was.

And suddenly he was terrified. Ice ran down his back from the base of his skull to the base of his spine. The day abruptly seemed to turn dark with threat. In a flash, all the anxiety of PTSD filled him, consuming in its voracity.

He didn't deserve any good in his life. He would just lose it, anyway. He always lost anything good. Always. Look what he had done to Carla. How he had driven her away. Now look what he had done to Wendy, taking her in a moment of desire that had overwhelmed his common sense, his decency....

God, if he had a decent bone in his entire body, surely he would not have made love to this innocent woman last night. Surely he would have pulled back. Surely he would have remembered how badly he might hurt her. How badly he always hurt everyone.

The weight of ancient guilt and old failings settled on him, crushing burdens of self-knowledge, self-judgment. Billy

Joe Yuma had looked at himself, and, as always, he judged himself a failure.

By the time they took a lunch break, Wendy was convinced that something serious was troubling Yuma. He had started the day so cheerfully, had even joined her in laughter, but the joy had waned, to be replaced by a quiet, even somber mood.

She wasn't surprised. She had expected him to have regrets first thing this morning. He was having them now. A difference of a few hours.

But actually facing the idea that he regretted their lovemaking was a lot more painful than she had imagined. She was afraid to look into his face for fear she would see loathing. Embarrassment began to make her insides squirm. What must he think of her, of the easy way she had given herself to him? He hadn't even needed to touch her. All he had said was that he was cold, and she had nearly thrown herself at him.

Oh, God. Suddenly she didn't think there would be a hole deep enough to hide in.

Throughout the afternoon, neither of them said anything. They walked side by side at times, at others single file, and no sound save their breathing and the tramp of their feet broke the forest's quiet. They might have been strangers, except that tension practically crackled in the air between them.

It was nearly sunset when they reached the site where Yuma had expected to find his friends. To the casual eye, it didn't seem as if anyone had ever disturbed this part of the forest, but Yuma inspected more closely and found signs that the site had been vacated in the last day. Squatting, he looked around at Wendy. Their eyes met, then skated away.

"They moved on. Guess I spooked 'em good with what I told them."

"Do you know where to look now?"

He nodded; he had seen the bent twigs that Cowboy had left behind, a sign readable only by one of the group.

"We'll camp here," he said. "There's water over that way." He pointed. "I'll go fill the canteens and scout for some dead wood."

With an aching, heavy heart, Wendy watched him walk away. How, she wondered, did a woman learn to live with the fact that she had exposed herself and all her vulnerabilities to a man who wasn't interested in her? How did she learn to live with the feeling that she had made a complete fool of herself?

Night had fully settled by the time they had dug a fire pit and cooked their meal. They sat facing the fire a few feet apart, and neither of them unrolled their sleeping bags.

They couldn't keep this up, Wendy thought as she sipped a mug of cocoa. They needed to talk, to air the tension. Needed to deal with whatever they were thinking and feeling. Bottling it up like this would only create problems.

But the mere thought of trying to discuss last night made her heart hammer so nervously that she could hardly breathe. It wasn't as if they were curled up in intimacy, all relaxed and warm and trusting. They were sitting apart, as if an invisible wall stood between them. As if they were in opposing armed camps.

And suddenly she couldn't stand it anymore. Rising, she set her cup near the fire and bent to grab her sleeping bag. "Let's zip these together."

"Wendy, I don't think—"

She turned to face him, and her expression silenced him. "I'm in no mood to be your guilt trip, Yuma. You'll freeze otherwise. If you can't bear to touch me, then—"

"Can't *bear* to touch you?" He tossed his own tin cup to one side and sprang to his feet. "What the hell are you talking about?"

"The way you've been acting all afternoon! As if I have something contagious!"

"Oh, damn...." He swore softly and stood facing her, hands settling on his narrow hips. "Baby, I—"

"I told you not to call me that! I'm not a baby! And obviously I'm not *your* baby. Just get over here and help me put these bags together so we can both sleep." Breaking off, she averted her face, hoping he wouldn't see how close to tears she was.

"Wendy, I'm sorry."

She refused to look at him, not wanting him to know just how weak she felt at this moment. She *wasn't* weak, and she wasn't going to accept anything less than having this issue settled. Certainly not an apology. "*Sorry* won't cut it, scout," she said, sounding very like her father. "We've gone a long way past *sorry.*"

"I know." He spoke grimly. "*Way* past. It's not that I don't want to touch you. It's not that you're contagious. It's none of that."

"Then for God's sake, tell me what it *is!*" Facing him at last, she didn't care if he saw the hurt that was mixed with her anger. Let him see it, she thought in sudden rebellion. He was so self-involved, it could only do him good to be reminded that other people had feelings, too.

"It's me," he said, dropping his hands from his hips to form fists at his sides. "I can't be what you need or want."

"Oh, really?" Sarcasm dripped from the words, concealing the hurt she felt. "And just what do you think I want and need? And how is it you know? What have I asked you for that you feel so incapable of providing?"

But it wasn't anything she had asked him for, and they both knew it. It was something *he* felt she *deserved,* something he felt incapable of giving to her. Rearing up to face him now were icons from his youth, misty mental snapshots of dreams unfulfilled. Ideas of what it would be like to have a family someday, be a father someday, a husband. He had failed at the husband image already, and he had been grateful ever since that he had not had children to suffer for it.

When he looked at Wendy, he saw a woman who deserved to have all those dead dreams of his fulfilled. She deserved a life that fit those mental snapshots he'd never been able to live up to.

It was not an easy thing to admit aloud. His fists knotted tightly, and he had to force the words through his throat, leaving himself raw in their wake. "I can't be what you deserve."

"What *I* deserve?" she repeated, her voice going suddenly quiet. "How about what *you* deserve, Billy Joe? Don't *you* deserve anything?"

His fists tightened even more, and he looked away for a moment before facing her again. "What I deserve doesn't come into it."

"No? Why not? Aren't you just as important as I am?"

"Wendy—"

"No, I'm serious," she interrupted. "I'm not sure where you got the idea you don't deserve anything. It doesn't matter, anyway. You deserve just as many good things as anyone else."

"You don't know what I've done!"

"I don't have to know what you've done! I know the man you are *now,* and he deserves the best of everything. Certainly he deserves the simple things that everybody else takes for granted."

"Wendy, I—"

"Oh, be quiet!" she snapped in frustration. "I've been listening to you for six years, and it hasn't done either of us a damn bit of good! Just help me get these damn sleeping bags together!"

Growing up the child of pacifist parents had long ago taught him to leash his temper. Only Vietnam and alcohol had been able to shatter his control. Vietnam, alcohol—and Wendy.

He closed the distance between them in two loping steps, tugged the sleeping bag from her hand and hauled her flush up against him. She tilted her head back and glared up at him, but not a flicker of fear showed on her face, something that he registered in the depths of his soul.

"Damn it, don't you dare manhandle me!"

"But that's what you want, isn't it?" he demanded. "You

just push and push until you push me past reason, past caution, past all my scruples and principles. . . .''

''Damn it, don't you lay *that* at my door! I'm not pushing you into anything! You're the one doing all the pushing, Billy Joe Yuma. You just keep pushing me away...and it hurts. . . .''

Her voice broke, and she quickly averted her face, but it was already too late. The firelight sparkled off the tears that filled her eyes, and he watched as one of them trickled slowly down her soft cheek.

''I haven't done anything this time,'' she whispered brokenly. ''Nothing except be here.''

It was true, he admitted. She hadn't chased him, hadn't set her cap for him—none of those things she had done six years ago. He was the one who kept closing the distance between them, kept touching her, holding her, kissing her.

Loving her.

''Damn it, baby,'' he murmured, his voice little more than a husky whisper. He was making her cry, and that pierced him in a way that little else had. Bending, he kissed the stray tear away, then dropped kisses on her eyelids, her cheeks, and finally her mouth.

Her response was immediate, welcoming. Even now, even when she was furious with him, she couldn't turn him away.

''Let's get those sleeping bags together,'' he whispered, his lips just brushing hers. ''Now.''

Chapter 10

The night was turning bitterly cold, the thin, dry air able to hold little of the day's heat. Before he joined Wendy in the sleeping bag, Yuma piled a couple of additional logs on the fire. When he crawled in beside her, there was no hesitation in the way he drew her back against his chest, in the way his arm locked around her waist and his legs tangled with hers. Over her head, he stared into the dancing flames of the fire.

"I lost my soul," he said after a while.

Wendy tensed a bit, then snuggled backward, letting him know silently that she was listening.

"At least, that's how it felt," he continued after a bit. His voice was low, rough, as if it were difficult to get the words out. "Even as I was doing it, I knew I was giving up something I'd never get back. But after you fly through heavy fire a few times with the red cross on your nose being used for a target, after you pick up the bleeding, mutilated kids enough times...well, things get kind of mixed up. Right and wrong don't seem so clear anymore. Nobody *else* seems to observe any boundaries... and your own get weak."

"I can imagine," Wendy murmured.

"It's just excuses," he said after a moment. "All of it. I should have stuck to my principles anyway. But I didn't. I got so damn mad that . . . I carried ammo. I told you. We'd drop off cases of shells, shove them out one side of the chopper while we hauled the wounded in the other side."

She covered his hand at her waist with her own and squeezed. That violation would be hard to live with. Hard indeed.

"I think the real clincher, though," he continued, "came in the camp. I learned to hate. I hated until there wasn't anything left inside me. So much for noble principles of turning the other cheek and loving your brother. I hated. I used to lie awake sometimes and just dream up ways to kill my captors. To torture them. That's when I really lost my soul."

"Yuma..." But what could she say? She let the word trail off as she faced the yawning chasm they would never be able to close. He could *tell* her. She could try to understand. But she would never, ever, truly be able to share his experience. She would never *truly* understand.

"Finally...finally the hate just burned me out." His voice had grown thick with repressed anguish, but he didn't care if she could hear it. Let her hear it. "I got to a place where I didn't feel. A place where I was dead inside. That's when I started playing the mind games. They got so they were more real to me than the camp."

She made a soft murmur to let him know she was listening. But what could she say? What could anyone say?

"When I . . . came home, the transition was almost impossible. The world—the real world—wasn't real to me anymore. I'd learned to live inside my head with an intensity that made everything else seem distant. Foggy. Carla picked up on that right away. At first she tolerated it, but when it kept on . . ." He left the sentence incomplete.

It seemed like a long time before he spoke again. Just about the time Wendy decided he needed her to say something, he began to speak again.

"It was...*safe* inside my head, you know? I was in total control. Nothing could hurt me. It was a kind of living death. I functioned, but I didn't feel, I didn't care, I didn't hurt. But that was too easy, I guess." He drew a long, ragged breath before he continued.

"I started to get these rages. Later, when I got counseling at the VA, they told me that was normal, but at the time I didn't know it was a sign of...well, recovery, I guess. I terrified Carla. I terrified myself. I lost job after job and started drinking, trying to drown the anger. Trying to stop the memories.

"Then I started having flashbacks. That was the last straw for Carla. She managed to stand it when she'd find me hiding under the shrubs in the garden, but when I blew up and started screaming on a public street because a car backfired... Well, I can't say I blame her. And at first it happened a lot. An awful lot. Finally I wouldn't even go out of the house, because I never knew when it would happen."

She squeezed his hand and bit her lower lip to hold back her tears.

"I couldn't leave the house, and I finally got so I couldn't answer a phone or the door, and had to keep the curtains closed. I was terrified out of my mind, but I can't even say what it was I was scared of. It's... I think you mentioned this to me. About how you just completely lose your sense of security."

"There was a guy at the VA hospital who couldn't leave his room."

"Yeah. That's it. I went through that, too. At some point or other, Carla left. To this day, I remember her telling me she was leaving, remember her crying her eyes out, remember knowing I'd broken her heart...but I can't remember when it was. Not the date, not the time of year, not even what year. And I can't remember feeling anything at the time. But now...now it seems like every time I close my eyes I see her standing there, and it hurts...."

Wendy turned within his embrace and threw her arms around his shoulders. "You're not to blame," she whispered fiercely, around a lump in her throat. "You're not to *blame.*"

The wind rustled in the treetops over their heads, and the fire popped loudly. Yuma stiffened briefly, then hugged her tighter. "No," he said. "I'm not to blame. I know that. But I still *feel* to blame. I always will. If I hadn't betrayed my principles—"

She pressed her fingers to his lips. "That's the nature of going to war, Billy Joe. Most everyone has to betray something. And that's why it hurts so bad when you come home. You have to live with the knowledge that you're capable of doing terrible things. You come back with your sense of self, your sense of right and wrong, all fractured. You're not ignorant or innocent anymore. But doesn't *now* count for something, too?"

"What do you mean?"

"Just that...if you can punish yourself for the rest of your life because of what you did as a young man, doesn't what you do now count, too? Shouldn't Billy Joe Yuma be proud of the man he is *now?*"

"Ah, baby, if only it were that easy."

She drew a shaky breath and brushed a kiss on his lips. "Nothing worthwhile is ever easy. But you're a good man *now,* Billy Joe Yuma. And that's got to count for something, too. You just keep telling yourself that, okay? And maybe you'll start believing it."

He had come to accept that he would never again feel that he was a good man. He knew himself too well to ever believe that again. Nothing he did now could erase the memory of what he had become back then.

But he was also human enough to be warmed by her belief in him. Human enough to want and need her faith in him. Human enough to need her caring and her love.

But honest enough to want to protect her from himself.

"Wendy...listen. Just listen. I'm...not sure what there is left inside me to give a woman. I'm not sure if there's anything left in there at all. I can't make any promises. I don't...trust myself enough to promise anything to anyone. But if there's anything left in there...well, it's yours."

Her arms slipped upward from his shoulders and twined tightly around his neck as she hugged him as close as she could get him. "You've always been enough for me, Billy Joe," she whispered softly. "The man you are has always been enough."

He wished he could believe that, but he had Carla's memory to remind him that it wasn't so. For now, though, he just let it lie. But in the back of his mind lay the conviction that Wendy, like Carla, would get fed up soon enough with his emptiness. With his guilt. With his craziness.

And then he would be alone again. As always.

Wendy knew she would never forget the hours that ensued. The desperation that had been part of their first coupling and the distance he had seemed to keep during the second—both were gone now. It was as if, in admitting his emptiness to her, he was no longer afraid to let her see inside him. And what she found was a tenderness that left her throat aching and her heart marked with his brand.

He touched her as if she were infinitely precious, his hands tracing loving patterns on her flesh as if his fingers were butterfly wings. The merest kisses of flesh to flesh built anticipation to a fever pitch of longing. And whenever she would start to reach for him, he would soothe her with a kiss, calm her with whispers, and then start building the hunger all over again.

If this was all he had to give her, she realized dimly, then he was going to give her the absolute best. That understanding filled her heart with an ache that merely intensified her yearning for him.

When she thought she could stand no more, he astonished her by sending his mouth on the same trip his hands had taken. Delicate kisses sprinkled her neck, her chest, her breasts. Gently, oh so gently, he drew her nipples into his mouth and suckled them to hard, aching peaks. When she clutched at his head, holding him even closer, a soft chuckle escaped him, a sound that warmed her through and through.

And then he traveled lower, dipping briefly into her navel in a caress that caused tremors to rip through her.

"Shh, shh," he whispered softly when she stiffened at the touch of his mouth on her most private flesh. "Easy..."

And then he compelled her to climb the mountain, one agonizing step at a time. Before long she forgot everything except the wild feelings he built in her, the hard ache that screamed for an answer. When she started to sob his name over and over again, he slid up over her and filled her aching, hungering depths with himself.

The ride turned wild, a bucking, fantastic, headlong rush up and over. Then, clinging tightly together, they drifted slowly off into sleep.

The following morning, Deputy Micah Parish straightened from a crouch and looked at Nate Tate. Behind Nate stood a half dozen more deputies, all armed with high-powered rifles.

"It's Teague's boot print, all right," Micah told Nate. There wasn't much of an impression in the mixture of fine dirt and pine needles beneath the old tree. Covered with frost in the early morning, it was nearly invisible. "At this point, I'd guess he's still nearly a day ahead of us."

"Damn." Nate swore with a vigor that was compounded of worry and anger. He still couldn't believe Yuma had taken Wendy. Hell, he couldn't believe Yuma hadn't *hog-tied* her to keep her from going. He knew damn well that the pilot had probably objected, but Wendy... Wendy was as stubborn as an army mule.

Worry was crowding his brain, making it difficult to think as clearly as he would have liked. Hell, he was worried out, he thought, tipping his head back and looking up at the pearlescent dawn sky. Worried what the hell was eating Marge, worried that his eldest daughter was going to get what she wanted in the form of one busted-up, broken-down Viet vet with PTSD. Worried that Teague would reach the vets first and all hell would break loose. Worried that Wendy might get caught in the crossfire. Worried . . .

Hell, *worried* wasn't a strong enough word. Patting his pockets, he found some antacid tablets and popped a couple into his mouth. About the only good thing he could say about the past few weeks, he thought sourly, was that he'd managed to drop fifteen pounds. And by the time he got this matter settled and his daughter safely home, he would probably drop another fifteen. He swore.

"Which way?" he said to Micah, who was one of the best trackers on the face of the planet.

Micah cocked his head toward the northeast. "That way."

"How's that match up with the possible hideouts Yuma told you about?"

"It's the right direction for one of them." Micah pulled a contour map out of his jacket and squatted to study it. "Yeah," he said after a moment. "I'd guess Teague has some idea where he wants to look. Which means at some time or other somebody must have said something about the places these guys hang out."

"I wonder who the hell could have done that?"

Micah shrugged and peered up at him. "You know how it is, Nate. Anybody who wanders in the mountains has probably learned something about these vets."

"Yeah. You're right." Smothering another curse, Nate shook his head. "Well, we'd better get a move on. Damn county's going to hell in a hand basket!"

"Your father is probably ready to kill me," Yuma murmured as he nuzzled Wendy's ear. The thin predawn light was barely enough for him to see the soft glow of her pale skin and the shadowy whorls in her ear.

"Why?"

"Because I didn't tie you to a chair to prevent you from coming with me."

"I'd have liked to see you try."

"I might have had some fun doing it."

A soft giggle escaped her, and she twisted a little so she could see him. "Is that the way your mind runs?"

"Wrestling with you, you mean? Isn't that what we've been doing?"

A laugh tumbled from her. "Fast thinking, Yuma. Fast thinking."

"I may be crazy, babe, but I ain't dumb." He kissed her soundly, liking the way she snuggled closer and closer. When he lifted his head, his voice had gone all soft and husky. "We can get kinky later on."

She caught her breath. "Promise?"

A slow smile spread over his face, transforming him completely. "Promise."

But it was time to get moving, so a short while later they climbed out of the warm cocoon of the sleeping bag and set about making a quick, cold breakfast.

"We should reach the next site late this afternoon," he told her. "Unless something has happened to spook them, they should still be there."

The weather had turned colder overnight, and the wind had strengthened, whipping through the treetops until it sounded like the constant rush of falling water. Despite her exertions, Wendy had to keep her down vest tightly zipped, and she pulled on her glove liners to keep her hands warm.

Their way grew steadily more difficult, becoming more of a climb than a hike. At places the terrain was so steep they nearly crawled. There were no vertical climbs, though, for which Wendy was grateful. She had some experience with rock climbing, but it wasn't anything she wanted to attempt with a backpack.

As the day wore on, they needed to take more and more frequent breaks. Muscles she had nearly forgotten she had began to quiver and ache from unaccustomed demands.

The sun had just disappeared behind the western peak when Yuma and she collapsed in the dim shadows beneath the trees yet again.

"Not much farther," he told her. "Fifteen, twenty minutes maybe."

"I don't see how *anybody* could ambush anyone else up here! My God, Yuma, they've got to have known we've been approaching for hours."

"We haven't exactly been trying to sneak up on them, Wendy. And there aren't that many of them. If somebody wanted to sneak up on them, they might just be able to manage it. But they picked this spot because it's so defensible. Chances are, if Teague gets anywhere close, they'll be able to surround him and stop him. I just don't want to see anyone get hurt."

"Me either." Which was the whole point of tagging along with Yuma on this trip. To make sure he didn't get hurt, and to be there to help if someone *did.* The first hour after serious injury was critical to patient survival. She only wished she'd been able to bring more than just the most rudimentary equipment. But she had her radio, and if there was trouble, she could sure as hell get the chopper in, regardless of whether Yuma's friends wanted it or not. And she would, if necessary. She'd already made up her mind to that.

"Howdy, y'all."

At the sound of the voice, Wendy's heart stopped beating. Yuma leapt to his feet.

"Cowboy, you son of a gun!"

Daring to turn her head, Wendy recognized one of the vets she had met the night Artie had broken his leg. The man was standing ten feet away, beside a lodgepole pine, a rifle cradled casually in his arm. "Your lady's right," he told Yuma. "We heard you coming hours ago." Then he smiled and winked at Wendy. "Got your breath back yet?"

Cowboy insisted on carrying Wendy's backpack the rest of the way, disregarding her protests. He gave the shotgun Yuma was toting a curious look. "Thought you didn't believe in guns, man."

"I don't. This is Wendy's. No way I was going to let her carry it."

"I can carry it now," Wendy insisted.

Cowboy chuckled and looked straight at Yuma. "Her gun, huh? Man, you got yourself a handful here."

Both men were laughing as they started up the trail. Wendy pretended to be annoyed by their humor, but in truth, she was so glad to hear Yuma laugh that she would willingly have played the fool a thousand times.

Yuma had been right about it being only another fifteen or twenty minutes. The last bit of the hike wasn't too strenuous, and at the end of it Cowboy led them into a makeshift camp in the middle of an open glade. Lean-tos had been hastily erected from pine boughs and tarps, a fire burned in a central pit, and a pot of coffee was warming beside it. There was no one in sight.

"Vance took a patrol out to look for Teague," Cowboy said. "They'll be back before full dark. Crazy and another team are scouting the area looking for the best defensive positions."

At Cowboy's invitation, Wendy settled on a stump near the fire and poured herself some coffee. It was hot, and as thick as mud from standing most of the day, but the warmth was welcome.

"Guess I should make some fresh," Cowboy remarked when he poured a cup for himself. "This looks pretty bad."

"It's hot," Wendy said, and received another smile. The man seemed much more cheerful today than the first time she had met him. "It's been a long time since I've been camping like this. When I was a kid, Dad used to bring us up here all the time. I'd forgotten how good even bad coffee tastes in the fresh cold air."

Cowboy chuckled, and Yuma smiled.

"I'll make fresh," Cowboy said again. "And maybe you're hungry?"

"I've got all kinds of dried stuff in my pack," Yuma told him. "Why don't you look through it and see what looks good to you. I imagine you guys are living off the land?"

"For now. We buried all the canned goods you brought up. Have to be able to move fast."

Yuma nodded. "Well, there's enough jerky in there for everyone. Coffee. Some other stuff. Wendy's pack is all medical supplies."

"Might need 'em if those jerks cause a lot of trouble."

"The sheriff is bringing some men up on their tail. Maybe he'll catch Teague before he gets here."

Cowboy shook his head. "Ain't gonna count on it, Yuma." He walked to the edge of the campsite and dumped the coffee in what was apparently being used as the men's garbage pit. Then he prepared fresh and set it in the fire to perk. "Those guys want trouble, they're going to get it."

Yuma looked across the fire at Wendy, their eyes exchanging concern. Then he spoke.

"I was kinda hoping I could talk you guys into trying to be sure *no one* gets hurt."

Cowboy looked up from poking at the fire, and his expression was grim. "We don't want to hurt anyone, man. You know that. But if those guys start shootin'...well, there's no telling what'll happen. Some of us might have flashbacks. You know how Crazy is about loud noises. And Boggs doesn't know where he's at most of the time anyway. One gunshot and it might be Nam all over again. You know that."

Yuma nodded. "But if you're all prepared..."

Cowboy shook his head. "We'll be prepared. For *anything.*"

And that grim statement seemed to close the subject. At least for now. Wendy looked at Yuma and found him staring somberly into the fire. He didn't like this at all, she realized.

"Look, man," Cowboy said, "I know it's against your principles. But it ain't against mine to shoot back when somebody's shootin' at me."

"It's not just my principles I'm concerned about. Things could get hairy for all of you if anyone gets hurt. You're just as likely as Teague and his friends to get arrested if someone is shot. The sheriff isn't going to treat you differently just because Teague came up the mountain after you. Shooting somebody is shooting somebody, and proving self-defense can be expensive, time-consuming and all but impossible. Are you prepared to sit in a jail cell for months while lawyers try to hash out who fired the first shot to the satisfaction of a jury?"

Cowboy looked him straight in the eye. "If that's the way it goes."

Yuma swore softly and sighed.

"Look, none of us wants to shoot," Cowboy said. "We came all the way up here hoping to evade Teague entirely. But if that guy gets here before the sheriff, and if he starts shooting, we'll do whatever is necessary to save ourselves. It's war, man. Teague has declared war."

And that was going to be the final word as far as Cowboy was concerned, Wendy realized. Nor did the mood alter when the two other groups of vets returned at sunset from their respective patrols. Vance's group had decided to plant a false trail that would lead pursuers into a deep ravine, where they could be surrounded from above. Crazy's group had ranged a half day out and caught no sign of Teague and his group, so they figured they were probably clear for another day at least.

Talk around the fire was tense as night settled more deeply on the mountains. These men were combat veterans, and Wendy had no trouble believing they had sounded like this around other fires in hostile lands.

They spoke of weapons, ammunition and strategies. They planned tomorrow's patrols. Teams were assigned sentry duty for the night. The fire, which had been kept small since dusk, was now only glowing embers, which were put out so as not to provide a beacon.

In the dark, they all crawled into sleeping bags and blankets. At the insistence of Cowboy and Vance, Wendy and Yuma spread their bags by the fire pit in the center of the glade.

"Safer there," Vance said. "We'll be able to protect you."

Wendy hesitated only momentarily before zipping the bags together. She and Yuma wouldn't be able to make love, but they *would* be able to snuggle and keep warm. Moonlight silvered the glade, providing barely enough light to manage by. After she slipped into the bag, Yuma followed her and drew her into his arms. A deep, satisfied sigh escaped her as she settled into his embrace.

"Sweet dreams," he murmured, and gave her a gentle kiss on her cheek.

But she didn't sleep immediately. Her awareness of him was too strong, nearly acute, and it kept her mind awake. That and the tension of their circumstances. Although the vets seemed sure that it would be another day at least before Teague could possibly find them, Wendy still found herself listening to every little night sound, wondering if a crack was a human foot on a dead branch or if each rustle was someone approaching.

Nor did it help to remember the bears that roamed these woods. As a child she had felt utterly secure in her father's protection. Adulthood had taught her that there was very little real protection in the world. Bad things could happen to anyone.

But at last fatigue caught up with her, and she fell into dreams of a smiling Yuma.

Yuma couldn't sleep right away, either. His mind wandered over all the mistakes of his life, not the least of them making love to Wendy. That, he figured now, was probably the biggest mistake of all, because for the first time in his life he had *willfully* done something for which someone else was also going to pay. All his previous transgressions had either affected only him or had been an unwilling result of his fractured mind. *This,* however, was in a class by itself.

This time he had chosen to do something that had serious ramifications for the woman lying beside him. It was no accident that he was the first man she had given herself to. No woman waited so long without a reason.

He could no longer doubt the depth and sincerity of her emotional involvement with him. That was bad enough. Worse was the realization that he had probably deepened that involvement by making love to her. Hell, *he* felt emotionally tangled as a result of their lovemaking. For an inexperienced woman, it was bound to be worse.

And now, looking at himself, he knew that he owed her whatever it was in him to give. Knew that he was going to blight her life by doing this. Knew that at some point down the road he was going to say or do something to drive her away.

So maybe it would be wiser now not to give her anything, regardless of what he owed her. Not to give her any hope that he might eventually be what she wanted. Sure, he owed her whatever he had. But, more importantly, maybe the thing he most owed her was to get out of her life.

But not yet, he found himself thinking. Not yet. Not here on this cold mountain. Later, when they got home, he would explain realities to her, but for now...

For now he needed her too much to let go. For now he could tell himself that up here in this strange place surrounded by all these hardened men, she needed *him*. That he gave her some sense of security, however meager. That he was of some use to her.

And, he told himself, she had waited so long to give herself to him, surely she deserved to enjoy what they had for a little while before he snatched it from her.

But just for a little while. He couldn't let it go on too long, or the wound he gave her would be too deep.

Maybe it was already too deep, he thought suddenly, with a chill that crept into his soul. Maybe he had already wounded her beyond repair.

Only time would tell.

In the morning, Wendy roused to find the camp already empty of everyone except herself and Yuma and Hotshot, who sat across the rekindled fire from her.

The two men were talking in quiet, low voices, and at first she let the buzz flow around her, not picking out any of the words, just enjoying the quiet sound of men conversing in the early morning.

The air smelled fresh and piney, cold clean mountain air that smelled like no other place on earth. She had forgotten how good a Rocky Mountain morning could smell, or how good the scent of freshly brewed coffee could be first thing on a cold morning.

Just as she was about to open her eyes and sit up, however, she realized that Yuma and Hotshot were talking about Hotshot's flashbacks. Her rising would interrupt the conversation, and from the sound of it the men were intensely involved in something important. So instead she lay quietly, pretending to sleep on. Her conscience pricked her—after all, this was eavesdropping—but the nurse in her was reluctant to interrupt an exchange so charged with intensity, one that both men seemed to need.

"You know how it is, man," Hotshot was saying. "I'm on Saigon time most of the time. Hell, right now, sitting here, talking to you and looking at your lady sleeping over there, I still feel... like things aren't right. Like they're slipping... Aw, hell, there's no words for it. It's like... like..."

"A distorted mirror, and you see two different things at the same time."

"Yeah. Sort of. And sort of like I slip back and forth between two places. My neck's crawling right now with the feeling that the VC might pop out of those trees any minute... yet I know they won't. I know that's past, man, but my feelings... don't believe it, I guess."

"Yeah." It was a single syllable that conveyed complete understanding. "I get the fractured feeling, too, still. Not like I used to. But sometimes I still get uneasy, unsure where I really am. But look, Hotshot, they have all kinds of new drugs now for this stuff. Mellaril. Haldol. Stuff they didn't have twenty-five years ago when you came home."

"Twenty-five years ago when I came home, the world thought only wimps had a problem, that real men didn't have flashbacks and nightmares." The words were bitter.

"But look at how it's changed. You can walk into any VA hospital now and tell them you have flashbacks and they'll take care of you. Right away. They'll try drugs. They'll try therapy. Relaxation techniques. That relaxation stuff really helped me. When the tension starts to build at the back of my head, I can usually stop it if I can just find a few minutes by myself. It gives *me* control, man. Me. Not the monkey."

For long moments there was no sound in the forest save the pop and crackle of the fire. Just as Wendy had concluded that it was time to let these men know she was awake, Hotshot spoke again.

"You make it sound good, Yuma."

"It's better than the alternative."

Hotshot chuckled softly. "Yeah. But you know, I don't believe in it."

"Don't believe in what?"

"That they can really do anything to put an end to this roller coaster. Hell, Yuma, you know there are guys who spend the rest of their days on the VA mental ward. I don't wanna be one of them. I'd rather spend my life out here in the woods than be locked up like that."

"Why should they lock you up?"

"Because I'm on Saigon time most of the time, man!" Hotshot sounded impatient. "Three quarters of the time I don't know what planet I'm on, let alone what country I'm in. You expect me to believe they'd let me walk away if their damn drugs and stuff didn't work? I can't risk it. I'll kill myself before I let anyone cage me again."

Another long silence, broken eventually by Yuma.

"You were caged?"

"Oh yeah. Bamboo cage, hanging from a tree like some kind of damn trophy. But I got away. After nearly a year."

"Yeah?"

"It was bad, though. Bad. Sometimes...sometimes I feel like I'm back in that cage, with all those guys poking at me with sticks and trying to make me scream. And there was that one guy who liked to play Russian roulette, only he pointed the gun at *me*."

Yuma swore softly.

"I had to kill three of them to get out of there. Damn it, Yuma, I was a pilot, you know? Up above it all. I didn't really see it...and then I had to kill those guys. It's different."

"Yeah."

"And they weren't the last ones. Getting out of there, getting back to our lines, there were more of them. It...did something inside me. I saw their faces but I had to kill them. I still see their faces. I'll always see them."

"I know, man. Believe me, I know."

"Yeah. You didn't come back so lily-white, either, did you?"

"No. I came back just as grimy as everybody else."

"But you never killed anybody."

Yuma was silent awhile. When he spoke, his voice was as rough as sandpaper. "Maybe I didn't kill 'em with my hands, Hotshot, but I killed 'em with my mind. And in the end, it's the same damn thing."

"Yeah." Hotshot made a soft sound somewhere between a snort and a despairing laugh. "I guess maybe it is." He swore. "You know, man, flying used to be the most beautiful thing in the world to me. I could get up there at thirty or forty angels with nothing around me but clear blue sky and feel as free as a damn bird. Even dogfights were just a big thrill, you know? My mouth got just as dry when it was war games as when it was the real thing. It was...clean. Sportsmanlike. Let the best pilot win. All that crap. It wasn't blood and guts and people screaming and crying.

"Then I had to punch out. I lost my wings and fell to the ground, man. And it was blood and guts and people screaming. Even the sky didn't seem clean anymore."

Listening, Wendy ached for the burden Hotshot carried, ached for the price he had paid and would continue to pay because he had done what his country had asked of him. He had been a good soldier, and in the end, to save himself, he had been forced to do things that still tormented him.

And Yuma, who had gone to save lives, had come out with his own endless dark night of the soul to burden him.

How, she wondered in anguish, had anyone ever thought war was glorious? How could anyone justify such nightmares, such atrocities to the mind and soul?

But surely, if a country were going to ask its young men to fight and die, it owed them more than a homeless future on the side of a cold, bleak mountain....

Yuma cleared his throat. "I can't guarantee the VA can help you, buddy. But I *think* they can. And I promise, if you want to go talk to them, I'll go with you."

There was a long, long silence. Then Hotshot said, "Thanks, man. I'll think about it."

He was closing the subject, Wendy realized. Nothing had changed his mind, but he was giving Yuma the only assurance he could. He would think about it. But he would never do it. Because he didn't believe there was any solution to his pain.

Wasn't that what Yuma had been telling her all along? No answer, no end, no cure. Yet here he was, trying to persuade Hotshot to get help.

Maybe, just maybe, Billy Joe Yuma still hoped. And if he still hoped, maybe he could still love.

Chapter 11

During the early afternoon, Yuma suggested to Wendy that they take a walk together.

"Head uphill man," was Hotshot's comment as the two started away from the camp. "Uphill and north'll keep you from getting between us and Teague."

The day was chilly, crisp. Throughout the morning low clouds had obscured the sky, but now the pale sun peeked through and gave the day a warmth that contrasted with the cold air.

When they got out of sight of the camp, Yuma took Wendy's hand in his, but he didn't speak, so she respected his silence while they walked.

Finally, though, when they were nearly a mile out, he leaned back against a tree and drew her into the V between his legs so that she lay against him. Bending, he pressed his face into the curve of her neck and held her fast, just held her, as if he needed to satisfy some deep need to be close.

"What's wrong, Billy Joe?" she asked finally, when the strength of his hold didn't abate.

"Nothing," he whispered roughly. "Nothing. I just... need you, baby. Damn, how I need you!"

There was little he could have said that would have stirred her as deeply as that declaration. Instead of denying her, denying he had anything to offer her, instead of fighting what he felt, he was simply admitting that he needed her. And not just physically, to judge by the way he was holding on to her.

Turning her head, she managed to kiss his neck. "I need you, too," she whispered unsteadily. "I've needed you for so long. I've never stopped needing you...."

His jacket scraped against the bark of the tree as he slid downward, taking her with him, until he sat on the ground with her lying between his legs.

Catching her face between his hands, he turned her mouth up to receive a devouring kiss. Warnings tried to sound in his mind, telling him that he was in grave danger, but for once he refused to heed them. He needed this. He needed this woman in ways he was past arguing with. And it was far more than her warm body and sweet loving he wanted. Deep inside was a craving for her smile, her laugh, her gentle words. Her *love*.

He didn't deserve it. He didn't deserve any part of her, and he was acutely aware of it, but he couldn't deny himself any longer. Whatever she chose to give him, he would willingly accept. Her touch, her voice, her sweet caring, all seemed to fill the emptiness inside him so that he didn't feel so hollow.

It felt as if something inside him were rupturing wide, cracking a shell so old it contained nothing but a dried-up void. Turning, he rolled them together onto their sides so that he could press her every inch to him, could fill himself with the feeling of holding and being held.

It had been so long since he had belonged to someone. So very, very long. And Wendy was so very generous, withholding nothing he might want or need from her. Her hands were everywhere, touching gently, urging him closer, waking the sweet, sweet yearning in him.

In broad daylight, beneath the sheltering arms of aged pines, they joined together on the bed of their discarded clothing. Without the shadows of night to protect their secrets, there were none. He traced her every line and curve with his eyes, his hands, his mouth. And then he endured the exquisite agony of having her discover him the same way.

Intimacy blossomed between them, and he forgot for a little while to remember his pain, to remember his emptiness and his guilt. For a little while she made him feel like a god among men, or better, like that ordinary man he hadn't been for so long. Like a man who was entitled to the love of a woman.

She rode him, and he loved watching her. A slender sprite, she seemed to him, delicately molded of flesh and sinew, a gift beyond words, a natural beauty to be appreciated. Even as the demanding ache built in him, he felt almost rhapsodic over the perfection of the woman who gave herself so freely to him.

When she collapsed on him, he jetted into her with mind-stunning force, then held her shaking body as tightly as he could while they found their way back to the present.

Then, reaching out a tired arm, he found his flannel shirt and pulled it over her damp body, shielding her from the chilly air.

Later they dressed. He propped his back against the tree, and she sat between his legs, leaning against his chest. Her hands rested on his upraised knees, and he covered them with his, lacing their fingers together.

The last time he had felt anything approaching this degree of contentment had been before Vietnam. Not since then had he known this gladness to simply be alive. Not since then had he rejoiced in someone else's existence the way he was rejoicing in Wendy's right now.

It wouldn't last, of course, but she had touched the young man in him, the person he had been before war had seared his soul. And for now he didn't even argue with himself about it.

Wendy turned her head and rubbed her cheek against his chest. A dream she had cherished for so long had now come true, and she couldn't help but revel in it. It wasn't perfect, of course, and she understood that at some point Yuma was bound to try to back away again, but for these precious moments all she wanted to do was enjoy the illusion of at last having her deepest wish come true.

Freeing one of her hands, Yuma touched her cheek with gentle fingertips and then tousled her hair. He wanted to say something special to her, something to let her know that she meant something to him, but the words wouldn't come. There were none, it seemed, that wouldn't imply commitment, and while he guessed that was exactly what Wendy wanted, the fact remained that he couldn't escape the feeling that he would be condemning her.

She thought, he was sure, that love could heal. And he was prepared to admit that perhaps it could heal *some* of his scars and wounds. But it couldn't heal them all. And it couldn't make a whole man of him. He couldn't promise never to have another flashback, never to go off the deep end again. He couldn't promise that he wouldn't wake some morning and be unable to leave the house. Hell, he couldn't be absolutely certain that he wouldn't go on Saigon time permanently. It wasn't likely, but there were no guarantees.

A man who had once lost his place in space and time could never entirely trust his mind again. And no matter how Wendy cared for him, no matter how willing she might be to take the risk, he couldn't commit himself to her when he wasn't sure of his own stability. He'd gone away from Carla emotionally and mentally, so far away that she had left him. Wendy didn't understand his fear that he might do it again, and that there was no guarantee in the world that he wouldn't.

But he couldn't let go, either. He couldn't refuse her, couldn't tell her to get lost, couldn't make himself stay away. Despite his every attempt to resist, she had managed to get under his skin and into his heart. Worse, she had given him back something of himself, a sense of being important. A sense of mattering. A sense that he *could* give joy and pleasure, a talent he had thought lost forever.

Wendy spoke on a soft sigh. "This is idyllic."

"Mmm. I could stay like this forever." As soon as he said it, he wanted to snatch the words back. It sounded too much like a promise, and he knew he shouldn't even imply that there could be a future.

"Me too," she said, and sighed again. "But I guess we'd better head back. If anything happens, I want to be where I can help."

"We need to talk about that. Cowboy's right about one thing, baby. If the shooting starts, some of the guys are going to be back in the middle of the war. They might not...recognize you. They might be shooting at anything that moves. So you'll have to stay clear. More, you'll have to stay low and look out if you get anywhere near the action."

"But if someone gets hurt—"

"Then crawl on your belly, babe. If you feel you *have* to get to someone, crawl. Stay low. Don't make a target of yourself, okay?"

"Okay. But you have to understand, one of the reasons I came up here was to help if someone gets hurt. The first hour after trauma is critical to the victim's survival. I won't risk my life recklessly, but I'm not going to hold back needlessly, either."

"I wouldn't ask you to do that. It's just...I've been watching you for a few weeks now, and you forget everything else when someone is hurt. You forget to look out for yourself. You're a real angel of mercy, no two ways about it, but, babe, that kind of tunnel vision can get you killed when people are shooting."

She turned to one side between his legs and leaned her head against his shoulder so she could look up at him. "I promise I won't risk my neck needlessly, okay?"

He looked down at her, his eyes skimming each smooth line of her face, and for a moment, in his mind's eye, he saw her as she had been six years ago, so eager, innocent and untried by life. So sure that everything would work out, that she could heal scars she couldn't even comprehend simply by loving him. Now she had lost some of that innocence, had faced some of life's incurable traumas, but she still looked out of eyes full of hope and confidence, eyes that promised to see only the good wherever possible... even in him.

He had a notion that she had seen things every bit as terrible as he had ever witnessed, but she had remained somehow unsullied by it. She had retained her incredible faith.

And in the end, perhaps more than his goodness, it was his faith he had lost. Perhaps that was what had really blighted him. He no longer believed that things would work out for the best. No longer believed that God noticed every sparrow's fall... or even cared.

What he had lost, he realized suddenly, was his faith in the goodness of his fellow man... his faith in his own goodness.

And maybe, he found himself thinking unexpectedly, you couldn't have goodness unless you believed in it. Looking down into Wendy's lovely, trusting face, he wondered if maybe, just maybe, she might give him back all the things he had lost.

It was a somber group who sat around the fire late that afternoon. Sentries had been posted along a perimeter several hundred meters out. The talk about plans had made little sense to Wendy. The men spoke in a kind of battlefield shorthand, using terms that were meaningless to her but evidently communicated a lot to them.

The faces tonight were different from last night, she noticed. The first time she had come up to the mountains with Yuma, she had gotten the impression of a small group of about ten men. Right at this moment, however, there were a dozen gathered around the fire, and only Cowboy and Hotshot were known to her. Thinking about it, she decided there must be nearly twenty men altogether, perhaps a stable group, perhaps a constantly shifting crowd as men came and went. Yuma would know, but this wasn't the time to ask.

How many men, she found herself wondering, were actually hiding out in these mountains when life became too difficult, or when reality slipped its gears for them? Maybe only this group. Maybe many, many groups scattered around.

She knew from her work in L.A. that homeless vets were entirely too common, but she hadn't really given any thought to the fact that there might literally be thousands of them scattered like leaves in the wind, hiding in small groups where no one ever noticed them. Like these men.

As night lowered its concealing cloak over the world, the men hastily prepared a hot meal, then doused the fire. The wind sighed through the treetops, creating a constant cascade of sound. Everyone headed swiftly for sleeping bags and bedrolls to escape the chilly night air.

Yuma wrapped Wendy in the warmth of his arms and held her close, but sleep eluded them both. They were both gripped by the sense that tomorrow would bring Teague and the confrontation. Under the cover of the sighing wind and rustling trees, it was possible to carry on a whispered conversation, and Wendy found herself turning toward Yuma and voicing her fears.

"I don't think Teague has a conscience," she murmured. "He'll shoot."

"I'm afraid you're right." He would have given anything to have hog-tied her to her bed at home so she couldn't be here now. All the independence he'd been willing to grant her before because she was a competent, capable adult suddenly seemed like foolhardiness. He should have called her father and let Nate put her in a cell. He should have found *some* way to keep her out of this.

But he hadn't, and now he was feeling like a failure because he hadn't protected her. All those arguments from her about being here in case someone was hurt—all that stuff he'd fallen for—sounded weak and flimsy now. He cursed his weakness, cursed his reluctance to force her.

"Damn," he muttered, "I wish you'd stayed home. I wish I'd *made* you stay home."

"And how were you going to accomplish that?" Before he could answer, she silenced him with a quick, hard kiss. "Shut up, Billy Joe. Don't make me angry. I'm twenty-four, old enough to make my own decisions about these things."

And young enough to make such a statement, he found himself thinking. Young enough to feel idealistic and indestructible, a truly dangerous combination. But argument now would serve no purpose...except possibly to wake everybody in camp.

Instead he chose another course, seeking to ease the tension he felt in her and send her to sleep. Pressing her face into his shoulder, he brought her to an amazingly fast and urgent climax with the touch of his fingers. She lay shuddering against him afterwards. Then, when he wouldn't let her touch him in return, she fell into a deep slumber.

He didn't sleep at all. Staring into the cold night over her head, he faced the long line of ghosts from his past and wondered what the hell he was going to do about the newest one: Wendy Tate.

"Teague's coming." Cowboy shook Yuma's shoulder just before dawn, dragging him from the troubled slumber he'd finally achieved into the ghostly light. "You and your lady better get ready."

While Wendy struggled to pull on her jeans inside the sleeping bag, Yuma hunted through the backpack for granola bars and poured her some coffee. The camp was silent, empty of everyone save themselves and Cowboy, who'd evidently been left to look after them.

"They're moving toward the ravine," Cowboy told Yuma. "They'll run into the trap in a half hour or so, if they keep moving. I don't know where the sheriff is."

"Probably right behind them," Yuma said as Wendy joined them at the small fire. He passed her the tin cup of steaming coffee and a granola bar. "Micah Parish is apt to be coming right up on their heels. That man tracks like the devil himself."

"Still, he's tracking," Cowboy said. "That's got to slow him down some. And we can't count on the sheriff getting here in time to prevent trouble. We're going to surround them and try to hold him until Tate gets here."

"You *could* just back off," Yuma said. "Lead Teague and his buddies back around to the sheriff."

Cowboy shook his head. "You know better than that, Yuma. We've given enough ground. We ain't giving any more."

"I'm not talking about giving ground, Cowboy. I'm talking about leading them into another kind of trap."

But Cowboy shook his head. "We already moved back twice. We gave the sheriff plenty of time to stop this. Hell, it's not like this just happened without warning. Tate could have stopped him somehow before he even started hunting us, if he'd really wanted to." He glanced at Wendy. "Sorry, Miss Tate, but that's the way I see it. Your daddy didn't do a whole hell of a lot to keep Teague from coming up here."

"He did everything he legally could," Yuma argued before Wendy could respond. "You can't throw somebody in jail for shooting off his mouth."

"Maybe not." Cowboy shook his head. "All I know is armed men are hunting us. That's war, plain and simple. If Tate gets here in time, fine. If not, we're defending ourselves. Hell, it isn't right that we should have to keep pulling back deeper and deeper into the woods, away from what little comfort we've got. How would you feel if *you* had to leave your home because some idiot with a gun had nasty ideas?" He looked at Wendy as he spoke.

"I know," she said quietly. "I know. I'd want to fight back, too."

"Damn it, Wendy," Yuma said.

She looked at him. "I'm sorry, Billy Joe, but I wasn't raised like you were. This is something we just won't ever see eye-to-eye on. A person has a right to defend himself and his home. That's how *I* was raised."

He admired her spunk. He admired her for standing up to him. But he also felt frustrated that she couldn't see his point of view. "Self-defense doesn't always require violence," he argued.

"Maybe," she said. "I guess it depends on how you were raised, doesn't it?"

He could see this was going to go nowhere. There was no way on earth he could prevent these men from reacting to Teague however they saw fit. All he could do was try to keep Wendy safe if trouble occurred.

And he was beginning to get the idea that it wasn't going to be easy.

Giving up the verbal battle, he hefted the backpack full of medical supplies and followed her and Cowboy down to the ravine, where the rest of the men were waiting to spring the trap.

He had no doubt that these guys could lead Teague and company right into a trap. Men who had been in the Special Forces, in Force Recon and Long Range Reconnaissance, knew how to lay a trail, how to lead the enemy. There was enough know-how among these men to draw smarter quarry than Teague into the maw of a trap.

And suddenly Yuma realized that for the first time in a quarter century he was praying. Actually praying that no one would get hurt today, that Teague would have enough sense to see that he was caught and lay down his weapon. That all the men with him would be so wise. That the vets wouldn't lose themselves in flashbacks and forget what was really happening here. That the entire matter could be resolved without bloodshed.

He wondered if heaven was listening.

"You stay here," Cowboy said, pointing to a cluster of boulders that created a small, protected space. "We don't want either one of you getting in the line of fire on this."

"But if someone gets hurt—" Wendy began.

"If someone gets hurt, you'll hear the screams," the man told her bluntly. "You'll know. The ravine's over there." He pointed. "Don't come until the shooting stops, though. I mean it, lady. Take care of your own ass, because nobody else'll be thinking about it...except Yuma, here." Cowboy turned to him. "Keep her out of it, man."

Yuma nodded. "I intend to. Believe me."

"What is it?" Wendy asked as she and Yuma settled in among the rocks. "Do I look incredibly stupid? Everybody thinks I need to be protected!"

"You look incredibly young, trusting and idealistic," Yuma told her flatly. "Nobody wants to see you hurt. That's all."

The rocks sheltered them from the bite of the wind and provided a backrest for Wendy. Tilting her head, she watched the dawn brighten the world from silvery gray to a brilliant pink as the rising sun illuminated low clouds from beneath. It would probably rain today, she thought. The weather in the mountains was wildly unpredictable, but the low, fast-moving clouds she saw overhead nearly always heralded rain.

She was almost afraid to look at Yuma this morning, she realized. Something had happened when they had made love in the woods yesterday. Something inside him that she sensed he wasn't very happy about. This morning there was a subtle irritation in his voice, an impatience that she had never before sensed in him.

His equilibrium had been disturbed, she thought. She had gone and done the very thing her father had warned her not to do. She had thrown Yuma off kilter. And maybe now his PTSD was acting up.

Gathering her courage, she looked at him and found he was staring at her solemnly. "What?" she asked.

He shook his head. "Just tense. The same old stuff, nothing new."

"The PTSD?"

"I guess."

"What does it feel like?" She half expected him to dismiss the question impatiently, but he never even blinked.

"Like something bad is going to happen. The way you feel when you've done something wrong and you know you're going to be found out. Anxious. Edgy."

Instinctively, hardly aware of doing it, she slid over until she was sitting right beside him. "You didn't do anything wrong, Billy Joe."

"No?" He shook his head.

"No. Not with me. I wanted you every bit as much as you wanted me. Probably a whole lot more. And I'll never regret it, no matter what happens."

Something flickered in his face then, but it was gone so swiftly that she couldn't decipher it. "Easy to say," he remarked, looking away.

That was when she realized he was fighting for control, trying to batten down the "monkey." It was a fight to maintain his grip on sanity, and she wasn't helping by talking to him. She made herself look away, forcing her attention to the wakening morning and rapidly scudding clouds.

Those clouds, she thought, might make it difficult to call in the helicopter if someone got hurt. Instinctively she started to turn toward Yuma to ask for his evaluation of the flying conditions, but she caught herself before she intruded.

She recognized the deep, regular rhythm of his breathing as being part of a relaxation exercise. Tucking her knees up under her chin, she closed her eyes and waited. It was disgusting, she thought, that so many people refused to recognize PTSD as a battlefield wound every bit as legitimate as a bullet hole in the chest or the loss of a leg. The horror of war did terrible things to minds, wounding the psyche and spirit beyond measure. Beyond repair. And those who took the longest to recover were those who had endured the horror over the longest periods of time. Especially those who had been taken prisoner and rendered utterly helpless for years.

Having worked at the VA hospital for the entire period of her training, she had some idea of how deep the wounds could be. She felt nothing but respect for Yuma, who had managed to pull himself far enough out of the morass of his pain so that he could function. So many never did. Never could. Billy Joe had an internal strength of mind and spirit greater than many, regardless of how he saw himself. An innate strength that allowed him to rise above his own wounds. A strength that was putting him back in the very same position that had caused the scars in the first place.

Every time he climbed into the cockpit of that copter, he had to be reminded of Vietnam, of his countless flights into battle. Every time he lifted that chopper into the air, every time he carried a wounded, screaming patient, he *had* to remember. He faced his nightmare daily, when he could have found easier ways of getting by.

And he came up here to take care of his friends, to help them, to encourage them. And now, when his worst nightmares must surely be staring him right in the face, he was here, facing them. Prepared to do what he could to protect his friends and to protect her.

Some people might think Billy Joe Yuma was weak, but Wendy knew better. He was stronger by far than most men. He had been tested more than most, and in the end he was living a daily triumph over problems that had driven equally strong men to suicide.

"Aw, hell," he sighed suddenly, and the next thing she knew she was being hugged to his chest. "Wendy..." He kissed her forehead, brushed her hair back and squeezed her closer. "I'm sorry, baby. I'm being a son of a bitch, and you don't deserve it. You should have somebody who's happy and excited and thrilled, not some idiot like me who's all messed up."

"Stop it. I don't want to hear it." Struggling against his hold, she lifted her head and looked him right in the eye. "You're exactly what I want. The only thing I've ever really wanted. I won't stand for you apologizing for anything, because there's nothing to apologize for. Nothing."

She really believed that, he realized. But that was because she was sure she would never regret giving herself to him.

He knew better. He knew how things that seemed so right at one moment could later prove to be disastrous. He knew how feelings and emotions could delude you, only to leave you feeling wounded later. He understood that later you could regret even the most wonderful things.

But there was no point in telling her that. She was in no state of mind to believe him. Besides, he didn't have the heart to destroy what she was feeling right now. Reality would impinge soon enough.

So he hugged her close and held his peace, and kissed her with all the warm, cherishing feelings she had evoked in him. And for now, just for now, he allowed himself to forget all his reservations, all his objections, all the million reasons why he should set her aside before he hurt her.

Because he *would* hurt her. It was inevitable. But right now he couldn't seem to make himself remember that. Right now he was just too desperate for her warmth and caring. Right now all that seemed to matter was the comfort she gave him. The sense that he was a man, and that he was worthy.

All of a sudden the morning quiet was ruptured by the shocking crack of a gun shot. Moments later there was an agonized cry.

Without even pausing to think, Wendy wrenched out of Yuma's hold and sprang to her feet, grabbing the backpack that contained her supplies. Because she had needed to bring I.V.s, it was heavy, and it momentarily knocked her a little off balance.

"Wendy, wait!"

Another shot ruptured the air just as Yuma grabbed her arm and tried to restrain her.

"Damn it, Wendy, they're shooting. You can't—"

"Somebody was hurt!"

"I know that. But it won't do him a damn bit of good if you get hurt, too! Just wait a minute!"

But she couldn't. The image of someone lying on the ground while an artery pumped out the last of his life was more than she could tolerate. With a jerk she broke free of

Yuma's restraining grip and began to run toward the ravine.

Yuma started after her immediately, but he covered only a few feet of ground before his foot snagged on something and he hurtled forward. With stunning force, his head hit a rock and the world turned black.

Wendy never saw him fall. She was totally focused on the shouts and shots ahead, intent on reaching the man who had screamed.

"Damn it!" Somebody swore and grabbed her arm, drawing her to a stunning, jerking halt. Looking up, she recognized Cowboy. He pulled on her arm, swearing softly as he dragged her down to a crouch. "Damn it, woman, you'll get killed!"

"Someone screamed."

"Boggs. He took a hit in the leg."

"Bad?"

"Artery."

"I have to get to him."

"You can't help if you get shot!"

"They won't shoot me. I'm the sheriff's daughter. None of those guys is that stupid!"

Cowboy shook his head. "Lady, I don't believe you! With all the bullets flying, *nobody's* safe. Where the hell is Yuma?"

"He was..." She looked back, and saw no one. "I thought he was right behind me."

"Probably tripped. At least he's not likely to be shot. You stay—"

The word broke off sharply as a man's cry ripped through Cowboy's words. "I'm dying. Oh, God, I'm dying."

Cowboy swore viciously, his eyes darting in the direction of the cry. The momentary distraction gave Wendy the break she needed. Jerking away from Cowboy's grip, she kept her head low and darted forward toward the groans.

She saw Boggs almost immediately. He was on his back, curled around himself as he pressed his hands desperately to the spurting wound in his leg. There was no mistaking the bright red of arterial blood, or the force of it. Without help, he would be dead in minutes.

"Medic," she screamed. "I'm a medic. Don't anybody shoot!"

Drawing a deep breath, she held up her hands, struggling to lift the heavy backpack, and hurried toward Boggs. "Don't shoot!" she called again.

And by some miracle, no one did. The forest grew silent except for Boggs's helpless sounds of pain. Reaching him, Wendy dropped to her knees and pushed his hands away from the wound.

"Lie back," she ordered. As soon as she got his leg straightened out, she laid her palm to the spurting wound and pressed down with the weight of her body. "Somebody come help me, damn it!"

But just then a bullet slapped into the dirt not far from her.

"Don't anybody move!"

Teague. She recognized his voice. "Damn it, Teague, if you prevent me from helping this man, you're committing murder!"

"You shoulda stayed home, Wendy, baby." There was no mistaking the sneer in Teague's voice. "I got a bone or two to pick with you."

"Well, pick them later. This man needs help now!" Looking around, she finally picked out Teague. He was standing between two boulders amidst heavy brush and was nearly invisible in camouflage. And he had the barrel of a rifle pointed straight at her. "What do you want?" she asked.

"Why don't you tell me how much you want me?"

She closed her eyes and tried not to gag. Teague's advances had always made her feel a little sick, but her reaction was even worse now. Having been loved by Yuma, she couldn't bear the thought of being touched by anyone else.

"Go to hell, Teague!"

He laughed. "Always a spitfire. You remember that time you kneed me? I don't forget things like that, you bitch."

Wendy looked straight at him and realized that this man intended to kill her. Right here and now, while she knelt beside Boggs and tried to stem the flow of his blood, Alvin Teague was going to kill her.

Yuma had absolutely no idea how long he was out. When he came to, he was vaguely aware of shouting voices, of a gunshot. Of a headache that threatened to split his skull.

Damn it. *Wendy!*

He staggered to his feet and had to wait a few moments for the world to stop spinning. The sound of another gunshot instantly cleared his senses. Wendy might be in danger....

He started hurrying in the direction of the voices. Wendy. He could hear her voice. It was raised and angry.

"Go to hell, Teague!"

He came around an outcropping of rock and halted so fast he nearly stumbled. Horror paralyzed him instantly as he gauged the scene. Wendy was kneeling beside Boggs, whose face was almost white as she pressed her bloody hand to a wound in his leg. She and Boggs were both looking toward a cluster of boulders.

And there was Teague. Pointing a rifle straight at the two of them. Looking at them with eyes as cold and hard as chips of ice.

There wasn't a doubt in Yuma's mind that Teague was capable of murder at that moment. Not a shadow of a doubt.

"Wendy." He barely whispered her name, but she heard him. Slowly her head turned, and she looked straight at him.

"Help me," she said. "I need a pressure bandage from the pack." She cocked her head toward the backpack that lay only a foot away from her.

"Don't move," Teague warned. "Don't anybody move."

"I have to, Teague," Yuma said, looking straight toward the man. "I can't let Boggs die." And he couldn't let Teague threaten Wendy, not if there was anything on earth he could do.

So he stepped forward slowly and just kept walking. The hair on the back of his neck stood up, but he ignored the chilling feeling and kept moving toward Wendy. He would place himself between her and Teague. That way, if the man pulled the trigger, she would at least have a chance to drop down before he could get off a second shot.

"Hold it where you are, Yuma!"

Yuma paused and looked straight at Teague. If nothing else, it allowed him to gauge the best place to kneel to protect Wendy. "I'm going to help her," he told Teague calmly, flatly. "Shoot me if you want, Teague. At least I'll die with a clean conscience."

Which really wouldn't be too bad, he thought, as he started moving again. Evidently Teague didn't want to do him that favor, because he didn't shoot.

Then, moving swiftly, Yuma knelt on Boggs's other side, facing Wendy, placing himself between her and Teague.

"Keep low," he whispered. "Don't give him a clear shot." Then he looked at Boggs and saw that the former marine's eyes were clear and alert, even though his face was a grimace of pain. He spoke his next words in a normal tone of voice so Teague could hear. "What do you want me to do?"

"In the backpack there are some pressure bandages. I need to get one on this wound so I can get an IV started. He's lost a lot of blood, and we need to replace fluids. Damn, I wish I had oxygen." The blood was no longer spurting up between her fingers, which was a good sign. If she hadn't needed to start an IV to keep Boggs from going into shock, she would have chosen to keep her hands right where they were so the bleeding couldn't restart.

"I'm reaching for the backpack, Teague," Yuma called out, then moved slowly, making sure his hand stayed in plain sight. His back crawled with the awareness of his exposure. "Keep me between you and him, Wendy," he whispered. "Don't give him a shot at you."

She looked at him from grim brown eyes, but she didn't say anything. Her mouth remained set in a thin, tense line.

"What are you hoping to accomplish with this, Teague?" Yuma asked as he put the pack beside him and began swiftly working the buckles. "The sheriff knows you came up here to hurt these guys."

"He can't prove they didn't shoot first," Teague said. "We came up here like good citizens to clean out this nest of thieves. There won't be any more robberies in Conard County after this."

"But these guys haven't robbed anyone. So there will still be robberies. And everyone will know it."

"No more robberies," Teague said again and laughed. "My baby brother is giving up his life of crime now. As soon as I take care of you and all these friends of yours."

His brother! Shock flooded Yuma, and he glanced at Wendy, but she was watching his hands as he pulled things from the pack.

"That's the bandage," Wendy said suddenly, keeping her voice quiet. "Can you wrap it around his leg above the wound?"

Following her murmured directions, he began to do as she asked. Boggs drew some sharp breaths but never made a sound.

"The robberies will stop," Teague repeated. "And the whole damn county will be glad to have these guys gone. They make everybody uneasy."

"Uneasy is no reason to kill innocent people, Teague."

"You make me uneasy, Yuma. And you're going to be dead. You got that little woman there eating out of your hand, but you treat her like dirt! Hell, she coulda had *me*."

Yuma lifted his eyes swiftly to Wendy's face and saw realization there. She had told Teague he wasn't half the man Yuma was, and now, because of one angry remark, people were going to die. He wanted to reach out, to somehow reassure her that she was not responsible, that she could have said the same thing to hundreds of other men without such disastrous results.

"Boggs hasn't done anything to you," Wendy said. She looked at Boggs. "I'm going to ask Yuma to apply pressure with his other hand way up here in your groin." She touched the area. "This should stop the bleeding while I put the bandage in place, okay?"

"Okay."

She guided Yuma's hand into position with her free hand. "Press hard. You'll probably have to lean your weight on your palm."

"Okay."

Straightening on his knees, he leaned down hard. Boggs groaned.

"Damn it," Teague said. "Don't you ignore me, woman."

"I'm not ignoring you, Alvin," Wendy said, watching intently as she lifted her hand from the wound. No spurting was apparent now, though there was a steady, slight ooze of blood. "I can work and talk at the same time." Swiftly she moved the bandage into place.

"You've been ignoring me for years!"

Wendy suddenly looked up, moving her head to one side so she could see Teague over Yuma's shoulder. At once she was looking straight down the barrel of his rifle. "So why hurt these men because you're angry with *me?* That doesn't make any sense at all!"

If he could have, Yuma would have resorted to violence right then and given Wendy a good solid shake. *Damn it!* Telling the man who was holding the gun aimed straight at her that he wasn't making any sense was enough to make anyone with sense want to shake her.

"Wendy!" he whispered sharply.

She glanced at him briefly, then returned her attention to the bandage.

"These guys are in my way," Teague growled. "Yuma's in my way."

It was a chilling revelation. Yuma felt his back prickle with awareness that a madman was holding a rifle aimed at his back.

"Okay," Wendy said. "Release the pressure." Yuma lifted his hand from Boggs's groin. "Good." The pressure bandage didn't immediately darken with blood, so the bleeding was controlled. "Now I need the infusion set."

Yuma pawed around in the backpack, finally coming up with the necessary preparations for the IV.

"Alvin," Wendy said as she wrapped a tourniquet around Boggs's arm, "we need to call the Medevac flight for this man."

"Right." Teague laughed.

Damn it, Yuma thought, admiring Wendy's cool as she went right ahead with the IV. Damn it, where were the other guys? Surely Teague ought to be wondering about them. But he seemed totally unconcerned. Could they all have been taken prisoner by Teague's friends? That didn't seem possible.

The woods were too damn quiet, he thought, looking up and around. His vet friends ought to be doing something if they were able to. But no one appeared to be doing anything. It was as if he, Teague, Wendy and Boggs were alone in the world.

Chapter 12

Wendy found a strong, stable vein in Boggs's arm, swabbed it and inserted the needle. Moments later fluid was flowing into Boggs, holding off the possibility of circulatory collapse from blood loss.

Once that task was accomplished, however, her hands were virtually tied. There wasn't much more she could do for him except get him out of here, and she couldn't call the helicopter unless Teague let her get the radio. Somehow she had to convince him to let her do just that.

But as she looked at him over Yuma's shoulder, she had the definite, queasy feeling that it was Teague's intention that no one but him would ever walk out of this ravine.

She had known the man was a troublemaker—he was always in fights, and he'd been in and out of jail—but there was no reason on earth to have guessed he could be a conscienceless killer.

"What do you want me to do, Alvin?" she heard herself ask. "What will it take to make you let Yuma and Boggs alone?" She heard Yuma swear viciously under his breath, but her attention was focused on Teague. Everything she had ever learned about managing people was on the alert right now, waiting for some indication as to how to reason with this man. How to keep him from getting to the point of pulling that trigger. If she could just hold him off long enough...

But that might be too long for Boggs.

Teague moved a little to the side to get a better view of Wendy. Even though Yuma's back was to the man, he knew it because Wendy's eyes followed the movement. At once he moved, too, placing himself as best he could between Wendy and Teague. If his body was all he could protect her with, he offered it willingly.

Wendy glanced at him then, and he saw from her anguished brown eyes that she knew exactly what he was doing. He suspected that she might have wanted to move again, to get him out of the line of fire, but she was holding the IV bag to keep the fluid flowing into Boggs, and she couldn't shift much farther.

For that small blessing he gave thanks.

"What do I want?" Teague laughed again, harshly. "What the hell makes you think I want anything from you anymore? You lost your chance, honey."

"Well, if that's how you feel, why don't you let me call the chopper? You can do whatever it is you need to do after Boggs is safely out of here."

"You think I'm dumb? Damn bitch! Nobody's walking away from here. Nobody but me and my buddies. They'll never find the bodies. Never."

Wendy shook her head. "Micah Parish is probably right on your heels."

Teague laughed. "Not likely. I know how to lay a false trail, lady. Been doing it for years. I expect he and your damn father are miles from here and heading in the wrong direction."

Yuma's stomach clenched uncomfortably even as he told himself that Micah wouldn't be misled by a false trail. No way. Not that man.

But even the best could be pointed the wrong way. Even the best.

Where were the other guys? Cowboy, Hotshot, Crazy, Vance and all the rest? Surely they couldn't all have been knocked out of action? Surely someone was left who could help them?

"What I want," Teague said finally, "is to never have to see your face again. Or his. So I think I'll shoot him first. He doesn't care about you. Not a bit. But you're crazy about him, and I want to see the look in your eyes when you watch him die."

Wendy drew a long, horrified breath and watched in disbelief as Teague leveled his rifle straight at Yuma's back.

"Teague, no..." she implored, her voice an agonized whisper. "I'll do anything...."

"Too late," he said, and took aim.

At that instant there was a shout. Suddenly and unexpectedly, Hotshot hurtled into the clearing and flung himself between Yuma and Teague just as Teague fired. The bullet caught him in the chest.

At the sound of the shot, Yuma instinctively fell to the side, grabbing Wendy's arm and pulling her down with him. She landed across Boggs's wounded leg, and he cried out.

"Drop the gun, Teague," said Cowboy's familiar voice. "All your friends are tied up, and you've got eight rifles pointed at you right now."

"Drop it, Teague," came Vance's voice from another direction. "I've got you covered, too."

"Me, too," shouted someone else.

There was a clatter as Teague's gun hit the ground.

"Wendy?" called Cowboy. "Wendy, Hotshot's been hit...."

Hotshot wasn't going to make it. The helicopter was on the way, but his chest was filling with blood, and Wendy didn't have the equipment to intubate him and drain his chest. Worse, he was coughing blood, a sign that the lung had been punctured. There simply wasn't going to be enough time to save him.

Hotshot knew it. He ignored Wendy, who was attempting to establish an IV, and focused on Yuma, who knelt beside him and gripped his hand.

"Why'd you do it?" Yuma asked tautly.

Hotshot coughed. "Man, I ain't got nothing to live for. Nothing." He paused, panting, a terrible gurgle in his throat. "But you do. You do."

Yuma swore softly. "You've got plenty to live for, Hotshot. Plenty."

But it was too late. Moments later Hotshot yielded his last rattling breath.

The sheriff hadn't been far behind Teague at all. Within five minutes of Hotshot's death, Nate and his deputies appeared. They had already run into the vets who had captured Teague's accomplices and were soon clapping handcuffs on Teague, as well.

As soon as the prisoners were secured, though, Nate's attention was all for his daughter.

"Are you all right?" he demanded of her. She was again beside Boggs, checking his pulse, watching for signs of shock. The IV bag was now hanging from a tree branch someone had thrust upright into the ground.

"I'm fine, Dad. I'm fine. Can you find out the ETA on the chopper?"

Nate turned his head. "Charlie? Radio the chopper and get an ETA, will you?"

"Sure thing, Nate."

Nate squatted beside Boggs and looked down at the man. "We'll get you out of here, friend. We'll get you patched up. What unit?"

"Third Marine Division, Force Recon."

"Force Recon, huh? You guys were something else."

Boggs managed a very small, very faint smile. "Yeah. Not too damn many lived to talk about it. You?"

"Special Forces. Force Recon gave us some of our training."

"Yeah. You were 'A' Team then."

"So was Parish over there. And Ransom Laird. You ever meet him?"

"Don't think so."

"Well, I'll tell you what, son. When we get you sewed up, I'll bring my buddies around and we'll shoot the breeze about the old days. How's that?"

"Sounds good, Sheriff. Sounds really good."

Wendy looked over at her father and felt tears welling in her eyes. She knew him as a parent, knew him a little as a tough sheriff, but this was the first she had ever seen of this side of him. Only by the grace of God, she realized suddenly, had Nate escaped Boggs's fate. Or Yuma's. And her dad knew it. It was apparent in the way he laid his hand on Boggs's shoulder and talked to him. Apparent in the ready way he reached out to the man's real pain.

Nate looked up and found her wet brown eyes on him.

"I love you, Dad," she whispered softly.

"I love you, too, honey," he replied gently. "And I've been scared out of my mind for you. Don't you ever do this again."

She gave a choked little laugh. "I sure don't intend to."

When the helicopter arrived, Dr. MacArdle was aboard, along with Sally Hawthorne, the nurse who was covering for Wendy. They got Boggs onto a stretcher and aboard, and arranged to make a return trip for Hotshot's body.

The rest of them were going to have to hike back out, the deputies and the prisoners.

That was when Wendy noticed that Yuma had vanished. She looked everywhere, trying without success to spot him. Finally she caught Cowboy by the arm. "Yuma?"

He jerked his head in the direction of the woods. "He took off that way."

"Did he say why?"

Cowboy shook his head. "Bet this set him off, but I'm not sure."

"You think it's a flashback?"

"I don't know."

"I have to find him."

Everyone was getting ready to leave, and it was obvious that her father didn't like the idea of her remaining behind.

"I'll stay, too," Cowboy said. "I'll see her back safely, Sheriff."

After a perceptible hesitation, Nate nodded. The frown he gave Wendy was a warning she knew from earliest childhood. She managed a smile.

"I'll be careful, Dad. Promise. Cowboy and Yuma will take care of me."

Minutes later she was walking off into the woods with Cowboy at her side. He carried a rifle and rucksack that she imagined contained whatever he considered necessary for survival. She carried her pack of medical supplies.

Cowboy knew how to track, and Yuma hadn't tried to cover his trail. Even Wendy could follow it.

"When we find him," Cowboy said, "you'd better approach carefully. He might recognize you and he might not. I know he's not a violent type, but there aren't any guarantees he won't strike out, anyway."

"I know. I've... worked with vets at the VA hospital."

Cowboy looked down at her. "You're really crazy about this guy, aren't you?"

"Forever, it seems." She shook her head. "He hasn't had a flashback in years."

"No, but he used to get 'em as bad as any of us. You know, he's got less to apologize for than most of us, but he sure lives with a bucketload of guilt."

She didn't say anything to that. There didn't seem to be any point. She figured that Cowboy probably knew more about Yuma than she ever would.

They found him finally, curled up under some brush. Cowboy hung back. "I'll just walk away a distance and give you two privacy," he said. "When you want me, whistle. You *can* whistle?"

She nodded.

"Just give a good piercing one, and I'll come at a run. Otherwise, I ain't here."

Wendy touched his arm. "Thank you."

He shook his head. "No need."

When the sound of Cowboy's boots had faded away, Wendy called out to Yuma.

"Billy Joe? Billy Joe?" He didn't respond. Tentatively she began to move toward him. "Billy Joe, it's Wendy. Can you hear me?"

When she reached him, she saw that he was curled up into himself, shaking. Forgetting caution in her concern, she dropped to the ground and curled herself around him, holding him tight.

"I'm here, Billy Joe," she murmured. "I'm here."

He turned into her, clutching her close, as if she were a lifeline. "I know it's not real," he said raggedly. "It's not real. That was a long time ago."

"That's right. It's over. It's not real. But it feels real, doesn't it?"

"Oh, God, yes!"

"We'll ride it out together, Billy Joe. Together. I'm right here, and I'm not going away."

He was struggling so valiantly against feelings gone wild, adrenaline surges beyond his control. PTSD didn't just flash memories up in the mind's eye, it brought all the feelings with it—the terror, the pain, the anger. When the flashback was strong enough, the body reacted as if it were happening right now.

"I hid for days in the undergrowth," he told her. "Days. I could hardly drag myself a few inches, because my hip was smashed. It rained. I drank water off the leaves. And I got so hot. Fever, I guess. I lay there for days, and I could hear them searching... I guess I must've gotten delirious and cried out. They found me."

Wendy squeezed her eyes shut, trying not to think about what a terrifying experience that must have been. All of it. She tightened her arms around him even more.

For a long, long time he said nothing else. She could tell he was trapped in memory. He would jerk and cry out, or swear viciously. She lost track of time, and it really didn't matter, anyway. However long it took, she was going to stay with him until he returned fully to the present.

All she could hope was that somehow her presence was comforting him as he struggled with memories of a long-ago war in a faraway land. She had worked with enough vets to know these were no ordinary memories that could be dismissed with a mental shift of direction. They were compelling, overwhelming, insistent. The sufferer could do nothing but ride them out.

Morning crept into afternoon, and the sun took the worst of the chill out of the air.

"I wanted to kill him."

The suddenness of the statement took Wendy by surprise. She tilted her head back so she could see him. His gaze was fixed on some invisible point. "Billy Joe?"

"I wanted to kill him. I wanted to gouge out his eyes and shove them down his throat. I wanted...to do terrible things."

"That's natural. That's perfectly natural." She didn't have any idea what he was talking about, but it hardly seemed to matter.

"He caned the bottom of my feet until they were raw," he said, his voice completely toneless. "Over and over again...."

Wendy's heart squeezed, and her diaphragm froze on a sob she didn't dare let escape. She couldn't imagine the nightmare paths he was walking; the glimpses he gave her were bad enough. "Oh, Yuma," she whispered on an agonized breath. She kissed the top of his head as she hugged him closer to her breast.

"I can't... Sometimes I just can't stop remembering," he said tightly. "Sometimes it just keeps coming and coming...."

"I understand. It's okay. Really, it's okay."

But finally the time came when he rolled away from her and lay on his back, silently staring up at the blue sky through the pine boughs. Wendy waited, aching for him, sensing that this flashback had cost him more than hours of agony. It had cost him his barely born confidence in his mental stability. And she suspected that there wasn't one reassurance she could offer that he would even listen to.

A long, long time later, he released a heavy breath. "Sorry."

"For what?"

"Flipping out."

"You didn't exactly flip out. And even if you had, it's understandable, given what was happening. Damn it, Yuma, why should you apologize because you're wounded? I could see it maybe if you'd shot yourself in the foot deliberately—"

"Damn it!" The exclamation interrupted her, and he sat up abruptly. "You don't understand!"

"Then why don't you try to explain?"

"I've been trying to *explain* ever since you set your sights on me, Wendy! I'm not normal. I'm not stable. I never know when I'll flip out! *I can't trust my own mind!*"

She drew a long shaky breath, knowing where this was going to lead, realizing that she was about to fight for her very life. "I can handle that," she said after a moment, managing to keep her voice calm.

"I can't." He spoke bluntly. Flatly. In a dead tone that terrified her more than anything else could have. He was distancing. Withdrawing. She recognized it. He was hurting so badly that he was retreating, separating himself from everything he cared about, anything that might wound him more. She couldn't allow it to happen.

"Billy Joe, you *can* trust your mind. You can trust it as much as I can trust my own! Damn it, you've seen me go over the edge remembering—" She broke off, emotion suddenly locking her throat. She had to take a couple of deep breaths before she could continue. "This is the mind's way of dealing with intolerable events. It's not some kind of abnormality. It's a healing process, awful though it is. It takes *years* to deal with some things. But it's getting better, isn't it? It doesn't happen as often, does it? And look at the stressors operating here today—"

"Enough." He cut her off with the one quietly spoken word. For a couple of minutes he didn't say any more. When he finally spoke, his voice was calm, reflective. "It doesn't matter, Wendy. Life is full of stressors. I freak out when a car backfires, when somebody slams a door, if I hear a gunshot. Hell, an odor can push me over. Every time I get into that chopper and smell the oil and fuel, hear the rotors wind up..." He shook his head.

"You manage it, don't you?" she persisted. "You sit there and smell the oil fumes and listen to the rotor whine. You look out of that cockpit the same way you did in Nam. The stick feels the same way in your hand, the sounds are the same sounds. And when we pick up the patient, you hear the same screams and smell the blood. But you handle it, Billy Joe. And in time you'll handle the rest. Just give it time."

"Time? It's already been damn near a quarter century! How many more quarter centuries do I have in my life? Damn it, Wendy, I'm forty-four. Nothing's going to change. Nothing's going to get better."

"But it already has! Look at you now! Six years ago you couldn't hold a job! Eight years ago you were an alcoholic! You haven't had a drink in how many years now? Are you going to sit there and tell me you aren't getting stronger? Are you going to lie to me, Billy Joe?"

"Come off of it! Better isn't cured! There's a whole big range between the two, and I'm a *long* way from cured!"

"Nobody ever gets cured," she argued softly. "Nobody. All of us get wounded by life, Billy Joe. What matters isn't what happened in the past, but what we do *now*."

"And right now I'm flipping out. My point precisely. So what am I supposed to do? Ignore facts?"

"I'm not asking you to ignore anything." She stared at his back for a long moment, trying to come up with some way of getting through to him. "When you were a POW," she said quietly, "how many times did you kneel in the dirt while somebody pointed a gun at your back?"

His head whipped around. "How did you know that?"

"You wouldn't be the only one who was tortured that way. You were put in the same position this morning. It seemed obvious to me."

He swore and looked away.

"Yuma... Yuma, you knelt there today with that gun on your back and you never let go. You moved to protect me, you never slipped into Saigon time.... You were magnificent."

"Oh, for crying out loud!"

"No, listen. Just listen. What you did this morning to protect me took a lot more guts than busting onto the scene with a machine gun. You placed yourself between me and a gun, between me and death. You placed yourself into a position that haunts your worst nightmares—no, don't bother to deny it—and you kept control in spite of what must have been the most terrible pressure to flash back. You can't tell me you weren't seeing flashes in your mind of all the times when you were trotted out like that and told you were going to be executed. That you weren't hearing the sound of a gun being cocked."

"Wendy..."

"Don't bother denying it, Billy Joe. The fact that you hung on until you weren't needed anymore tells me that when the chips are really down, you *can* control yourself. How much more can anybody do? You can rely on your mind in the crunch. Not everybody can say that."

"Pollyanna."

"I resent that!" Her temper flared with white heat, nearly blinding her. She didn't think she had ever known a man this stubborn, this... blind! Why was it so impossible for him to see his own goodness? His own strength? He might not be the only man in the world who would have made a human shield of himself, but he was probably one of a very, *very* few who could have done so given his background.

But it went beyond even that, and Wendy knew it. He had seen Boggs wounded, had seen Hotshot killed. Had faced the fact that another man had chosen to die in his place. Only a monster wouldn't have been moved by what had happened this morning to two of his friends. So the nightmare had extended beyond the threat of execution, had reached out of the past with all its blood and gore to mark the present with real injury, real death. Real loss. She seriously doubted that Yuma would be the only one to experience fallout from today's events. She expected that her own reaction would set in once she felt safe to unwind, and probably any number of the other vets were suffering, too.

But he couldn't see that he was no worse, no weaker, than any other man. He couldn't see that he was just an ordinary man who had been wounded by extraordinary events.

With a sigh, she lowered her chin to her knees and considered for the first time that Billy Joe Yuma might be truly unreachable. That, despite her every effort, he might not be able to free himself from guilt enough to accept the good things that life offered.

For the first time she truly despaired. For the first time she acknowledged that she might well never be able to give him enough, love him enough, argue with him enough, to make him feel worthy of her. For the first time she acknowledged that there might be no hope.

Billy Joe Yuma would slip away from her because he believed he was not good enough for her. He was slipping away even now, considering today's events to be the final proof of his unfitness. There was no argument she could make that could ever persuade him to see himself differently.

Reaching out, her eyes filling with tears even as she did it, she drew him toward her. "Make love to me, Billy Joe," she whispered tearily. "Make love to me."

One last time. She never spoke the words, but they hung in the air even so. He heard them, too, she could tell. It showed in the way his face tightened, the way his eyes narrowed in renewed anguish. This was farewell, but neither of them spoke a goodbye.

He hesitated, but only briefly. Leaning over her, he found her mouth with a kiss so exquisitely gentle that it felt like the brush of butterfly wings to her. "Wendy," he whispered against her lips, and in the single word was a wealth of unspoken feelings.

Feelings seemed to reverberate in the air around them, all the emotions that would be left unspoken, all the yearnings that would never be met, all the possibilities that would never come to be. All the sorrow that awaited them both.

It seemed to focus them intensely in the moment. Yuma knew that never in his life, not even as a very young man, had he been this exquisitely aware of the textures, tastes and heat of a woman. The brush of his lips against her cheek brought him the texture of satin, the warmth of living flesh, the sweet scent of her clean skin.

Suddenly conscious that they were at the edge of a clearing, he rolled them deeper into the brush and brought an unexpected, delightful burst of laughter from Wendy's lips. Suddenly the darkness was gone and the afternoon was ablaze with the light of life and passion.

"You're beautiful," he whispered, cradling her face in his hands. "So beautiful."

"I'm plain. Ordinary."

He pressed his thumb to her lips and shook his head. "Beautiful. Body, soul and mind." Gently he rained kisses on her face until her eyes fluttered closed and her mouth began to seek his. Only then did he kiss her, taking her mouth with erotic tenderness in a slow, lazy kiss that built and built until it was as if his tongue stroked her inside from head to toe. Her fingers clutched at his shoulders, trying to draw him closer, nearer, trying to bring him down to her to satisfy her aching need for his weight.

But he remained propped on his elbows, resisting her plea. This was to be the last time. This had to be perfect, a dream he could cherish through the cold empty years to come. Every sensation, every scent and sound, had to be imprinted on his brain so that it would never be forgotten. He was branding her on his memory.

Suddenly her eyes flew open, and in their warm brown depths he saw the anguish and the understanding. Her clutching hands relaxed, and she sighed, giving herself up to the process of drawing out each moment, each caress, each sensation, into an infinity.

The last time.

Weaving a memory of rainbow hues and exquisite sensation, they journeyed slowly, as if they had a lifetime ahead of them, because they would not have that lifetime together. Each caress became an end in itself, every sigh or moan a culmination.

Slowly, slowly, he unzipped the front of Wendy's jumpsuit. On each inch of newly exposed skin he pressed a warm, wet kiss, tonguing her just enough to taste her sweetness, to make her shiver. When the zipper was down far enough, he pulled the fabric to one side and bared one small, soft breast. The chilly air stiffened her nipple immediately, and when he blew a warm breath across her, she shivered and moaned.

"Ask me, baby. Ask me," he whispered roughly. He needed to hear her pleas, needed to store up the sound of them forever in the treasure chest of his mind. On cold nights in years ahead, he would replay it all, but most especially her breathless pleas.

"Please, Billy Joe," she whispered. "Kiss me...oh, please..."

He closed his mouth over her nipple with the most exquisite care and gently tongued her. A soft whimper escaped her, and her entire body arched. Her fingers plowed into his hair, holding him closer, begging for a deeper, harder touch. "Please," she whispered. "Please. More...oh, please..."

He gave her more. He gave her as much as she could stand, until she was clawing at the ground, and then he moved to her other breast, treating her to more of the exquisite torment.

In some part of his soul he acknowledged that giving her up was going to be absolutely the hardest thing he had ever done. No loss, no sacrifice, no suffering, had ever equaled what he was about to do to himself. And the fact that he was doing the right thing was going to be cold comfort in days to come.

But he yanked his thoughts away, refusing to allow the foreshadowing of pain to color the joy of the present.

Taking care, hurrying not at all, he helped her sit up and slip out of her jumpsuit. Before she lay back, she wrapped her arms around his neck and leaned into him, pressing her face to his neck.

"Oh, Billy Joe," she whispered, unshed tears apparent in her ragged breath. "Oh, Billy Joe..."

He spread his palms on her bare back and stroked her soothingly, lovingly, aware of each delicate vertebra, each fragile rib, as he ran his hands over her. Small, soft, exquisitely formed. His throat tightened with yearnings that could never be satisfied because he was so unworthy.

Finally, as if she sensed the moment had to end, she lay back on her jumpsuit and held out her arms. Then, button by button, she undressed him, revealing the strength of bone, muscle and sinew that was Billy Joe Yuma. Her hands touched him lovingly, memorizing him in an unmistakable way.

Taking her cue from him, she taunted and tormented his nipples until ragged moans were escaping him and his hips moved restlessly. Overhead, a bird called, and clouds scudded through a blindingly blue sky, and he knew he would never again hear a birdsong or see racing clouds without thinking of Wendy, of her hands and mouth on him, tormenting him, teasing him, driving him to the brink of ecstasy and then holding him there.

He would never again smell the rich scent of pine and loam without thinking of her. He would never feel the brush of cool air on his skin without remembering. More than Wendy herself was being engraved on his heart and mind.

He nearly cried out when she took him into her mouth and gave him an intimate kiss born of her feelings for him. She cradled him gently in her palm and loved him in a way that deprived him of breath, of awareness, of any thought save making her his.

When she would have lain back to receive him, he turned her over and guided her onto her hands and knees. Then he took her from behind and wrapped himself around her so that he could caress her intimately all the while he thrust deeply into the place she had made for him.

The consuming eroticism of it left Wendy gasping for breath. With one hand he caressed her breast, tugging gently on her nipple. With the other he touched her between her legs, giving the most maddening caresses to the sensitive knot of nerves there.

Sexual tension drew her taut, causing her to arch her head back as the feelings rocketed through her, hot, sweet and consuming.

He murmured something rough and hot, and gently bit her shoulder as he drove deeply into her. He was, she realized dimly, making sure she never forgot these moments. As if she could. The pleasure he was giving her seared into her brain. Hot, aching waves of need surged through her in a hypnotic ebb and flow, each time peaking higher and higher.

"Yuma... Yuma..." She hardly had breath to squeeze that much out.

"I know, baby," he gasped. "Let it happen...sweet baby, let it...happen...."

She didn't want to. She fought it, wanting to cling to these incredible feelings as long as she could. Fought it, knowing that once it was done, she and Yuma would part. This was his final gift to her, and she wanted to squeeze every single second out of it before he was gone for good.

The chilly air seemed to vanish. The heat between them was animal and sweet, aromatic with their scents, hot enough to bathe them in sweat.

"Wendy..." Yuma sounded almost desperate. Anguished.

"Not yet," she gasped. "Not yet."

"Baby...please..." She was killing him, and he was loving it. He was going to explode, bust something permanently, be damaged forever...and he didn't care. It was such sweet, sweet torture.

But finally... finally he felt her stiffen and arch, felt her grind herself hard against his hand, felt the rippling contractions within her.

He exploded, and reality vanished in a blast of white heat.

I love you. The words trembled on her lips as they had so often in the past, but she left them unsaid. Six years ago he hadn't believed them. Now he simply didn't want to hear them. Nor could she inflict any more pain on him.

It was over. Dry-eyed, she lay on her back and stared up through the branches at the sky. It was over. He was sending her away. And she no longer had the heart to fight it. There was, in any event, nothing to fight. Nothing but phantasms from the past that, like shadows, could not be banished.

A huge wound gaped deep inside her, the place where Yuma had oncc been. Only now, in the final wrenching moment of accepting his loss, did she realize that she had never in all these years stopped loving him. He was so much a part of her that she hadn't even realized she had been carrying him with her every moment.

Now there was not even the vainest of hopes left. If he could reject her now, when she had made it plain that she wanted him despite his illness, despite his flashbacks, then what was there left to say?

Slowly she turned her head and looked at him. He was watching her, his expression absolutely flat. He had moved himself beyond feeling, she realized. He had cut himself off. How she wished she had that ability.

"I'll walk you back out to the car," he said. As if it were not a rugged, two-day hike.

Wendy shook her head. "You don't have to. I marked the trail."

"You can't go alone. If you slipped and got hurt, you'd be a goner."

"Then I'll ask Cowboy to go with me." Tears were stinging her eyes, and the ache in her heart threatened to kill her, but she knew the break had to be clean. Two more days in his company would kill her, now that the end had been reached.

He nodded finally. "All right. I'll be out in a couple of days. I have to... think."

"Sure." Sitting up, she reached for her clothes and began to dress with movements made awkward by her trembling. "I... um... I'll see you when you get back."

"You bet."

She glanced over her shoulder at him and found that he had looked away and was staring off into the woods, as if he had forgotten all about her. No goodbyes, she thought. None. She couldn't stand it, and she suspected the distance he had just donned was tenuous at best. It would only hurt them both to drag this out.

Drawing quick, deep breaths to hold back the tears, she pulled her boots on and laced them. Then she rose.

"See you," she said, amazed that her voice didn't break.

He nodded but never looked at her.

"Yeah," she said and turned. When she reached the clearing, she put her fingers to her mouth and let out a piercing whistle. Half a minute later she heard the crash of boots in the underbrush, and Cowboy appeared.

"Ready?" he asked.

"Yeah. Do you mind walking me out to where we left the car? I marked a trail...." She couldn't make herself finish. Compressing her lips, she looked away.

"I don't mind," Cowboy said with surprising gentleness. "I don't mind at all. Come on, Missy. We'll get you home."

No such place, Wendy thought as she went with him. Billy Joe Yuma had just seen to that. There would be no home for Wendy Tate.

Chapter 13

Cowboy didn't say much at all until the next afternoon, when they were less than a mile from the road. He had been a solicitous companion, looking out for her every step of the way with a gallantry that was downright old-fashioned. He'd been pleasant, but quiet.

But when they were nearly at the road, he brought up the subject that Wendy hadn't once been able to put out of her mind during their entire trek.

"He needs a good shake-up," Cowboy said.

"Hmm?"

"Yuma. He needs a good shake-up. Man has his brain in a rut so deep he can't see over the top. Somebody needs to kick him out of it."

Wendy sighed. "Easier said than done."

"Maybe not." He fell silent for a while, then spoke again. "Might be easy to shake him free now. Man's crazy about you. Any fool can see it."

"Not me. Not him."

"Oh, he knows it, Missy. He's just being so damn noble nd self-sacrificing it's enough to make a body want to omit."

Wendy might have laughed at that had she not felt so niserable. She managed a small smile, though.

"That's been his problem all along," Cowboy contin-ed. "Man keeps wanting to be perfect. Now, nobody's erfect. Nobody. But he won't settle for less."

"Not from himself, anyway."

"Well, maybe we can convince him you're settling for less nan him."

Wendy halted and looked up at the gruff combat vet-ran. "What do you mean?"

"Thought you'd have figured it out. I have some busi-ess in town that needs tending. Mind if I hitch a ride?"

"Of course not."

Cowboy smiled slowly. "Thanks. And maybe I can re-urn the favor. When that sorry so-and-so gets his butt back civilization, maybe you and I can do some hanging round together. I don't clean up so bad. Maybe we can onvince him he has some competition."

Wendy stared at him, amazed he would make such an of-er. "Cowboy, I can't lie."

"Nobody has to lie. Nobody has to say a thing. That man so crazy about you, all he'll need is to see us together a ouple of times. If that don't wake him up, then it's hope-ss for sure."

They resumed walking. After a bit Wendy said, "I don't now. It doesn't seem honest somehow."

"What's dishonest? I buy you dinner. Maybe take you ancing at the hall on Friday night. A couple of friends can o that, can't they?"

The more she thought about it, the more she felt she had othing to lose. What good was it going to do to mope ound anyway? If Yuma thought she was moping over him, would just go on another guilt trip for sure. If he thought e was having fun . . . well, it might work. At the very least it would leave him free of guilt. And she honestly didn't want him to feel guilty. He already felt too much of that.

"All right," she said. "If you're sure about this."

"I'm sure," Cowboy said with unmistakable determination. "He's a good man, Missy, and he's paying for crimes he never even committed. Chaps my butt to see it, if you want the truth. If we can knock some sense into him, I'm all for it."

Wendy almost cried then. These men loved Yuma, she realized. Hotshot had flung himself between Yuma and a bullet, and now Cowboy was prepared to go out of his way to see that Yuma came to his senses. "You're a good man, Cowboy."

He waved the compliment aside. "A man does whatever he can to help his buddies. That's all."

That, Wendy thought, was one of the best philosophies she had heard in a long time.

She and Cowboy had dinner with her parents that night. Marge Tate was a lovely woman of forty-five, with coppery hair and a figure that belied giving birth to six daughters. Tiny, compact, she was a bundle of energy and always had a place ready at her table for an extra mouth. Cowboy looked a little overwhelmed by the exuberance of the six Tate girls, the youngest of whom was Krissie, twelve, and the oldest of whom was Wendy, but they soon convinced him that they weren't dangerous, and before long he was laughing and relaxed.

Alvin Teague was being charged with first-degree murder in the shooting of Hotshot, and attempted murder for Boggs. His friends were all being held on lesser charges as accessories, and his younger brother had been arrested in connection with the thefts at the outlying ranches. Nate allowed as how he thought they might actually get the county cleaned up for good.

And Hotshot would be buried tomorrow.

Wendy instinctively looked at Cowboy, knowing he had lost a friend, but Cowboy remained inscrutable.

"There'll be a memorial service," Nate said. "And some of my deputies are planning to go."

"I'm going, too," Marge said calmly. She did not look at her husband. "He may well have saved Wendy's life. Poor man."

Noticing again that strange tension between her father and her mother, Wendy looked from one to the other but kept silent. She had long ago learned that whatever occurred between her parents was private, and that neither of them would tolerate intrusion.

"I'm sure Hotshot is happier now, ma'am," Cowboy said gruffly. "He was...barely hanging on. I always expected him to step out in front of a train. At least he got to get out and do some good at the same time."

Wendy saw her mother glance at Krissie, but the youngest daughter seemed oblivious to what was being said.

"Sorry," said Cowboy.

Marge gave him a warm smile. "Probably nothing she hasn't heard elsewhere already. Coffee and pie?"

After dinner, Wendy drove Cowboy out to the motel where he had booked a room.

"Will you be all right?" she asked him before he climbed out of the Wagoneer. "You have my number."

He turned and looked at her fully. The autumn night had long since darkened the land, and the green-and-white neon from the motel created crazy patterns on his face.

"I've been all right for some time now, Wendy. Seriously. You just get into a habit of living a certain way, and somebody has to look after those guys when they go off the deep end up there. But maybe it's time I came down myself. Gonna give it a try. You let me know when Yuma shows up, and we'll go out for dinner."

"Why don't you just let me cook dinner for us tomorrow night? I'd like to."

After a moment, he smiled and nodded. "Sure. That'd be great. See you at the memorial."

* * *

The day was cold, gray, bitter. The mourners at the graveside were surprisingly many. Most of the vets had come down from the hills to be there. Many other local veterans from many other wars also turned out to honor the last act of gallantry of one of their own. Many of Nate's deputies were there, too, along with Nate and Marge.

Wendy and Cowboy stood together, near the other men from the mountains. Dry-eyed, she listened to Reverend Fromberg read scripture and pray. She hadn't really had the opportunity to know Hotshot, but she'd listened to him talk to Yuma that one morning, and she felt she had some idea of the man he had been, the agony he had suffered. And she could only feel that Cowboy had been right. Hotshot had found the only peace he could ever have.

It was appalling to think, though, that there were so many others who could hope only for the same peace. Appalling to count the real cost of war in terms of lives blighted forever. The veterans who had died at least had a memorial. Those who had lived were left to remember and grieve.

Glancing up, she drew a sharp breath as she saw Yuma on the other side of the fresh grave. He wore his usual sage-colored flight suit covered by a leather flight jacket. His ears looked red from the bitter wind, and he was staring down into the open grave as if he might well jump in with Hotshot.

Cowboy heard her indrawn breath, and he reached out, taking her arm and tucking it through his. "It's okay," he murmured.

Okay? Wendy wondered wildly. Twenty-five years after the damn war, it was about to claim yet another victim, this time a woman who had been in diapers when it had been going on. She still remembered the acid in Yuma's voice when he'd pointed that out to her six years ago. The way his words had cut at her soul, making it clear there was a chasm of time and experience between them that could never be bridged.

But they *had* bridged it. Perhaps Billy Joe Yuma had been a POW when she had been toddling around in diapers and learning her first words. Perhaps he had been brought home from captivity the same day she had entered nursery school, but what of it? Time had closed that gap, time and closeness and understanding.

What stood between them now was the shadow of a war and a man's stubborn belief in his own unworthiness. Not one other blessed thing. And there wasn't a single thing she could do about it. You could prove to a man without arms that he could still make love. You could prove to a man without legs that he could still be mobile. You could convince someone who was blind that he was perfectly capable.

But you couldn't convince a man of his own goodness.

Battling tears, she threw a rose into the grave and turned away. Cowboy was right beside her, his arm wrapped protectively around her shoulders. As if she were the bereaved, when, in fact, it was exactly the other way around. Cowboy was the bereaved. All the men in their tattered camouflage clothing and boots were the bereaved.

But they parted before Wendy and Cowboy, then followed them from the cemetery.

There had been no wake, but now a group of ragtag veterans made their way to Houlihan's, with Wendy in their midst. In the back room they pulled tables together and clustered chairs around and called for the beer.

One after another, they rose to toast lost comrades. Hotshot was first. Cowboy rose, glass in hand, and began to talk about the man Wendy had never known.

"Hotshot," he said slowly, "was really Lieutenant Commander Royce Applegate. He was a Navy Top Gun, and he flew off a carrier in the Gulf of Tonkin for three tours before he was shot down. He was the guy who flew in fast and low when us grunts needed some strafing done, the guy who blew the hell out of the NVA when they had us pinned down. We'll never know how many of us he saved on those screaming runs he used to make. He was an ace, one of the best dogfighters, they say. In the sky, he was untouchable."

Cowboy shook his head a little. "I don't even know how many medals he got, and he probably wouldn't want me to say anything about it, anyway. He was a hell of a pilot and a hell of a man, and his only failing was that he had a soul too good for the job he finally had to do."

He raised his glass. "To Hotshot."

Wendy lifted her glass, careful to barely sip the beer. From the look of it, these men intended to toast themselves right under the table.

Crazy stood up and offered a toast to the hospitalized Boggs. Then Vance reminisced about Artie. And after that she didn't recognize any of the names mentioned and toasted, but the stories began to take on a crushing similarity as she realized how many of their comrades had committed suicide.

Of course, she reminded herself, they were only toasting fallen comrades. But that still didn't deprive the moment of a certain ghastliness. Finally, unable to listen to any more, and feeling that she was really out of place and probably inhibiting the expressions of grief these men needed to make, she slipped on her coat and left.

Outside, the late afternoon had grown windy and dark, looking truly wintery. Not until she pulled up in front of her dark duplex, though, did her own crushing grief assail her. Somehow she had moved through the last couple of days on automatic, but now awareness returned.

She had lost Yuma.

All at once her diaphragm froze in a painful knot and she couldn't breathe. And then a huge, helpless sob rolled right up from some deep well of grief and ripped her defenses wide open.

She couldn't stop the tears. She couldn't stop the sobs. She sat hunched over the steering wheel in the cold and cried and cried and cried. She wept until the skin around her eyes felt sore and her face felt raw and the sobs just kept coming.

Suddenly the car door opened. Startled, she jerked upright and found herself looking at Cowboy. Oh, Lord, she had invited him for dinner. How could she have forgotten?

"Aw, Missy," he said gruffly. "It'll get better. Just you wait and see." Reaching in, he wrapped his arms around her and drew her against his chest in the same comforting way her father often did. He smelled faintly of beer and the cold night air. "He'll come to his senses. You'll see."

He held her that way for several minutes while she regained control. Then he solicitously helped her from the vehicle. Arm firmly around her, he guided her up the walk and took her key to unlock the door for her.

"I'll cook," he said. "You just tell me what you want me to do."

And suddenly Wendy laughed. It was a small, weary sound, but it was genuine. "You're a real sweetheart, Cowboy."

"Just keep it to yourself, okay?"

Out in the shadows near the street, Yuma watched the scene unfold. *You're a real sweetheart, Cowboy.*

Something inside him felt as if it were being torn in two. He hadn't been able to believe the way she had ignored him at the cemetery earlier, the way she had clung to Cowboy and then had left with him, all without saying a word.

And that bastard Cowboy! It sure hadn't taken him long to move in! Damn, he must have sweet-talked her nonstop from the moment he started walking her out of the forest.

His hands tightened inside his jacket pockets, and he felt the white heat of a familiar rage. It was the rage he had learned first in Nam, learned first at the sight of the broken, bloody bodies, then had relearned at the hands of his captors. It was a gut-deep, soul-deep urge to kill, smash, destroy. Get even.

Tightening his hands even more, he forced himself to turn and walk away. Rage could only destroy, never mend. He had understood that from his earliest youth; it was a lesson brought home again and again by his parents. He had learned to control that rage, had controlled it even in the prison camp. He would control it now because it could only hurt Wendy or Cowboy, two people he loved dearly.

But, God, the spear of betrayal twisted in his gut like a burning brand. Only a couple of days ago Wendy had loved him as if he were the only man on earth, as if she would die without him. Now, already...

But hadn't he wanted that? Well, sure. But Cowboy was no better a bargain than Yuma was himself. Both suffered PTSD, though Cowboy seemed to have been handling it pretty well lately. Both men carried crushing burdens of guilt, neither one seemed to have what a woman would need.

What the hell was wrong with that woman? he asked himself angrily. How could she want to throw herself away like this?

He paced the entire length of Conard City as the afternoon deepened into night. The bite of the wind grew cruel, a harbinger of approaching winter. Lights winked on in residences, a homey sight that always made him feel lonesome when he saw it.

All right, so he'd freaked out a little up on the mountain. That wasn't a crime, was it? Not considering what had happened. Wendy had been right about that. He'd been hanging on to the present by a thread while he relived some of his worst experiences. And losing Hotshot like that... He'd lost other friends that way, with bloody holes in their chests, drowning in their own blood. Nor did it help to realize that the other man had died in his place.

Thinking about it now, calmly, he could see that he had been pushed by an extraordinary set of circumstances that weren't likely to occur ever again. That he need not fear for his stability. That he *was* in charge of the monkey, not the other way around. Wendy had been right about that, too. About how he kept control when it really counted. How he climbed into the Huey time and again and flew out to aid the wounded. If he could do that, well . . . maybe he was pretty much recovered after all.

Of course, that didn't deal with the rest of it.

Reaching the railroad tracks on the far side of town, he turned around and began to walk back the way he had come.

The guilt. The guilt that plagued him and drove him to deny himself and punish himself endlessly—even that was beginning to loosen its throttling grip. He was just so used to thinking in a certain way about things that he hadn't even realized he didn't feel that way any longer.

It was as if he had gotten so used to an old song that he couldn't hear that a new one had begun. As if he had fallen into a mental rut and couldn't see his way out of it. The litany was just that: a litany. A string of words and protests recited by rote.

Because he had realized this afternoon as he stood beside Hotshot's grave that he—along with all the other vets—was paying endlessly for a war long over, for crimes committed out of necessity, for horrors he had been caught up in but hadn't created. Their country said "go," and they had gone. They had stepped onto battlefields steeped in gore and done their best to stay alive and serve their country.

And when you put men in that position, you took away all civilized restraints. Kill or be killed was a very primitive, very potent, driving force. And afterwards, when they came home and returned to civilized norms, they had to live with memories of savagery that conscience could not condone. Many simply flagellated themselves for the rest of their days. Some were completely broken.

And some, like him, were a little bit crazy, a little bit unstable, a little bit guilty and a little bit lost.

But that was no crime, was it? And why did he persist in feeling guilty for the hate and anger he had felt? Why did he persist in feeling like a murderer because he'd had a very human wish to get even with his tormentors? Must a man pay for his feelings, too?

The wind gusted suddenly and blew some leaves across his path. It was cold out here, he thought. Cold and lonely.

And the only thing on God's earth that was keeping him out here alone was himself.

Wendy didn't let Cowboy cook dinner. He wanted to help, though, and he was handy enough. While she pan-fried chicken, he sliced vegetables for a salad.

"Yeah, I was married," he said when she asked about it. "Most of us were, at one time or another. PTSD isn't an easy thing for a woman to live with. Figure I gave my wife her own case of it. She never knew when I was going to come unglued, or go into a screaming rage and start smashing things. Not much of that you can ask someone to take."

"And now? How do you think you are now?"

"Better." He looked up from the cucumber he was slicing and gave her a faint smile. "A lot better. I got through that mess up on the mountain without slipping my cog. At least not much."

"Yuma—" She cut herself off and bit her lip.

"I know. But he hung on until it was over. And it's been an awful long time since he flashed back. Besides, he was the one under the gun, not me. If I'd been kneeling there with Teague's rifle aimed at the back of my skull, I'm not sure I wouldn't have freaked out right then."

He cocked his head. "I'm not sure I didn't, a little. I mean, it was like some of the things that happened back in Nam. I probably *was* a little bit here and a little bit there." He shrugged. "For once it wasn't inappropriate. Probably why it didn't much show. Anyway, don't worry about Yuma. He's got it all together as much as anybody else on the planet. There isn't one of us who's perfectly sane, is there?"

Almost in spite of herself, Wendy laughed. And it was during that moment of camaraderie that Yuma opened the back door and stepped into the kitchen.

For a long moment the three stood frozen, caught in a tableau. Yuma looked from one to the other, then spoke stiffly. "I came to get my things."

Wendy drew a sharp breath and looked wildly at Cowboy, who gave her a small, encouraging nod. Yuma never took his gaze from Wendy, and he didn't miss the way she looked to Cowboy for support. Something inside him suddenly felt as if it had been sundered.

"Umm...can't you stay for dinner?" Wendy asked in a breathless rush.

His first instinct was to say no in a fit of jealous irritation, but there was no way on earth he was going to leave these two alone to get any more intimate.

"Sure," he said, closing the door behind him. "Thanks."

"Good," Wendy said. "Uh, the potatoes are ready to be mashed...?"

"I'll do it," Yuma said instantly. In case there was any doubt that he knew his way around the kitchen. Which was really childish, when he thought about it. The most childish impulse he'd had in years. And he didn't like the way Cowboy was grinning at him.

It wasn't until after dinner, though, that things grew really tense. With the meal no longer an excuse for anyone to linger, with the dishes all washed in record time because of all the helping hands, there was suddenly no reason for either man to stay...at least, no reason other than Wendy.

She looked at Yuma. "You said you wanted to get your things."

He looked at Cowboy. "In a minute."

Cowboy smiled faintly and turned to Wendy. "I'd better be heading back now. Don't forget our dinner date tomorrow night."

They hadn't made any such plans, but Wendy managed to smile and nod. "Six?"

"Six. See you then." He nodded at Yuma, grabbed his jacket off the back of a chair and headed for the door.

Wendy followed him, murmuring the things a hostess murmurs to a departing guest, but never once suggesting he stay longer. She and Cowboy both knew better, even if Yuma didn't.

And then, finally, she was alone with the man who owned her heart, body and soul. The man who didn't want them.

"I'll make more coffee while you pack," she said, forcing herself to act as if she didn't care that he might really be moving out. As if she didn't desperately want him to stay.

"Thanks. That sounds good."

He watched her brush past him in the narrow hall and vanish into the kitchen. He had to do something, he told himself. But what? After all his protests and all his determination to stay away, there didn't seem to be an easy, obvious way to change course.

Or even a believable one.

Listening intently, Wendy waited for the sounds that would indicate that Yuma had moved down the hall to his room and was packing. She heard nothing at all, which meant he was standing in the hallway, exactly where she had left him.

Her hand trembled as she slipped the carafe onto the warming plate, and the glass clinked noisily. Leaning forward, she flipped the switch and listened to the first hiss as the pot heated up.

"Wendy."

She was so tense that she jumped and whirled around at the sound of her name.

"Sorry. Didn't mean to scare you." Yuma stood looking at her from hollow green eyes, his expression almost grim.

"You're packed already?" she asked when he said nothing.

He drew a long breath, so long that she heard it and realized he was as tense as she was.

"I'm an alcoholic," he said. "I always will be."

"I know."

"I might fall off the wagon sometime."

"You might." Her heart had begun a steady, heavy pounding as she listened. Why was he listing his shortcomings? Hadn't he already done that ad nauseam?

He frowned. "You don't believe that."

"Oh, I believe it," she said promptly. "I'm a nurse, remember? I know there's no cure."

"Good." He scowled at her. "I had a flashback just the other day."

"Extraordinary circumstances."

"Damn it!" The curse escaped him explosively. "It could happen if a car backfires. It could. It might! It probably will!"

"If it does, then it does!" She scowled right back.

"You don't understand what it's like to live with it!"

"For you?"

"For somebody who loves me!" He bellowed the words, and the glass in the window over the sink rattled.

"Thank God," she said. "I was beginning to think you didn't believe me!"

The statement clearly confused him. He froze, his mouth open on a word that never emerged. After a moment he asked, "Didn't believe you about what?"

"That I love you."

Now he really looked floored. "Why wouldn't I believe that?"

"Because you kept on giving me all the reasons why I couldn't possibly love you!"

"That's different from believing that you *do!* Not that you've said so in recent memory!"

"Damn it, I don't believe you! All this time—"

He interrupted her ruthlessly. "Do you?"

"Do I what?"

"Love me?" He nearly bellowed the words.

"Of course I do!" She glared at him, hardly able to believe the ridiculousness of this entire conversation. "I never stopped loving you."

"Wendy, I..." He stepped toward her, but before he could speak, she was plunging ahead.

"I could hardly tell you, could I? I mean, every time I turned around you were telling me why I shouldn't, why you couldn't, why—"

He closed the distance between them, swept her into his arms and sealed her mouth with a hot, wet kiss. When he felt all the tension slip out of her, felt her sag into him as if she wanted to melt, he lifted his head and made his own breathless declaration.

"I love you, baby. I love you beyond belief. I was crazy to think I could ever let you go."

In that instant everything inside her grew silent and still. Reverent. Filled with awe as her own personal miracle came true. Finally, in a hushed whisper, she asked, "Billy Joe?"

"I love you," he repeated, understanding her need because it exactly matched his own. "I love you."

Then, bending, he swung her up into his arms and turned, heading for the bedroom.

"Billy Joe! Put me down. You'll hurt yourself!"

"It's high time I made love to you in a bed," he said roughly. "Comfortably. In the warmth. In privacy."

He shouldered his way into her room and lowered her carefully to her double bed. With hands that trembled, he stripped away her clothes in a rush, then carelessly tossed his own aside, coming at last to rest beside her.

She turned into him, wrapping herself around him in a way that made his throat lock and his heart pound. The gesture was so giving, so welcoming. He knew he would never forget it. Never. Nor would he ever forget how it made him feel.

Wrapping his arms around her, he hugged her back. "I can't... I can't give you up."

"I'm not asking you to." Reaching up, she touched her palm to his cheek. "You don't have to give me up."

"When you didn't speak to me earlier, at the cemetery...? When you walked off with Cowboy...I thought you might never speak to me again. And all I could think was—Damn it, Wendy, if you're going to throw your life away, throw it away on me!"

Astonished, she nearly gaped at him. "Throw my life away?"

"That's right. I mean, if you're set on having some broken-down vet, then you may as well—"

She clapped her hand over his mouth to prevent him from saying another thing. "Don't you dare, Billy Joe. Don't you dare finish that thought. I'm not set on having *some* broken-down vet. There's only one vet I want, and he's far from broken-down!"

He caught her chin in his hand and turned her face up so that he could study her expression. "You mean that, don't you? You really mean that."

She nodded.

"Oh, my God," he whispered. "Oh, my God."

All of a sudden she was crushed to him, held so tightly she could barely breathe.

"Sweet mother," he murmured, "I must have been a good boy sometime or other. Ah, Wendy, Wendy... baby, I love you. I love you."

She wasn't quite ready to be happy yet, though. Even the intimacy of their warm, naked flesh pressed so enticingly together couldn't quite make her forget that there was something else she needed, too.

"What does that mean, Billy Joe? That you love me? What are you going to do about it?"

He laughed then, a warm, unexpected sound. "Marry you, of course. You can't back out now, Wendy. I won't let you."

"I wouldn't even try." She pressed a kiss on his shoulder, then tilted her head back so they were eye to eye. Her heart was suddenly galloping so hard hat she wasn't sure she would be able to force the words out. "And... children?"

He closed his eyes, and his head made an instinctive movement to one side. He was going to say no, she realized with a deep pang. He wasn't going to agree to have children. She didn't know if she could handle that.

Suddenly his eyes opened and looked straight into hers. "And children," he agreed. "As many as you want. As many as we can manage. I... always wanted kids."

She drew a sharp breath. "Really?"

A slow smile spread across his face. A slow, happy smile, unlike any she had ever seen on his face before.

"Really," he said huskily. "If I don't die first of happiness. And, babe, you've made that a distinct possibility."

Because he was lost no longer.

* * * * *

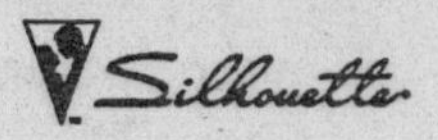
Silhouette